# ASHES TO ASHES

# ASHES TO ASHES

RAVEN BOWER

ISBN: 978-1-958414-19-4

Hydra Publications

Goshen, Kentucky 40026

www.hydrapublications.com

*To my husband, Greg. His unwavering support and caring is the most invaluable thing in the world. Love you, Darlin!*

# CHAPTER ONE

*Snap!*

Harley lifted her tactical boot and lowered her torch toward the cave floor, cussing under her breath. Yeah, she'd stepped on something, all right. Ribs. Human ribs. "Homey. Gotta love the décor. It's all sorts of fuzzy."

She hated caves, particularly this one. Shaped as if a gigantic tapeworm had eaten its way through the stone, the middle section rose four feet above her head while the sides tapered into small, bone-filled crevasses. A dark crack slithered down from the ceiling, vanishing into the crevasses. Where did they lead? To nowhere? The abyss?

*To rats?*

Harley grimaced and swept the crackling flames in an arc in front of her at knee level. Bones, too many to guess the body count, covered the grimy cave floor. Ribs, femurs, shattered skulls, and fractured spines lay strewn in a macabre, haphazard mess. Scraps of clothing wove through the bones in frayed, bloodstained ribbons.

"No feces," Cerise, Harley's partner, said. She'd whisked her platinum blond hair back into a ponytail. A neat yet carefree look that Harley envied. Whenever Harley pulled her hair back, she looked like a drill instructor. Then again, Harley's upbringing hadn't allowed for learning the gentle arts, like styling hair or applying makeup. "Do you still think werewolves did this?"

Cerise dropped into a smooth crouch. Her butt hovered inches away from a tangled mass of spines heaped as unceremoniously as a pile of discarded shrimp tails. Wedging her torch into a rib cage to free her hands, she gripped a pair of tattered jeans with her leather-clad fingers and dug into the pockets, searching for identification.

"Could be that they learned some hygiene." Harley blew a dangling strand of auburn hair out of her face, wishing she'd chosen a cute, hair-always-out-of-your-face pixie cut instead of keeping it on the long side.

"And the likelihood of that is?" Cerise asked.

Harley frowned. Cerise was right. Notoriously dirty creatures, werewolves dropped their intestinal burdens anywhere the urge hit them, including next to their food. They weren't concerned about eating E. coli infested flesh or nuggets of their own steaming shit for that matter. Werewolves also didn't operate on the waste-not-want-not principle. They left chunks of rotting flesh, bits of organs, and shanks of hair amongst their victims' bones.

This lair was too clean. Each bone was meticulously stripped of meat and there wasn't an organ or hair to be found. The only thing left to rot was the bloody clothing.

*Can't expect them to Hoover blood out of fibers, now, can we?*

"More likely than werepumas forming a pride." Harley wiggled her boot between two broken rib cages then stepped forward, searching for an intact skull amongst the remains. "If this is a singular puma, it's one fat ass cat with midnight cravings that'd put Garfield to shame. Think it got into the catnip?"

"There are exceptions." Cerise tugged a wallet out of the shredded jeans and flipped it open, indulging in her morbid and mentally unhealthy habit of collecting victims' IDs.

"Will you leave that for the cleaners to handle? We're not supposed to rummage through the remains of stolen lives. We're supposed to stop this shit from happening."

*We failed every one of these people.*

Harley strained to see through the shadows. She wanted to saturate the cave with light to defuse the shadows, to reveal what might be lurking within them, and to help her find an intact skull in the mess. She considered snagging the flashlight from her belt loop. Fire was cozy but couldn't compete with the flashlight's powerful beam, but it wasn't the wisest of ideas considering what they might be up against. No were species feared flashlights, but most shunned fire. If this was a were-puma lair, as Cerise believed, the torches could multi-task as weapons. If there was one thing that Harley believed without a doubt, it was that there was no such thing as too many weapons.

"I'm not sure I trust the cleaners, either," Cerise said.

"You've watched ten too many conspiracy shows," Harley said. "Now, put that down." She moved her foot to the side and slipped it under a stack of thighbones as she picked her way through the human debris.

"Just because it's a conspiracy theory doesn't mean people aren't conspiring." Cerise rocked back on her heels and held the ID up to the torchlight. "A Mr. Kent, from Sweetwater."

"Speaking of." With a gloved hand, Harley plucked a skull out of a tangle of bones. Licked clean of flesh, the smooth skull gave her a lopsided leer dotted by cracked and missing teeth on a fractured jaw. Empty eye sockets stared up, accusing. The flesh of the victim was long since digested, but she made a promise to the lingering soul, *We'll find them. They'll pay.* Harley ran her thumb over the chipped cheekbone. How had this happened under the local slayers' watch?

The simple answer was – it shouldn't have. They were outfitted with enough do-dads, weapons, and snitches that detecting and stopping monsters before they killed too many people, or killed at all, was the norm rather than the exception. And yet, she stood amongst a boneyard of who knew how many bodies.

People who shouldn't have died. Although, in this case, the dead should consider themselves lucky.

*Better dead than were'd.*

Humans contained enough beast as-is. Humans infected with the were virus danced within the halls of madness. The animal within devoured their human faculties. It ripped compassion and rational thought out, replacing them with violence and predator cunning until nothing remained of the human except a facade worn to creep close to their prey. A vile camouflage.

Theories written by mystics claimed that decent, moral weres existed, weres who possessed supreme wills and could be allies in humanity's battle for survival. But years of experience taught Harley no such thing existed. As usual, the Church's mystics had sucked on a few too many bongs.

"Don't start," Cerise said.

"If the local slayers get bent about this little excursion of yours, I'm blaming it on you." Careful not to jostle the fragile skull, Harley turned the sightless sockets into her palm. There was one indisputable way to distinguish a werepuma kill from that of any other were. Once she proved pumas weren't the culprits, they could figure out what actually *was* responsible for the death piled in the cave. It wasn't werewolf, but it had to be something and that something wasn't human. "Going to tell them you hauled me here at gunpoint. It was trespass or have my spicy brains splattered across their pretty soil."

"Uh-huh."

"Hm. This could be the work of a troll," Harley said. "They're voracious and like dingy ass caves."

"They also make werewolves look like Martha Stewart. Plus, troll stink is something you never get out of your nostrils."

"Point." Harley skewed her lips to the side. "Though, we shouldn't rule out a manic fae cult, one determined to put Manson to shame. I hear they're competitive like that."

"They took his cash." Cerise snorted in disgust and dropped the wallet. It hit the floor with a thunk. "Thieves."

Harley barely heard her. Buzzing, the sound of a million shit-frenzied flies echoed in her head as she stared at the skull. This was no werewolf lair. It wasn't a troll, or ghast, nor the dumping ground for a rabid Charles Manson cult.

"Houston," Harley whispered.

"Find something?"

"We have a problem." Harley probed a finger into one of two punctures at the base of the skull to make certain they were real and not a trick of the flickering torchlight or her imagination running amok, tainted by Cerise's mad theory. Her finger penetrated the empty hollow where the brain once resided. She twisted her finger, feeling along the ridge. It was no illusion. They were standing smack in the center of a werepuma lair. No doubt about it.

The skulking predators came at their victims from behind. Swift and silent, they pounced on their prey, snaring them with sharp, curved claws before the person even realized they were being hunted. Then, *snap*. With a singular, powerful bite to the back of the head and neck, their prey was dead.

"Minimum fuss, little muss," Harley muttered. "All nice and feline tidy."

"Ha. I was right, wasn't I?" The triumph in Cerise's voice grated on Harley's nerves.

"This shouldn't happen." A hollow pit formed in the center of Harley's belly, sucking the warmth from her body like some demented black hole. "How the hell did we miss another pride forming?"

"We didn't. Not our turf, remember? And incidentally, *I* didn't miss it." Cerise came up beside her, examined the holes, and then gave a pleased nod.

Harley set the skull back amongst the bones. Had she placed it with the right remains? She wasn't sure. "Sorry."

Given the chaotic sprawl, there was no way to sort the remains without a forensics team or two. But the victims would never have that final luxury of entering eternal rest intact. Once they secured the cave, they'd have to call a cleaner team. The Church's cleaners were disturbingly thorough. After they finished, the police could coat the area with luminal, fluorescein, or whatever else they wanted to use and find nothing. Not a trace of blood. Not a fleck of bone. Not a single cell.

As if none of these people ever existed. Their deaths washed from the scene with no more thought than one would give to swatting a fly.

"Almost wish I'd been wrong." The satisfaction in Cerise's voice faded as the weight of their discovery settled. She tugged her silver crucifix, edged with frilly silver loops, from beneath her peach cotton shirt and slid it up and down the silver rope chain.

"Just because it's a werepuma pride, doesn't mean it's Niko's." Harley twisted Cerise's favorite phrasing against her. It gave her some small, petty satisfaction when Cerise favored her with a rare glower. Her gray eyes looked ethereal in the torchlight.

"Doesn't mean it's not." Cerise scanned ahead and then made her way deeper into the cave. She moved carefully to avoid stepping on the dead.

"If it is, then that means someone in the Order released them and that's not in the realm of Realityville."

Cerise shrugged. "There's been a lot of weirdness lately. I wouldn't be so sure."

"Is this adventure really about Lars?" Harley asked. Born two years apart, Cerise and her brother were tight as crocodile scales. Unfortunately, he and his partner disappeared somewhere in Colorado, deep in the Rocky Mountains.

Cerise's shoulders stiffened. "One minute, their signals registered everything as normal and dandy, the next...*poof*. Gone. How do you explain that?"

"They ran into some mountainous version of the Bermuda Triangle?"

Cerise turned, slowly, spreading her arms to the side. "It's impossible. Our chips do not just stop transmitting."

"Improbable. Not Impossible." Harley rubbed her left shoulder. The hard edges of the chip the Church used to track their whereabouts and monitor their physical status pressed against her fingertips. Built to withstand the slayers' brutal lifestyle, the chips transmitted, even in remote areas, via satellite link. If a slayer was injured or died, the chip would emit an emergency signal so they could be rescued, or the body located and given a proper burial. "Time anomalies have stopped transmissions before."

"Blocked. Not stopped." Cerise's brow furrowed. "Unless... Lars recognized something was wrong in the Order, too. If he did, he might have removed his chip."

"If that was the case, he'd have told you, wouldn't he? Given you a warning, or something, right?"

Cerise bit her lip and thought for a moment. "Either way, we don't leave slayers behind. Dead or alive."

Cardinal Germaine had said all the right things to Cerise: oozed apologies and sympathies, sent handmade Belgian chocolates, and a thick, handwritten, incense-scented letter expressing his deepest regrets. But until Lars's body was found, Cerise would never accept her brother's death. *Supposed death.* It was clear Cerise blamed the Church for his disappearance or at least for losing track of him.

"Maybe they lost him," Harley said. "Or I don't know, maybe he found a way to remove his chip without it alerting the system. None of this means there's rampant corruption in our ranks. It means mistakes happened. Tragic, yes, indicative of slayers gone bad, no."

Cerise turned away, rubbing her temples.

Harley sighed, then continued, "Look, I'm not convinced he's dead, either. Lars is tough. If anyone can survive out there without support, he can. Maybe he's somewhere that's blocking the transmission. Deep underground or something. You know, like where you're leading *us*."

"Then, why isn't there an exhaustive manhunt?"

"There was. They didn't find anything."

"I don't believe that."

"Hey, I offered to take our banked vacay time so we could go hunting for him. But nooooo —"

Cerise shook her head. "The trail starts here."

"Kinda a contorted path of reasoning, don't you think?"

"Lars would want me to follow my instinct, and my instinct says something is wrong. Very wrong. If we can figure out what, we can prepare for what might await us in Colorado."

Harley sighed. She knew the sting of despair, and the balm of a friend's strength. If Germaine hadn't been there for her so long ago, where would she be?

*Probably at the bughouse flicking lint at the walls. One of the lost. The straight-jacketed. Pitiful and forgotten.*

That's where society hid people who saw things that, supposedly, "weren't there." Ha. As if humans had the right to contain the universe in safe, neat theories.

Despite Harley's bloody baptism into the world of monsters,

at least she knew her parents' fate. Cerise had no such closure with Lars. It must have been driving her nuts. No matter where the adventure led, she'd support Cerise because that was what slayers did. That's what friends did. Even if it got them in trouble. Germaine would eventually understand.

*He'll probably cut me off from those lovely chocolates for a while, though. Damn.*

Harley inhaled a resigned breath, flanked her partner, slid her .45 Smith & Wesson out of its holster, and chambered a round. It didn't take magic bullets to kill a were, only a shit ton of damage to major organs, with the heart and brain being prime targets. Still, she erred on the side of overkill and laced her hollow points with silver, anyway.

Cerise raised her eyebrows and glanced down at the pistol. "That's not your tranq gun."

"If this *is* the start of a pride, I'm sending them to hell, not to take a damned cat nap."

"The Powers That Be won't be happy, and I don't think batting your baby blues will get us off their skewering stick this time."

"We've given the white coats enough weres to play with; they don't need more." Harley didn't want to give any weres, puma or otherwise, to the white coats—scientists hired by the Church to create a drug to reverse the turning process. They were also working on an antiviral cure that could be secretly released to the public and provide immunity to the were virus. Noble as their cause may be, Harley would rather kill the weres and let the white coats study their corpses instead of snarling beasts. It was safer for everyone. "Besides, blood is blood. Whether they syphon it from a fresh corpse or a live subject, it's the same damned thing."

"Brought this, too." Harley patted the matte black Vamp Buster grenade, complete with an outline of a silver fang to distinguish it from the other grenades that graced her hip.

"Those are for vampires. We're dealing with weres."

"I consider them more of a multi-purpose tool. The Swiss Army knife of the grenade world."

Cerise shook her head. "The latest kill is two days old. Niko and his pride are gone."

"He was never here." Harley took a deft stride over a knot of leg bones and stepped in front of Cerise, taking point. She'd see her partner through this mess, but that didn't mean she'd cater to insanity. "Nothing breaks out of our sanctuaries. Ever. These are new kitties. They're inexperienced, sloppy. Niko would stay under even *your* radar, like he did before."

"Just because he's loose," Cerise quickened her pace to reach Harley's side, "doesn't mean he broke out. And this time it feels different. As if he doesn't want to hide. As if he wants us to find him."

Harley gritted her teeth. "Start one more sentence today with 'Just because' and I'll give you a nose full of muzzle."

"Always the threats, never the nose job." Cerise examined her nose with her fingertips and frowned. "Could use one, too. I got my dad's nose, Lars got Mom's. How unfair is that?"

"We should call for backup."

"I didn't see any fresh kills. They've abandoned this lair. We're safe."

Harley poked her torch ahead and pressed her back against the damp, cool wall of the cave. To her right was a tunnel that ran straight for a few feet, narrowed, then bent into a sharp left turn. There, the ceiling sloped down in a claustrophobic pinch.

"Tennessee. Spelunkers' paradise. Yay," she muttered. "Why would anyone willingly traipse into caves for kicks? Mystifying. Tons of rock looming overhead, waiting to crush bone and flesh into tiny blobs. Everlasting darkness. Desolation. Yeah, no. I'd rather be cruising around Disney World. Almost."

"It's Mickey, isn't it?"

"Creepy ass talking mouse freaks me out."

"This is a perfect layover spot for Niko." Cerise tiptoed through the bones. She hadn't drawn her pistol or tranq gun. Harley would have settled for either, as long as it did damage. "Lots of places to hide, gather his strength, and more pumas."

Irritated at her partner's fixation with the impossible, Harley glowered at her. "Weapon. Now."

"They're not here." Cerise strode into the tunnel. "Let's get this sweep over with so we can start tracking. I want proof before we send word to the other slayers."

Maybe she was right about the werepumas abandoning the cave. Pumas were territorial creatures. They would have attacked before she and Cerise got anywhere near the entrance. They wouldn't tolerate trespassers, particularly not on their feeding grounds. If they'd abandoned this lair, and she called in backup, she'd never hear the end of the teasing.

Cerise's words floated across her mind in an ominous warning, *"There are exceptions."*

"Fine." Harley followed her partner down the tunnel. Though Cerise and common sense told her that, besides the dead, the place was empty, she didn't holster her pistol. What Germaine called her God-given instinct, and she called her "ping," hummed in her head. "I'll still take safe over rational any day."

Bending her knees, she crouch-walked through the narrow curve. Strands of her hair brushed against the ceiling, tugging lightly on the gritty surface.

*Probably spiders, mites, and all sorts of shit down here. Rats. Maybe rats.*

She didn't mind normal arachnids or insects. Some of them were even cute. There was nothing cute about beady-eyed, scaly tailed rats.

*Rats don't live in caves. Do they?*

"Seems it opens up farther ahead," Cerise said.

"It better." The last thing she wanted was to worm her way through more itty-bitty, soul-crushing tunnels. "Watch it," she ducked her head forward as the ceiling clenched lower, "openings are juicy ambush spots."

Cerise chuckled. "Remind me to talk to Germaine about getting you some anti-paranoia meds."

"Funny." The only thing Harley needed, other than getting back to the great wide-open, was a bottle or two of stiff rum. Spiced and dark. On the rocks. Her shoulder scraped on the unforgiving tunnel wall.

*Nix the rocks. Neat. Definitely neat.*

"I'm out." Cerise's voice echoed.

"Next time you get the hankering to go off turf," Harley squirmed her way through the last few feet of the narrow tunnel, "we go to Hawaii or something. Capture some merfolk. Maybe a megalodon. Some place with lots of alcohol and cabana boys in thongs. They can feed us grapes after a successful hunt."

"Didn't think you were into umbrella drinks."

"They can fan me with palms just as easily if I'm sipping a coconut filled with rum as some sugary slosh." The word slosh echoed and faded as Harley slid out of the tunnel into a vast cavern. "Eh, roomy."

"What do you say to a quick walk-though and call it done?" Cerise tried to brush the cave grime off her tan pants but only smeared it into the fabric. Giving up on her primping, she shuffled forward a few steps, mindful of the glassy pools of water that dotted the low spots of the uneven floor.

Harley lifted her torch to decipher the cavern's size. The darkness swallowed the light outside of the small circle that radiated a few feet around her. Endless black spanned above her in a starless, foreign sky. The only visible location markers were the walls that stretched out to either side, but the dark gobbled them up, too.

"I don't like these walls. We are in so much shit." Harley stepped closer to the rough, water-hewn wall, searching for scratch marks.

"Since when are you a cave critic?" Cerise turned full circle. Her torch held at arm's length as she strained to see in the meager glow.

"Looks to have ledges." Harley ran her fingers across the cragged stone. It was easily climbable, especially for a werepuma. She gripped her pistol, slid her finger on the trigger, and pointed the muzzle at the ledge, staring down the sight. If she saw the slightest hint of movement, she'd drain the clip so fast the lead would touch end to end as it left the barrel, blasting anything in its way.

Cerise's chuckle echoed through the cavern. "Come on."

"Yeah." Harley clomped through the puddles to Cerise. This place was wrong on a level that didn't involve the threat of crushing stone or even rats. They needed to get out. Yesterday. "Quickie sweep and we're out of here." But as the words crossed her tongue, they tasted of a lie. She had a queasy feeling getting out wouldn't be as simple as getting in.

*So should have called for backup.*

"Keep the circles touching." Cerise motioned with her free hand. "We'll keep that wall within sight as a guide. I wouldn't want to get lost in here."

"What, you don't want to play Marco Polo with me? That hurts."

*And whatever else might lurk in here.*

Harley kept the light of her torch slightly overlapping Cerise's as they moved forward. It increased their visibility range, but not by much. The flashlight's weight tugged at Harley's hip. She could use it. It'd cut better through the dark, or maybe a dark this deep would devour even the high-powered flashlight.

*That'd be freaky.*

She debated keeping two weapons, the torch and her .45, or opting for one weapon and more light. After a brief hesitation, she left the flashlight in her belt loop.

*When in doubt, use disproportionate force.*

And she was in serious doubt. With each step into the cavern, her senses pinged louder, sending electric jolts through her veins. Something was out there. Silent. Watching. Waiting.

*Go ahead, I'm ready, you pervy felines.*

But they had to be gone, right? Could be a horde of hungry rats, though, feasting on the leftovers.

*Shouldn't have watched* Willard. *Evil rat movie.*

"You can play that with Max tonight." Cerise flashed a lecherous grin.

*Ugh. Max.*

If she missed yet another date, he'd be beyond angry.

"Is he still mad at you for missing the cruise?" Cerise asked.

She shrugged. "He wasn't amused that I'd choose to wrangle a PR nightmare instead of spending a romantic weekend in the Keys." Of course, the PR bit was a lie. She couldn't tell him what she'd really been doing. He'd believed her fabricated cover story, but he'd think the truth was a lie or that she was insane. Cute as he was, his ordered, lawyerly brain couldn't reconcile her world.

*Ping. Ping. Ping.*

A movement flitted at the corner of her eye.

She pivoted, swiping the torch at the wall.

Nothing.

"It wasn't your fault." Cerise slowed her pace to meet Harley's. "When imps slip out of hell's gates on our watch, who else are they going to call?"

"Ghostbusters?"

"Yeah." Cerise chuckled. "Not sure their vacuum hoses could withstand the onslaught of imp teeth and claws."

An icy chill ran down Harley's spine. The hair on her neck prickled. Tiny icicles raced across her skin.

"Hold on." Harley took a few cautious steps forward, closer to the wall. There in the flames' flickering light, a bump protruded from the cavern floor. Whatever it was, the torchlight glimmered off its surface. It was motionless and wet.

"What is it?" Cerise closed the distance between them.

"Don't know." Harley walked closer, keeping her torch low to illuminate the floor. At her peripheral, she could see that Cerise's light continued to overlap with hers. Cerise might not take situations as seriously as she should, but she never neglected one of the top rules drilled into their heads during training, never split up.

She edged closer. Slashes of white jutted out from the wet lump of red.

*Ping. Ping. Ping.*

The bump's ragged top line trailed down to a skinless neck and a head, long blond hair matted with chunks of flesh splayed across the floor.

Harley froze. Her throat constricted.

The bump, partially hidden in a shallow puddle, was the half-eaten corpse of a woman.

*Half-eaten. They're still here.*

"Houston..."

"What did you find?"

Flakes of stone skittered off the cavern wall and fell like grainy snow on Harley's shoulders.

"We're in deep shit."

~

"I DON'T SEE why you can't do this without me." Father Francis gripped the oak rail so hard the flesh under his fingernails paled.

He stared down the concrete steps flanked by thick stone walls. It reminded him of the gaping gullet of a hungry beast. Down there beyond the stairwell, *they* waited. His collar felt tight, as if the fabric were shrinking, choking him. With his free hand, he stuck his finger under the black and white collar, pulling it away from his sweat slicked neck.

"Only you," Ian said, "and your slayers have the access codes, remember? You haven't been giving them out to others, have you?"

"Of course not." Technically, Cardinal Germaine possessed a master code he could give his inspectors, but Francis didn't correct Ian. He didn't like Slayer Ian any more than he liked the creatures that lurked below. It was something about Ian's eyes, a darkness that slithered below the surface, flitting into view only to disappear as if it never were, leaving you to wonder if you'd seen it at all.

"We gave you ample notice of this inspection, Father."

"Yes, well..." Frances let his words trail off. That vexing man would accept no excuses.

Harley and Cerise, the slayers assigned to his church, usually managed the inspections and opening the doors for the feeding and cleaning crews. They watched over the activities, ensuring no one was hurt, and above all, that nothing escaped. Francis hadn't ventured there since his third day as the Pastor of St. Ambrose, and he had no desire to go there now. While other sanctuary priests found honor and purpose in guarding the innocents from the vicious creatures locked in cells under their churches, Francis found no joy in his duty, only fear and misery. He'd never aspired to be a sanctuary priest and had requested several transfers, but once a sanctuary priest, always a sanctuary priest.

*Until death.*

He shuddered.

*How many of my brethren have died at the claws of their wards?*

Surely, there'd been a few. Tight as their protocols were, mistakes happened. When dealing with beasts who knew only destruction and death, those mistakes were often fatal.

"Be thankful in your prayers tonight," Ian said, "that you don't have to deal with these abominations out in the wild." He leaned forward, looming so close the priest felt squashed between the lethal slayer and the dank stairwell that led down, way down to where the beasts lived.

"They can sense fear, you know," Ian said. It would have seemed a statement of fact if Ian's voice wasn't so low and whispery. "Fear is death."

Francis's clammy palm slid across the rail, and he forced himself down a few stairs.

*Ian wouldn't bully Harley this way.*

Harley often teased Francis about his fears, valid fears, but her teasing was always in jovial humor. Ian was someone he wished Harley was here to deal with. Not him.

Ian stalked close behind, keeping only one stair between them, his muscled body blocking Francis's escape route to the sacristy. To safety.

The closer Francis got to the solid steel door at the bottom, the more his hand trembled upon the rail. He attempted to gather the shreds of his courage, but his body refused to obey, reacting on primal instinct that his mind couldn't override.

"According to my records," Ian said, "Harley signs the inspection reports. Where is she?"

*My God, I wish she were here.*

"She and Cerise are in the field." *Two more steps...* "Investigating."

"Interesting," Ian said.

"Why's that? It's what they do, isn't it?" They'd reached the small alcove at the bottom of the stairwell and stood before the impenetrable door. Freshly polished metal gleamed in the dim light, permeating the air with an odor akin to engine oil. His stomach churned. The walls leaned in, threatening to crush him.

"There have been no recent activities in their area."

Francis stiffened. How would Ian know that? Though slayers banded together to combat major threats, each pair patrolled a specific area. Other slayers didn't butt in unless invited.

"I could have heard them wrong," Francis said. "Maybe they're training."

A heavy silence hung for a moment.

"You don't know where your slayers are?" Ian asked. "You are supposed to know their whereabouts at all times. It's protocol."

"I–I'm sure it's written somewhere." It wasn't. He worried about Harley and Cerise. Prayed for them when they were out on missions. He'd love to know where they were in case a situation spiraled out of control, but Harley rarely did things the way they ought to be done, and arguing with her was its own form of torment.

*Utterly futile, as well.*

"You're not a very good liar, Father," Ian whispered.

Francis repressed a shudder.

Ignoring the slayer, he placed his palm against the glass surface of the biometric reader and a green LED blinked on the keypad, backlighting the numeric keys.

*What was that code?*

He'd used it once. Since the Church assigned the codes, the numbers had no innate meaning to him. They weren't anyone's birthday, anniversary, or even the text speech that Harley called "leet."

With a wrinkled, jittering finger, he plugged in what he thought was the right code.

An LED flashed red.

Jiggling around some numbers, he tried again. Red flashed in the dim landing.

"You're going to lock us out," Ian said.

"Ah. I remember." At least, he thought he did. Trying again wouldn't hurt. At worst, the system would swing into lockdown. Then, they'd have to wait for Harley to return, which suited Francis just fine. He entered the code.

Unfortunately, the display scrolled, showing his name, the date, and time. Another LED flashed green.

Thick metal clunked inside the door. There was a series of whirls as the mechanisms disengaged, then the locks released and the seal shicked free.

Ian reached around him and grabbed the door. "Priests first," he said as he pulled the door open.

"You enjoy this entirely too much." Francis hesitated on the threshold, staring down the stone corridor. The last time he'd crossed it, he'd almost died. If it weren't for Harley's quick reflexes, he'd be rotting in the cemetery out back.

*Stuck here forever.*

"Go on," Ian said. "I'm sure your friends miss frightening your cassock off."

It was wrong to hate. Hate was the tool the devil used to divide the people, so Francis refused to hate anyone, even Ian. At that moment, however, he disliked the man with a severe passion.

"You don't have to tolerate it much longer." Ian stepped forward, corralling Francis forward, leaving him no other option than to enter the corridor.

"Does that mean they approved my request? I'm getting transferred?" Francis glanced back at Ian.

The slayer shrugged and gave him a sly, knowing smile.

Francis was a man of peace, prayer, and tranquility, but he sorely wished Harley was there to punch that smile off Ian's face. Knowing he wouldn't get an answer, Francis shuffled down the corridor, his back rigid, hands twitching.

He stopped before the secondary barred steel door, and after a long pause, withdrew the keys from his pocket. They clinked in the silence.

"They're quiet," Ian said. "Too quiet."

"Harley said they've been this way for a few weeks." Francis unlocked the barred door, swung it open, and stepped aside. "Slayers first."

A heavy, brooding storm of silence hung in the sanctuary, as if the creatures knew something they didn't. As if biding their time for the storm front to break loose and...

*And what? There's no way they can escape.*

But hadn't that very scenario plagued his nightmares ever since his assignment to St. Ambrose? Hadn't one of them almost escaped because of his bungling? And hadn't it almost killed him?

Ian strode past him.

Father Francis didn't follow. He stayed on the threshold, hidden from the evil that lurked within the cells.

Ultra-modern versions of dungeons, the sanctuary boasted a line of cells on either side of a wide hallway. Thick metal walls shielded each prisoner from the others. The same metal, a specialized alloy designed to withstand the strength of the beasts, comprised the barred fronts. The slots between the bars were too thin to reach an appendage or claw through. Tested extensively by the Church, the metal was nearly indestructible. The only way to weaken it was with an acid the white coats invented for emergencies. Each sanctuary church kept several vats full, which could be piped into a sprinkler system and released, though Francis was at a loss as to why such a system was necessary. Over history, the Church had spent countless dollars, and its slayers had shed oceans of blood in pursuit of those creatures. Why destroy it?

Ian strolled down the hall, conducting a quick head count, penciling check marks on his paper as if the creatures within the cells were inventory.

*Deadly inventory.*

"Two goblins. A fae. Troll. A wererat." Ian peered closer at a cell to the left and then counted. "Didn't your last inspection show three vampires?" He flipped through the pages on his clipboard. "I don't see a requisition form from the white coats."

"I, uhm, I'm not sure." His stomach flipped. Vampires. Of all the creatures Harley captured, they were the most odious.

"The paperwork says three. I only see two."

"It has to be in there. They can't escape." Francis mopped the beading sweat off his forehead with the cuff of his sleeve.

Ian turned his head, giving Francis a wicked smile. "They can't?"

"W–with all of our precautions and, and..." A vampire, loose in his church? Free to attack his flock? Good God. It couldn't be.

Ian laughed, but Francis sensed more cruelty in it than mirth. "Take it easy, Father. All three are here."

Anger flickered within him. Heat rushed to his face.

*Peace to all. Accept and* love. *Even,* especially, *the difficult ones.*

Except, no. He was pretty sure he hated Ian.

*Lord, forgive me.*

"Stick golem, devil, ghoul." Ian proceeded down the hallway, checking, and counting. Most creatures Harley and Cerise had recently captured were there, except for demons, imps, and other small or wispy beings, like murderous apparitions. They kept those at other sanctuary churches that possessed the supernatural confines to keep them secure. A few times a year, the Church would cull the stock, bringing the white coats fresh test subjects. Or if the sanctuaries became overcrowded, they'd order selective executions.

Finally, Ian reached the end of the hall. "Everything is accounted for."

"It wasn't too long ago when slayers killed these creatures outright," Francis said. "I'm curious. When did the Church decide to keep these things alive? Is the gain worth the risk?"

"Have faith," Ian said. "Cardinal Germaine knows what is best."

"Do you honestly believe we can save them?"

The wererat snarled, breaking the eerie silence.

Francis took a step back, edging into the stairwell landing.

"Possibly." Ian stared into the wererat's cell, his shoulders squared, challenging it.

Keeping weres confined was dangerous. Their energy, their hatred of humanity, and their viciousness grew as weeks passed into months and months into years. Harley told him stories of some weres confined for decades, their minds reduced to feral insanity, their behavior so unpredictable even the white coats eventually put in paperwork to have the beasts put down. Sometimes, Cardinal Germaine approved their requests. Other times, he didn't.

Francis drew a breath then eased it out in a soft humph. "The animal has sway over them. They're more beast than man."

"Yet they serve their purpose in helping formulate cures that one day will grant redemption for others."

"The bloodshed, the potential for escape. Is it worth it?" Francis asked.

"What risk isn't worth taking to save a soul?"

# CHAPTER TWO

Harley didn't bother to brush the damp flakes off her shoulders because things were about to get a lot messier than a case of pseudo dandruff.

"They're on the ledge." Harley backpedaled away from the cavern wall and the partially devoured corpse. There was a soft whisk from behind her as Cerise finally drew her pistol. "When we get to the truck, I'm creating a new rule: no entering strange, dark areas without weapons drawn and ready, period. Because this."

She thrust her torch in front of her and tracked the sight of her .45 along the light's edge, searching for a clear shot. The spit in her mouth evaporated, leaving her tongue as dry as the Atacama Desert.

Five pairs of cold, golden eyes and one pair of green flashed in the light.

*Shoot.*

Her trigger finger twitched. She clamped her jaw and fought the urge to squeeze. Six werepumas with home court advantage vs. two slayers with limited ammo. It didn't take Stephen

Hawking to figure out that every bullet must hit its mark, or they'd be kitty kibble.

*Not today.*

Using the torch as a shield, she backed toward Cerise.

Feline eyes blinked in and out of the darkness, their bodies insubstantial shadows.

*Damn it.*

A soft, menacing growl. A werepuma crouched. Its wicked, curved claws flexed and bit into the flaking stone. Emboldened by their superior numbers, the pumas' innate fear of fire wore thin.

Harley sensed Cerise a few inches away and halted.

"Six." Harley shut her mouth before the rest of her statement trailed out her lips, *That I can see.* Some things didn't need saying, for sanity's sake. "Not enough light for a kill shot."

*What if there's more?*

Harley didn't want to think about the enormous cavern behind them, or the other ledges that might span throughout it, serving as convenient perches to God only knew how many murderous felines.

"We're in a giant puma version of a murder hole," Harley said.

"I hate it when I'm right."

"We'll correct that dangerous habit later." Harley nudged her partner and then glanced to the narrow passageway which led back to the bone-littered room and the exit.

Cerise gave a slight nod.

If they could get back through the tunnel before the pumas totally lost their fear of flames, the narrow tunnel would force the kitties to enter one at a time, swinging the odds in slayer favor. Plinking them off one by one was a safer, more effective use of their ammo than fighting the entire pride in an open cavern. Still, werepumas were cunning. Their lairs boasted at least two entrances, sometimes more. If the other entrances didn't exist naturally, they'd create them to avoid being cornered. Man, she hated smart monsters.

A snarl. Another set of feline eyes lowered as the puma settled into a squat, a hair away from pouncing. She'd prefer not to be standing there when the entire pride leapt on their heads. Their fear of fire may have been waning, but she'd bet they weren't ready to get up close and personal with the flames. She shifted her weight, drew her torch down, and readied for a throw.

In unison, the pumas' gazes flicked between Harley and the torch, trying to preempt the trajectory of her throw.

With the pumas' attention diverted, Cerise launched her torch at the ledge. It arced up, reaching its apex between them and the werepumas. The flames whooshed, and the torch spun in a plummeting circle of fire.

Harley shoved her torch into Cerise's free hand.

Cerise snickered then dashed for the tunnel, lighting the way for Harley, who was the better shot. She jogged backward, keeping her .45 aimed at the pumas.

The torch completed its final flip, and the tawny blurs scattered in a fit of pissed off hisses. Muscles bunched beneath bristling fur as the werepumas leapt from their perch, desperate to avoid the fur-devouring flames.

"Sucks to be flammable, doesn't it?" Harley said.

The torch clattered against the stone, rolled, and came to a tentative rest at the brink of the ledge.

Harley tried to line up a shot, but the pumas were too fast, and the chaotic sputtering of flames cast jarring, distracting shadows. She couldn't get a kill shot. Cussing, she lowered the pistol to chest height and swept it left to right, ready to fire if opportunity presented. Since the pumas lost the ledge, now the attack would come from ground level. She might not have the overwhelming advantage she'd prefer, but they'd climbed a few rungs up on the survival chart.

"Come on," Cerise called.

Harley risked a glance back. Cerise stood in front of the tunnel opening where they'd entered. Now, it was just a short wiggle through the claustrophobic passage, and they'd pluck this pride down by half, one pretty hollow point after another.

"Go." Harley waved Cerise forward so she could get a head start. If she could see Cerise's light, she could find her way.

Cerise shook her head and held the torch up as a guiding light.

*Must chat with her about following orders after this snafu.*

Besides Germaine as the Order's official leader, there was no ranking system amongst slayers, nor was there any dramatic age difference between her and Cerise. Still, most slayers granted some deference to those with more experience. Cerise gave her exactly none, even though Harley had been the youngest slayer ever inducted into the Order, and she'd been training with swords when Cerise had been playing with her first mascara wand.

Angry hisses and furious roars reverberated through the cavern. It might be her imagination, or echoes, but it sure sounded like more than six kitties gathering in the dark.

Harley picked up her pace.

A gloom darker than the cavern's stygian black gathered in the tunnel behind Cerise. The shadow stepped out of the tunnel, towering over Cerise's head. Torch light shone off its broad chest, scintillating over shades of sand and gold fur. Brilliant amber eyes locked on Cerise, their gaze void of fear, hesitation, or emotion. The puma would experience no more remorse killing Cerise than a cat would disemboweling a plump mouse. To weres, humans were just sweet, meaty morsels.

*Bloody and raw, no cooking required.*

"Get down." Harley set sights on the werepuma's heart.

Cerise tilted her head then turned toward the tunnel instead of dropping.

*Yeah, we're so going to have that chat.*

Though significantly smaller than the were, Cerise blocked enough of the creature's body that Harley couldn't take a shot without risk of hitting her. There were areas in the human body that a solid bullet could pass through harmlessly and carry on, hitting another target. Given Cerise's refusal to cooperate twice so far, Harley wasn't incredibly concerned about her partner experiencing some pain.

*It'd serve as a tutorial via lead moment.*

The paperwork she'd have to wade through afterward would be immense. Still, she would have considered it if she'd loaded her.45 with solid rounds, which she hadn't. One benefit of hollow points, besides their innate stopping power, was that they generally stayed inside whatever they hit first, doing massive damage rather than passing through. A benefit in close quarters that eliminated collateral damage, but a severe drawback in this case.

"Cerise. Get d—"

Muzzle fire burst from Cerise's pistol. Shots roared, bouncing from wall to wall through the unknown depths, pummeling Harley's eardrums like a mad, hammer-happy troll.

Harley winced. She'd never opened fire in a cave, but the way things were going, there'd be a hell of a lot more.

*And I didn't bring earplugs.*

The werepuma drew its bulky arm up, curved claws glinted in the torchlight.

"Son of a..." Harley rushed sideways, hoping to get a better shot.

Claws streaked down.

Another flash of muzzle fire.

Cerise tried to pivot, but she'd waited a fraction too long. Her torch jarred out of her hand and clattered to the damp floor. Blood splattered and sizzled, spraying into the flames.

*No, no, no.*

Harley couldn't tell if the blood was Cerise's or the puma's.

*Did she hit it?*

Cerise wobbled and then dropped with a sloshy thud beside the torch.

With a clear line of fire, Harley aimed at the puma's thick chest and squeezed the trigger in lightning procession.

*One, two, three.* Harley tallied the spent bullets. There were few things more frustrating in battle than an empty click that ought to have been a beautiful bang. Guts and gore splattered across the tunnel rim. The werepuma's final scream pierced through her ringing ears. The creature staggered, crumpled against the wall, and slid to the floor, its head hanging limp on its chest.

Behind Harley, a chorus of hisses arose from the pride.

"Cerise, get up." Harley ran toward her.

Cerise stirred. Her pale, blood-soaked hand twitched toward the torch. She tried to grab it; her fingertips overshot and knocked into the handle. It spun from her fingers and rolled into a puddle.

The flames fizzled out.

Darkness descended.

*Crap.*

She couldn't turn on her flashlight until she'd reached Cerise. That would buy them the most time because not even pumas could see in that darkness. They could still hunt by their acute hearing and scents, but she could use the lack of visuals to her advantage. She dropped into a low crouch and duck-walked toward Cerise. Cold water splashed up, soaking her jeans, and chilling her knees and shins. Hopefully, the pumas would assume she'd remained standing and attack using that assumption, leaping over her instead of onto her.

The growls ceased. Smug purrs vibrated through the lightless murk.

*Now, that's all sorts of comforting.*

The pumas thought their dinner was served.

*Yeah, yeah. Try it, shit whiskers.*

"Have I mentioned," Cerise's whisper hardly concealed her pain, "I really, really hate being right?"

"Prove it." Harley made her way to her partner's side, using Cerise's voice as a guide.

"What?" Cerise grunted.

Harley tamped down a rising wave of worry.

"You never said we'd be the main course for hungry kitties today." Harley slipped the heavy flashlight out of its holder.

"Details."

The purring grew closer. The pumas were entirely too pleased with the situation, and Harley felt the irresistible urge to rectify their arrogance by raining some leaded hell on their dinner plans.

"Yeah, well, that's where the devil is." Harley clicked the flashlight on, flooding the spot with a brilliant bluish-white light. It hit their sensitive eyes.

The pumas hissed and retreated. Unlike fire, pumas weren't afraid of the light, so the flashlight would only be effective until their vision adjusted. Then, the attacks would begin.

Harley blinked, acclimating her eyes.

After the haze passed, the first thing she saw was red. Lots and lots of red. It covered the cavern floor, crept along the nooks and crannies, then seeped into the puddles.

Blood. It oozed from the gaping wounds slashed across Cerise's belly.

Harley took a quick glance at her partner's face. Tense, slick with sweat, and vampire pale, Cerise was ready to go shocky.

*Damn.*

"You can only boast being right all the time," Harley tried to engage Cerise in conversation to take her mind off the pain, "if we're downing shots at some backwoods bar tonight."

Cerise's laugh sounded too much like a sob for Harley's taste.

She didn't have time to assess the wound, but Harley had been in enough battles to know what she could fix on site and what was a "get to the hospital, stat" wound. It was the latter with post haste. The only relief was the wounds were from claws, not teeth, and there were no signs of were drool anywhere near open flesh, so it was unlikely Cerise was infected with the were virus.

The whole insta-death via gut wound was a Hollywood invention. In reality, it took more time, and a lot more pain, before the victim faded into the great beyond. But it was still a race against the reaper.

*Not today. Not Cerise.*

"If we're chunks digesting in cat bellies tonight." Harley shrugged off her shirt. Cold, damp air raised the hairs on her arms. At least she'd worn a tank top so she wouldn't be running from weres in just her bra and stretchy jeans like some C class horror flick. "Then I get the joy of reminding you that you can be wrong."

"If we're..." Cerise bit her lip as Harley helped her up into a sitting position, "being di...gested, that means we're dead."

"I'll haunt you." Harley whipped her shirt around Cerise's belly and tugged it tight.

Cerise yelped.

Ignoring her partner's pained gasps, Harley used the arms of the shirt to secure it around Cerise's abdomen. Pain was a small price to pay to keep one's innards where they belonged. She slipped an arm under Cerise and gripped her close. "I'll have eternity to tease you about this. It'll be fun."

"I can't—"

"Up." Harley popped to her feet, bringing Cerise along with her as quick as a nurse ripping off a tacky bandage.

Cerise choked back a scream and slumped heavily against Harley's side. "You coulda gone slow."

"Hear that?" Harley waited a moment for Cerise to listen to the silence.

"Fast works." The steel leaked into Cerise's voice. "I like fast."

"Hold this." Harley pressed the flashlight's butt end into Cerise's hand and held it there until her chilled, blood-slicked fingers gripped it.

"Going to pull a bunny out of your tank top?" The beam bounced erratically on the floor.

The skin across Harley's scalp prickled. A subtle shift of air behind her.

*It's time.*

The faint sound of a ripple lapping against the edge of a puddle.

"Flash to the rear." Harley turned toward the entrance.

"Oh, shit," Cerise groaned.

Feline eyes flickered in the jittery light. The pride had circled around and now six muscular werepumas stood between them and the tunnel. They flexed their claws in anticipation. Drenched from the puddles, the sharp, curved points gleamed.

She could handle a few of them with Cerise down, but six?

*We're gunna die.*

"I got this." Harley backed away, hauling Cerise with her. She yanked the Vamp Buster grenade off her belt, pulling the pin with a smooth whisk of her finger.

"You're not—"

"*Mazel tov.*" Harley tossed the grenade toward the pumas. The metal cylinder hit the ground with a clink and rolled between their paws.

Harley turned her back and squeezed her eyes shut, covering one ear with her free hand, and hunching her shoulder upward to protect the other without loosening her hold on Cerise.

"Seriously?" the Vamp Buster detonated in a horrendous boom, drowning Cerise's voice. Though the rowan wood slivers, which caused excruciating pain to vampires, would be wasted on the weres the bright light would temporarily blind them and the explosion would put them off balance enough to even the odds for a while.

Harley tugged the flashlight from Cerise's hand and swept the beam over the area, assessing the new situation. Even with their golden fur smoldering and their senses stunned, the weres stumbled toward them.

"Well, aren't we ambitious?"

"Thank God we're not in the Alps," Cerise said.

"Don't want to snowboard with me?"

"We can't make it past them."

She was right. The risk of being bitten was too great, and bitten was worse than dead, and dead sucked enough. In fact, the entire situation was one big wad of suckage.

"Sure, we can." Harley felt Cerise stiffen. "Just not through there."

They hurried deeper into the cavern. If a secondary exit existed, sticking to the wall was the only way they'd find it.

"Over there." Cerise slowed and pointed.

Harley squinted. Ahead of them was a jagged crag in the wall. Wide at its base, it stretched eight feet up, where it narrowed into an ever-slimming crack that disappeared into the darkness where her beam couldn't reach.

Angry growls echoed through the cavern. The Vamp Buster's effects were wearing off.

"There's another ahead." Harley shifted the flashlight beam between the two holes; both were natural and could either lead them to the freedom of the forest or deep into their graves.

"Which is out?"

"Stay put." Harley took Cerise to the first opening and propped her against the wall. "Don't go anywhere."

Cerise narrowed her eyes.

Harley ran to the far tunnel and a few steps in. No light ahead. No nothing. It looked like a tunnel, just like any other tunnel.

"Damn it."

One must be an exit, but which? If she chose the wrong one, they'd die.

"Of all the..." she muttered a litany of cusses. A tunnel that led outside would have a breeze, right? She smelled nothing different there. She licked her finger and held it up, testing if she could feel any wind. Then, she took several deep breaths to memorize the scent, ran back toward the first tunnel, and passed Cerise.

"What are you—"

"Finger test." Harley dashed into the tunnel and filled her nose with the scents. It was almost the same as the other. Fresher? Maybe. Possibly. She wasn't entirely sure. Was that a hint of oak leaves or wishful imagination?

She licked her finger again, evaluating the air. Like the other tunnel, there was no light, no breeze, no sign other than what might be a wisp of outdoor scent, that the tunnel led anywhere near the surface.

"It's this one." Harley jogged to the cavern and slipped her shoulders underneath Cerise's arm, supporting her weight.

"And you know this how?"

"Fresh air." If they were going to die down there, then she'd rather have Cerise die brimming with hope while showering the weres in a rain of brass and lead.

*I can live with that, errrr, die with that. Whatever.*

"A-ha." Cerise leaned heavily on her. Blood soaked through the which Harley had tied around Cerise's waist.

She pulled Cerise against her to keep her steady. Warm blood seeped onto her tank top and pants.

She glowered at the tunnel. *You best be the way, damn it.*

"Don't go growing a beard. Not sure...Max would...appreciate it," Cerise said.

"What?"

"Gandalf."

Growls. Closer now.

"Come on." Harley helped Cerise into the tunnel.

They shuffled through the twists and turns until Harley lost all sense of direction. The only thing she was sure of was they were being followed and the kitties were treading ever closer.

They rounded the nth curve and ran smack into a boulder. Blood smears marred the side.

Harley followed the trail up. The pumas must have dragged victims in through that route, so presumably it led out.

*Or to a gruesome pantry or secondary dining area...*

"There's an opening." Harley set the flashlight down, its beam pointed at the boulder. "At the top. Let's get you through it."

Wherever the opening led, they'd find out soon enough.

"You go." Cerise sagged against the boulder. Blood oozed from her belly and dripped onto her tactical boots. "Give me my pistol. I'll buy you time."

Harley glowered at her. "Fuck you. You talked me into coming to this Godforsaken hole. Now, I'm getting *us* the hell out."

"Someone...has to make it back. Let the others know." Cerise's face gleamed ghostly white, nearly translucent in the bluish light.

"Yup and we will." Harley crouched and grabbed Cerise's legs, using the action to fight the panic that rose like a relentless flood. *You won't die down here. I won't let you.* "Now, quit your damned whining."

Harley hefted her up and pushed her through the opening.

Cerise gasped in pain.

The hair on Harley's neck stood on end. The pumas had caught up.

"Use your flashlight. I'll be right there." Harley pushed on the soles of Cerise's boots, helping her to scramble over to the boulder. "Don't wait. Keep going, I'll catch up."

Cerise yelped. Good. She'd made it to the other side.

"Lost your ball of yarn?" Harley pivoted and dropped to one knee, raising the pistol's muzzle in a fluid motion.

A tan blur flew from the dark. The were leapt, its golden belly stretched over her head.

She took aim at its muscled chest and fired.

*Four. Five.*

She pushed off, rolled beneath the were's rear paws, and came up in a crouch behind it. The were slammed into the boulder and slumped, twitching, on the tunnel floor. Prodding it with the toe of her boot, she checked for any indications of retaliation.

There were none.

Another were down, more headed her way and only five rounds left in her magazine.

A spitting hiss from behind.

Harley whirled.

Claws swiped at her face.

She leaned backward, narrowly avoiding a lethal blow.

"Son of a bitch." She bowed her head, bent her knees, thrust the Smith & Wesson's muzzle up, jammed it under the were's chin, and pulled the trigger.

*Six.*

The shot echoed down the tunnel, and the bullet knocked the were back and splattered a motley mix of its blood, brains, and skull across the wall. It weaved on its feet.

Harley shimmied to the side to avoid being squashed by its death throes.

The were lost its balance and thumped to the ground next to its companion.

"Duck," Cerise yelled.

Harley dropped, catching herself on her toes and fingers, hovering inches from the musty floor.

Gunfire blasted over her, hitting a skulking werepuma square in the chest and head.

"Nice." Harley popped up and scrambled to the boulder. "See, I ducked, like my partner said. Why didn't you go, like *your* partner said?"

"Scared of the dark?" Cerise offered a wan smile. "That and I remembered this." She waggled a small package with a tiny timer.

"Brilliant." Harley climbed up the boulder, snatched the mini explosive, and wedged it into a crack at the top of the tunnel. "Let's get the hell out of subterranean Dodge."

She set the electronic timer and skidded down the side of the boulder.

"Ten...nine..." She grabbed Cerise and half dragged, half carried her away. "Eight... Seven..."

"Why must you do that?" Cerise held her belly tight, trying to keep her guts inside.

"Four...Got my ammo...Three...count in my...Two... head."

Even when they were safely out of the blast's range, she didn't slow her pace.

"One." Cerise finished the count.

A deafening boom roared through the trembling tunnel. A hot puff of air blew past them, dust churned and eddied, rock chips plinked on their backs and thighs.

Coughing and hacking, they shuffle-ran through the tunnel.

With each step, Cerise grew heavier and her feet dragged.

"Could carry you," Harley said, "we'd go faster."

"Hear that?" Cerise's voice was raspy. Weak.

Harley strained to listen.

Soft huffs behind them.

"Shit. Some of the pumas must have slinked out before the explosive went off." Harley looked over her shoulder, twisting to pull the flashlight beam into the pitch. Glowing eyes. All amber.

*Where is the green-eyed puma?*

"There's hope," Cerise said.

"Not from the view back here."

"Ahead. Smell that?"

Harley doubled her efforts and concentrated on moving forward. Sure enough, the crisp scent of pine, oak, and humus whirled in a breeze.

"Light." Harley barely slowed. She reached down, swooping Cerise up into a carry.

Cerise cried out, clutching her stomach.

"Sorry," Harley didn't look down at her partner, afraid of what she might see in Cerise's face, "this *is* faster."

Cerise groaned.

*Plop. Plop.*

Blood splattered freely on Harley's boots.

"Hold on. We're almost there."

"Follow...these assholes...to Niko. Kill them. With...or without me." Cerise's words slurred.

Now wasn't the time to correct her. A pride existed. Yeah, they'd proven that way beyond doubt. That Niko had escaped? They weren't even close to proving that. Harley promised, nonetheless.

"We will." Harley stumbled into the fading light of the forest. Birds chirped and sang, sneaking in their songs before nightfall, unaware of the furry danger charging from below.

"Find Lars." Cerise's head dropped onto Harley's shoulder. "He'll help you."

"We'll find him together." Harley gently set Cerise down.

Cerise wobbled and swayed.

Harley kept a grip on her, helping to stabilize her balance. Slowly, she let go of her partner and snagged one of her green grenades. If Lars was dead, they were both going to meet him soon if she didn't stop the pumas from following.

"Promise." Cerise touched Harley's face. Her strength waning, her bloody fingertips slipped, leaving a blood trail from Harley's cheekbone down to her jaw.

"Yeah, promise. And you'll be with me, damn it." Harley yanked the pin out of the grenade. "*Mazel tov.*"

She lobbed the grenade into the tunnel then whirled. Grabbing Cerise, the two jogged fast as they could to shelter before it exploded.

With an oomph, Cerise's legs went out, her knees buckled, and she nearly slipped from Harley's grip.

Harley tripped over Cerise's feet, stumbled and they fell.

*Boom.*

The ground vibrated. Dirt and rock spewed from the tunnel in a roiling, noxious cloud. Harley rolled on top of Cerise, shielding her from the brunt of the debris. Stones pelted her back and scraped across her arms and legs. She tucked her head down.

Too late.

A stone crashed into her head. Stars flashed in her vision. Wet warmth flowed down her face, and darkness threatened to overtake her.

Cerise's elbow jabbed weakly into her ribs. "Ele...phant..."

Harley rolled off her and carefully prodded her head with her fingertips. Yup. Blood. A rising bump. The skin on her temple curled back and in a jagged tear. Harley's stomach churned.

"What is it you...always call me?" Cerise tried to sit up then sobbed and plopped onto the ground.

"A ninny." Harley fought through the dizziness and struggled into a crouch. She helped Cerise to her feet and stared into the forest. "Where the hell are we and where is my truck?"

"That way." Cerise pointed for a fraction of a second. Then, her hand fell limp to her side. "You are directionally...impaired."

"It's unnatural to have a built-in compass." Harley twined her arm around Cerise and headed in the direction she'd pointed. At least the forest offered a better chance of survival than the squishy, dingy caverns.

They trudged on. Thick ferns lashed their legs, and low-growing vines hooked their ankles. Dry, sun-deprived branches scratched their arms and snared their hair.

Harley tromped through it all, bearing most of Cerise's weight upon her shoulders. A spot of blue peered through the leaves. "Not much farther."

"I could go on for...miles. You're the slow one."

"Uh-huh." She hauled Cerise to the passenger's side of her Tahoe and settled her into the seat. Sweat poured down Cerise's pale face, and her arm flopped across her stomach. "You're not allowed to die in my truck." She pulled the seatbelt around Cerise and snapped it in place."Behind...trees...coming."

Harley hit the rear release button on the fob, tossed the keys in Cerise's lap, and slammed the door shut. She dashed to the trunk, yanked the back door open, and grabbed her beloved machine gun.

"Because it pays to be prepared." Harley released the safety. "Lock down."

As soon as she pushed the door closed, the locks clunked into place. At least Cerise listened this time.

Harley drew a deep breath and let it out in a slow whoosh, emptying her body of anger, of rage, of everything other than survival.

"Here, kitty, kitty."

Tree limbs shook under the werepumas' weight, dislodging a spate of falling leaves. Like fanged golden leeches, the pumas hung from the branches and trunks, snarling down at her. Among them, clinging to a pine toward the rear of the group, was the green-eyed puma.

"This mouse bites back." She winked at Green Eyes and raised the machine gun's muzzle. They didn't look scared. They should have been. Then again, they didn't know what surprises she'd loaded for them.

Two pumas leapt closer, one on either side, attempting to flank her.

"Merry fucking Christmas." Harley lit it up. Rapid fire clattered through the forest. Bullets hit puma flesh, ripping and rending through their hides, sprinkling the bark with blood and chunks of gore.

The pumas screeched and clawed at their bodies where the bullets had penetrated, their claws gouging their own muscles, tearing them into jagged strips.

One by one, the werepumas on the front line fell onto the soft padding of decaying leaves writhing in a mass of muscled agony.

Green Eyes yowled and sprang back.

The others hissed in anger but followed its lead.

"Aw. Tired of your presents so soon? They were custom made just for you." Harley strode forward and released another barrage of death.

The pumas retreated farther and farther until they were out of her sight and out of her range. It'd be easiest to track them and put them all out of the world's misery now, but doing so would cost precious time that Cerise didn't have.

"That's right. Run, kitties. Run. We'll play again later." She waited. Listened. In the absence of gunfire, the forest fell into a hushed quiet. She drew a breath of smoke-tinged air and knocked on the Tahoe's rear hatch. It clicked open.

"What...did Fern put in those bullets?" Cerise asked.

"She didn't say. You'll have to ask her when we restock. And boy howdy, are we restocking for armafuckinggedon. Damned weres." Harley carefully returned the machine gun to its place in the back. "Hang their furs on my wall. Could use a cozy blanket, too."

"Someone...in the Church. Behind this." Cerise slumped against the seat, her dimming eyes searched for Harley's. "Stop them."

"Haven't I made you enough promises today?" Harley smiled at her partner, but it did nothing to lighten her heart. Cerise was dying. Even if Harley could bestow the speed of Hermes on her truck, she wouldn't get her to medical help in time. But damn it, she'd try.

She slammed the window shut, ran to the driver's side, and flung the door open.

"Just one...more..." Cerise struggled to push her hand over the center console toward Harley. Entwined in her bloody fingers was her crucifix, the one Lars had given her upon her entry into the slayer ranks.

"Such demands. Yeah, I promise." Harley slipped her leg into the truck. A branch snapped in the forest.

Cerise's fading eyes widened. "Behind you."

Harley pivoted, dropped into a crouch, and reached for her Smith & Wesson.

Before she could draw the weapon from its holster, a burly werepuma was upon her. Its claws swiped down.

Harley rolled. Claws whisked above her head.

*Cerise.*

She had to force the creature away from her partner, kill it, and then get to a hospital. She rose to her feet and slid the .45 out.

The were turned. Its thick, stubby maw gaped at her, teeth bared as it hissed.

"You're out of lives." Harley lifted the .45.

A series of cracking brush came from the side.

A heavy body crashed into her with the weight and fury of a Mack truck, slamming her against the Tahoe's unforgiving metal. Her finger automatically squeezed the trigger, but her shot went wild. Hot flames of pain ravaged her ribs and arm. Musky werepuma stench invaded her nostrils and churned her stomach.

The puma turned. Its wide hand spread over her neck and closed around it, ripping her off her feet.

Harley gritted her teeth and pulled the .45 up.

But before she could fire, its other paw plowed into the side of her head.

Pain exploded behind her eyes and down her neck. The world darkened and careened out of control. A groan. Hers, though it seemed to have come from some other place and time, somewhere far away.

Shots rang through the woods. Each report sent a jab of brutal pain through her skull.

*How many?*

The paw that clenched her neck abruptly released.

She fell to onto the leaf-strewn ground and crumpled against the tire. Spikes of pain shot through her ribs. Darkness rimmed her vision.

*Cerise?*

A flash of black to the side, then a set of unfamiliar brown eyes blurred out of focus, smearing into blackness.

Not Cerise.

# CHAPTER
# THREE

Ian leaned against the wall. The chill from the cinderblock leaked through his thin jacket to his shoulder and down his arm. He liked the cold. The dark. He was at ease in the windowless room, lit only by the singular beam shining from the flashlight set in the center of the floor. It pointed upward, spot-lighting broken ceiling tiles. Particles of disturbed dust danced in the concentrated beam flowing in lazy pirouettes. Inside this forgotten womb, his prey was shielded from the passage of time. She wouldn't know how long she'd been unconscious: hours, days, weeks. Nor would she have any indication of time. Whether it was day or night. The distortion would add to her confusion, and his delight.

He loved abandoned buildings, like this factory, set in a deserted industrial park amongst others of its kind, each in its own unique state of disrepair. No smoke rose from the tall, black tipped stacks. No semi-trucks rumbled in line loaded with crates filled with parts. No employees punched their timecards or whittled the tedious hours away with work and chatter. Industry's busy sounds had forsaken these walls, but he would bring new, vibrant, violent sounds here.

And death.

He would grant purpose to this place again, if only for a night or two. Everything needed a purpose, didn't it? What others considered an eyesore, he saw as a repurposed playground, where anything was possible, where sins were committed with no eyes other than the angels' to bear witness. They would watch stoically, raising neither hand nor sword to stop him. They'd bless the spirit of his prey as it departed its mortal cage, or they wouldn't. That was their decision to make. Afterward, he would kneel before them and pray. He'd ask for forgiveness, and they would grant it. They understood in times of grave spiritual warfare, warriors must commit heinous deeds to ensure the survival of the soul, of purity in the name of God to save His people from themselves.

They'd chosen Ian for those tasks because he was strong and cunning. He possessed the tenacity to commit the acts required to spare the flock of the Lamb. God instilled within him the joy of the hunt, the senses of the predator, and the ability to harden himself against the pitiful cries of his prey, the enemies of the light. Then, He'd seen fit to bestow upon Ian the willingness to sacrifice bits of his soul and risk perdition for the salvation of his brothers and sisters.

*Selflessness, such a rare gift. Thank you, Father.*

His cell phone rang, disjointed, surreal, in a room with nothing other than predator, prey, and a lone point of light.

"Your Eminence," Ian watched his prey's shadowed face and hoped she'd stir, "I was about to call you."

"Where is Harley?" Cardinal Germaine's ominous tone confirmed what Ian already suspected. He was growing impatient for news.

He'd never understood the cardinal's love for Harley or his

enduring faith in her. Though her accomplishments as a slayer were indisputable, she was a threat to his mission and, therefore, a threat to God's flock. The cardinal should order her elimination, not coddle her. In some ways, Ian knew Harley better than the man who'd raised her. No matter how pure Ian's intentions were in his tough-love approach to bringing those who'd lost their faith back to their shepherd, Harley would never accept it. She'd fight, and the very skills that made her their most valued slayer would become a liability. If allowed to live, she would delay their plans and, possibly, thwart them altogether if she rallied the more soft-souled slayers to her banner to form a resistance. What would the cardinal do then? Would he side with him or Harley?

If he couldn't turn the cardinal against Harley, he'd have to lie about her fate because he didn't intend to bring her back alive. It was yet another minor sin he would pay to save countless souls from hell's fires.

"I found their vehicle—" Ian said.

The cardinal interrupted him, "I didn't send you out there to find her truck. I sent you to find her."

Ian bit back an unwise quip. The cardinal was a powerful man with the ability to demote him, or make him disappear, with no reprisal from the law or the Church. There were other slayers whom the cardinal relied upon, and any of them would eagerly replace him as the cardinal's go-to-man. They'd have no compunction about killing him and ensuring his body never surfaced. Because he found the idea of his own death unappealing, it was best to pander to the cardinal's needs, even if it meant lying.

A whimper from the corner. His prey twitched. She would soon reach consciousness and realize the depth of her unfortunate situation. He'd have to finish the conversation with the cardinal fast. It wouldn't do to sully the cardinal's ears with the sounds of God's dirtier work.

"There was much blood, your Eminence and—"

"From Cerise, not Harley."

"I'm sure you're right, but—"

"So why haven't you located her?"

"It is as we feared," Ian said, even though he couldn't be certain until he'd discussed it with his prey. It was as accurate a statement, as any and logic would support it, if the cardinal pondered the truth of his words.

There were two ways a slayer's chip would cease transmitting. It could be removed and destroyed, messy but doable. Or the signal could be scrambled, possibly blocked, by electronic means. Ian believed it to be a case of the latter. Only one group possessed the capability to block their transmissions, the Cerberus Foundation. Considering the prey he'd captured, Ian had no doubt that Harley was with agents of Cerberus. What he didn't know yet was where or why.

"Explain," the cardinal said.

"I found a third set of prints at the scene, big, a male most likely. It appears he has removed both Harley and Cerise from the forest."

If he thought Cerberus would kill her, Ian would consider it a favor and wouldn't bother searching. However, he suspected Cerberus was aware of his activities. Perhaps they'd even deduced parts of the grand plan. If that was true, they wouldn't kill Harley. Not right away. They'd question her. Ian knew well how much sensitive information people would reveal under duress and pain. He couldn't allow it. He must find Harley before they forced her to divulge information that would hamper the mission. Then, he'd kill her himself and place the blame on Cerberus, negating two threats with one lie.

"So, she is in the enemy's hands," the cardinal whispered, his voice laden with sorrow.

"It would seem." Grit from years of neglect crunched under Ian's feet.

"Use whatever means necessary to find her and return her to me safely." There was a soft click as the cardinal disconnected.

"Oh, we will do just that, won't we, dear?" Ian tucked his phone in its holder and smiled at the cuffed, quivering woman huddled in the dank corner.

Catching her had proven amusing. Cerberus trained its healers in tactics and defense. They weren't as versed in combat as their warriors, but their heightened sense of danger proved most invigorating in a hunt. He'd thought he'd have to circumvent one of their warriors because the enemy rarely ventured out alone. They usually paired healers with formidable warriors, but he'd seen no sign that anyone accompanied her. A shame.

He twisted the chunky silver ring on his finger, wishing he'd had the opportunity to outsmart a Cerberus warrior. It would make the torture more fulfilling if Ian knew her partner was out there in the night, searching for her, stewing in the knowledge he'd failed in his duty even as Ian tormented her, coaxing forth screams from her raw throat.

*Ah, well. Next time.*

Ian released his knife from its sheath and crouched before the woman, exhilarated at the fear in her wide eyes. By night's end, she'd tell him every shred of information he ordered her to and then beg to tell him more. She'd offer everything freely, hoping the pain would end. And it would. Eventually.

"We'll start slow." He slid the wickedly honed edge under the top button of her shirt and flicked his hand, cleanly shearing the button from the thread, revealing unmarked tender flesh. It wouldn't stay that way for long.

She spat. Warm spittle splattered over his face.

He laughed. "Yes, do fight. It'll make it all the sweeter."

# CHAPTER FOUR

It was the kind of hell only those who'd been through it understood. The limbo of the lost. The hell of not knowing. Brahms rubbed his face, barely able to feel his numb cheeks. His brain buzzed with fatigue, and the constant chatter in the safe house blurred into a dull drone. He couldn't follow the conversations if he tried. The only thing he wanted to do was fall into a dreamless sleep and forget.

Though that wouldn't happen any time soon.

Fellow Cerberus agents drifted around the house, moving from the open-planned living room into the kitchen and back again. Laptops took up every available surface and lap. Phones rang. When people caught his eye, they looked at him with compassion or pity.

Brahms didn't know which was worse.

Yet another day passed into night, and he was functioning on several gallons of stiff coffee and sheer stubbornness.

The fate of his partner, Livia, haunted him. Each time he relaxed enough for his eyes to drift shut, her smiling face and the echo of her broken promise floated into his mind, dispelling sleep, but not the growing exhaustion. It'd been three days since her disappearance, and the once quiet safe house had turned into a hive of activity. Fellow Cerberus agents came and went, phones rang, and the secure internet line was in constant use. Every agent and their devices focused on two things: determining where the pride of werepumas had fled and finding Livia.

So far, there'd been no breaks on either front.

Brahms had searched every area between the safe house and town, not just the obvious route Livia would have taken, but also the meandering ways, in case she'd sneaked in some sightseeing. Or accidentally wandered off the grid or broken down. But even with his tracking skills, powerful sense of smell, and understanding of his partner's habits, he'd returned empty handed. Without any hint of Livia. When his fellow agents arrived, they'd searched, too, thinking they'd spot something important that he, in his emotional and tired state, had missed, but they'd returned without answers as well. Perhaps what his grandfather once said was true. That truth reveals itself in its own time, not that of the seeker. So, those who sought, he'd said, must foster patience. Brahms did his best to follow the ways his grandfather taught him, to keep the knowledge he'd passed on burning bright as the sun so one day so when he had children of his own, he could pass that light to them, keeping it kindled through the generations. But when despair threatened to swallow that sun whole, casting him into the forgetfulness of depression, the dark threatened to devour those valuable lessons.

Unable to tolerate the slightly ordered chaos that filled the living room and kitchen, Brahms slipped into the dim bedroom, where Cree and her partner, Thayer, were tending the wounded slayer. As he entered, the scent of orange, lavender, cloves, and basil wrapped around him, easing the tension from his weary head.

He could sleep in there.

Swathed in the soothing scents of Cree's herbs and muted light. There was an overstuffed chair in the corner that looked awfully tempting. Unfortunately, he didn't trust himself alone with the slayer. She could lead them to Livia. She had to. He wanted to shake the slayer awake. Get her to tell him where his partner was. Yet Cree insisted on letting the slayer rest until she awoke naturally. It was a waste of time that could mean the difference between life and death for Livia.

Cree held her hands over Harley's ribs and quietly chanted. Petite with a serene face and a wild mass of mahogany hair that she attempted to tame with colorful ribbons that sometimes matched and other times clashed with her bright clothing. She was Cerberus's best healer in the area. She and Thayer were the first agents that Fain, the head of the Cerberus Foundation, sent after Brahms contacted him about Livia's disappearance and the slayers he'd found in the forest.

Fain had ordered Cree to bring the slayer back to health so they could gather more information. Fain's wording had been clear on that point and vague during the rest of the conversation, particularly when Brahms asked questions about what he planned to do next. Brahms suspected he wanted something else from the slayer, something beyond information.

*More mysteries.*

"Still no word?" Thayer asked. Dark-haired, tall, and stoic he possessed a professional air more befitting a suit and tie than jeans and T-shirt. If it wasn't for his thick chest and uncanny grace, like the great cats, Thayer could be mistaken for a vacationing businessman. In a way he was. He manipulated stocks with such accuracy that some Cerberus agents thought he tapped into black magic to make his predictions. Those rumors had no basis. Most people simply didn't bother to look past Thayer's brooding personality and fiery moments of temper to see the honor deep within. Brahms would have staunched the whispers and sideways glances if he weren't sure, for undisclosed reasons, Thayer wanted distance between himself and the others. Brahms respected him too much to tear down the barrier he'd chosen to build. A seed required time to germinate. When Thayer was ready, he'd act.

"Nothing." Brahms shook his head and stared at his cell phone's screen, willing it to ring and show Livia's goofy picture of her making a peace sign while sticking her tongue out. He'd called her and left messages, which he rarely did. Unlike Thayer, he didn't care for technology, gadgets, or things that removed the human aspects from communication. He preferred to talk to people in person. Or at the very least, talk to them over the phone. Not to some digitized recording.

The last day he'd seen her, Livia promised she wouldn't leave the safe house. Brahms had believed her. Partners were supposed to trust one another. There shouldn't be any reason not to because they were expected to be honest with each other. Yet shortly after he left to investigate the allegations of a werepuma pride, she'd done exactly what she'd promised not to do. She'd headed out to get pizza, of all things. And they only knew that from the note she'd left propped against the toaster. But she'd never made it to the pizzeria, never made it back to the safe house. No Jane Does had turned up in the morgue or hospitals. No one they'd interviewed claimed to have seen her. It was as if she'd walked out the door and vanished into the mists.

"It's not your fault." Thayer leaned against the back wall and crossed his arms. "You told Livia to stay here, where it was safe. She ought to have listened." He skewered a glare at the notoriously rebellious Cree.

"I shouldn't have left her." Brahms sank into a chair. There, deep in the soft cushions, he felt the weariness seep from his bones. He should force himself to sleep. Perhaps within his dreams the spirits would speak and give him a trail to follow. A clue. Something. Anything. "Protecting her was my responsibility."

"She shouldn't have broken her word." Thayer raised a wide hand to stop Brahms from arguing. "You were following Fain's orders. A werepuma pride is a grave threat to people, especially children, anywhere within several miles of their lair. There was no other way to assess the situation without sending you out to investigate. You blend better in a forest than any of us, that's why Fain chose you."

"Still..." Brahms let the words trail off. The hungry maw of guilt gnawed at his stomach.

"You had no other choice," Thayer said. "Woods filled with werepumas was no place for Livia. Her healing skills are powerful, but her fighting skills are abysmal."

Cree grabbed a bundle of basil and shook the leaves as she passed it over Harley's body from her head to her feet. Her soft chant came to a crescendo and then ended in a whisper.

"Besides," Cree said, "if you hadn't gone when you did, this one would be dead."

He glanced at Harley's pallid face, offset by the billow of deep auburn hair that glimmered with a copper sheen. "For all we know, we're spending our energy to save the very person who's been killing our people."

"She was in the forest when Livia disappeared," Cree set the basil on top of a bowl filled with fragrant liquid, "remember? So, she didn't abduct Livia."

"Maybe not Livia, but," Thayer drew his palms over his close-cropped hair, "she is the cardinal's most trusted slayer and the closest thing he could have to a daughter without having sired one himself. If the cardinal is involved in this—"

Brahms interrupted, "He is."

"Then, it's likely Harley is involved, as well," Thayer said. "To what level, we've yet to determine."

Cree tisked. "You both judge too quick."

"Or maybe you're too trusting," Thayer said.

Brahms agreed with Thayer, but he chose the wiser path and didn't voice it. Many Cerberus agents had lost their lives and even more had shed blood or suffered grievous wounds unnecessarily because of the slayers' recent antics. The number of rampaging monsters running loose had surged within the last few months, and the body count, many of whom were mundanes who didn't realize they were causalities in a centuries old war, rose along with it. The Cerberus Foundation had traced the beasts to the Church's sanctuaries. Someone was setting them free, and if it continued, they'd soon live in a world where people again feared the night and the bloodthirsty creatures who lurked within it.

While there was no proof Harley murdered Cerberus agents, her closeness to the cardinal was proof enough she was involved in the release of deadly monsters and attempting to throw the world back into the dark ages. If that happened, Cerberus would be sorely outnumbered and out clawed. Even if they formed a resistance and pooled resources with similar groups, the death toll would be staggering. And if the entire Order of Slayers were involved?

*Then, we're the walking dead.*

"We must tread carefully," Brahms said.

Cree tilted her head. Coiled strands of brown hair and multi-colored ribbons dangled down her shoulder. "How we treat Harley might influence whether the slayers join or oppose us."

"Assuming there're any decisions left in that regard," Thayer said.

"I'm amazed," Cree said, "your negativity hasn't eaten you alive by now."

"Is there any magic you can work to help Livia?" Brahms asked, attempting to derail their banter before it turned hostile.

"She read the signs—" Thayer started.

Cree smacked him on the arm and gave her partner a dark glower of warning.

"You are not to speak of what is mine." Cree's voice was low, ominous.

"If you know something of Livia's fate," Brahms said, "say it."

Cree waggled her finger in Thayer's face. "Don't do this again. I'll tell when the time is right for telling."

"Brahms." Another agent poked her head into the room. "Fain is online. He wants to talk to us. *All* of us," she emphasized and then hesitated long enough to ensure Thayer understood skipping the meeting wasn't an option before she returned to the living room.

"What will you tell him about the slayer?" Brahms asked Cree.

"Her name is Harley. She'll be fine and awake this night." Cree tucked the white sheet under Harley's chin.

"Coherent enough to talk?" Brahms asked.

"Talk? Yes," Cree said. "Give you the answers you seek?" She shrugged. "You'd have to consult with Celeste for that."

Brahms waited until Cree and Thayer were out of the room before reluctantly parting with the soft cushions. Standing there a moment with his eyes closed, he called upon the spirit of the grizzly bear who resided within him. He brought it close enough to the surface to feel its power surge through his veins and muscles. He tapped into its strength, using it to thwart the exhaustion that clouded his mind, and then let it return to its lair within him to rest. Soon, he'd need every ounce of power it had to fight the darkness that threatened to engulf the world.

He found everyone gathered in the living room around the TV, which was connected to a laptop to serve as a giant monitor. On the screen, Fain's shaggy brown hair and angular features distorted into blotches, part of the security software designed by Cerberus to keep prying eyes and ears out of their business. Eavesdroppers wouldn't be able to untangle the mangled video, so Cerberus agents' identities would remain secret. The audio, also irreparably distorted to disguise voices, contained a piggy-back signal only their devices could decrypt. Because those signals fed false information to anyone listening, their enemies were never quite aware of what Cerberus was up to.

"I hear Slayer Harley has vastly improved," Fain said, "thanks to Cree's healing touch."

How did he know? Cree only allowed himself and Thayer into Harley's room, and neither spoke about her condition.

*Celeste.*

Fain's beautiful, if strange, sister. Everyone in Cerberus knew of her and most had met her either over the phone, computer or, rarely, in person. Fain didn't allow her to venture out into the world. He kept her secure in the library, built like a vault, beneath the Cerberus Foundation's main headquarters, protected like a precious jewel.

She seemed to tolerate it, though he couldn't fathom how. A cage, no matter how plush, was still a cage.

"Yes," Brahms said. "The slayer's wounds were severe, but Cree's healing has brought her back."

"Now, on to a matter I believe weighs heavily on your mind," Fain said. "Celeste located Livia, and our recovery team has successfully returned her to headquarters."

"She's alive?" The burden of guilt lifted from Brahms's shoulders. His muscles slackened, and if there'd been an unoccupied seat around, he'd have sagged into it.

"She was..." Fain's voice trailed off and for a second, silence reigned. "She was branded."

Cree lifted her hand to her chest, clutching it tight.

*Branded. No. No. No.*

His partner, dead. Worse than dead. Tortured, raped, branded, and then left out to rot. The killer's message clear with each murder; to him, the victims were little more than trash.

"You're sure?" Thayer asked.

"Unfortunately, yes." Celeste took her place beside her brother. While Fain's image remained distorted, Celeste's came across the connection as clear and real as if she were standing behind a freshly cleaned window, not hundreds of miles away, in front of a computer screen.

She tucked a wayward strand of honey blond hair behind her pale ear. Her spun gold eyes glanced over the room, hesitating for a fraction of a second on Thayer before moving on to the others. Her perpetually placid expression didn't change, and few would have noticed the slight hitch in her gaze.

Thayer's dark eyes narrowed, and he turned on his heel, stalking to the end of the room, as far away from the computer as he could without melting into the drywall.

Cree spared her partner a quick glance before settling her attention back to Celeste.

"Despite this tragedy," Celeste's warm voice drizzled out of the speakers, "it is imperative Slayer Harley regains her health and remains unharmed."

Thayer's back stiffened, and his hands clenched at his sides.

"Her people killed Livia," Brahms said.

Cree whapped his arm, hard. "More listening, less talk."

Celeste chuckled.

"We don't know what Slayer Harley's involvement is yet," Fain said, "if she's involved at all. Until we do, you are to treat her fairly, as a guest of the Cerberus Foundation."

"She's Germaine's most trusted slayer," Brahms said. "How can she not know?"

"Trusted, yes," Celeste's voice was barely audible. Even Thayer turned his head to hear her better, "to capture or kill the beasts, not to release them. I don't believe Harley would—"

"We have no proof she wouldn't," Brahms said. "Besides—"

"I understand your pain," Celeste said, gently, "but punishing the innocent will not bring Livia back. Now, allow me to finish."

"I'm sorry." He lifted his hands in a gesture of submission. If anyone could divine the truth amidst the tangle of lies, it was Celeste. Rumor had it her magic and Fain's talent as a warrior were angelic gifts from their mother's side. Whether there was truth in that, he didn't know, but if he had to imagine what an earthbound angel would appear like, it'd be Celeste. Though Fain was as far from angelic as one could get without joining the dark side. "Forgive me. I'm tired, angry, and shouldn't be talking."

Celeste favored him with a soft smile and then continued, "As much as Cardinal Germaine trusts Harley to complete her tasks as a slayer, I believe it would be nigh impossible for him to convince her to release the very creatures she's sworn to destroy."

"While I will not divulge information within her domain to tell," Celeste said, "I will say she has suffered as each of us has. She is a dutiful slayer and her dedication to her calling is personal. You must trust me when I say any anger cast at her is misplaced. Even so, I have released her file to the three of you." Her gaze rested briefly on Brahms, Cree, and Thayer.

"Then why was she out in the forest meeting with Niko's pride?" Brahms asked. It was a remote possibility the slayers were not only releasing the beasts, but also collaborating with them to fray the fabric of ordered society. It would be an insane alliance doomed to implode, but it was not impossible.

"Slayer Cerise died, did she not?" Celeste asked, softly.

"Dealing with the devil has its consequences."

Celeste's smile was sad, her eyes veiled, unreadable. "Sometimes, the truth is simpler than assumptions."

*She knows why they were there.*

During his years of friendship with Celeste, he realized one indelible truth about her, what the mage knew and what she deigned to tell were often two entirely different things.

"But you can't say she's not involved, as a matter of fact?" Brahms asked.

Celeste's voice lowered, musing to herself as much while replying to him, "Can anyone's heart be truly known by another?"

Thayer muttered under his breath.

Though she couldn't have understood Thayer's words any more than Brahms, Celeste glanced at Thayer, and a brief flicker of hurt broke through her placid expression before she walked silently out of view.

"Harley is our guest." Fain took control of the meeting and the screen returned to its blotchy look. "But that doesn't mean we don't want answers. Do what you can to convince her of our stance without giving too much away. Get what answers you can and then release her."

Brahms nodded. Celeste was usually accurate in her convictions, but this time Brahms felt she was making an error. But arguing with Fain would gain him little more than a reprimand or worse, he'd take Brahms off the mission, and someone else would seek justice for Livia's murder.

"Everyone else," Fain said, "return to your posts and continue with your respective missions. Thayer and Cree, you are to remain with Brahms and follow this through. When we locate the pride, we'll inform you. If anyone finds the werepumas before we can, do not, I repeat, do not approach without proper backup."

"Understood," Cree said.

Fain tapped a button on his keyboard to sever the connection, and the screen went black.

Brahms stewed, shook his fellow agents' hands by rote, and nodded as they offered their condolences before they left.

Within moments, the bustling safe house plummeted into a sullen silence that rang louder than the chatter.

He needed out. Needed the woods. Grass. Air. Anything except the confines of four walls and carpet.

"Slayers killed Livia and," Thayer said, "for some unfathomable reason, Celeste is protecting this one. Why?"

"There is nothing wrong with Celeste's heart." Cree glowered up at him with a wicked glare.

"Except that it is born of ice," Thayer said.

"Some people just don't understand forgiveness," Cree said. "Or necessity. Sacrifice."

Thayer spun on his heel and strode out of the safe house, slamming the door behind him.

Cree stared at the exit for a moment and then turned back to Brahms. "Celeste does as she does and says as she says for reasons. You trusted Fain enough to swear your allegiance. Are you now wavering over a singular death?"

"She was my—"

"And she knew the risks. As do we all."

# CHAPTER FIVE

Pain ricocheted through Harley's skull.

*Hangover. Ugh. Great.*

Her mouth felt dry and tacky. How much had she drunk and with who?

*Max?*

No. Max didn't party. He schmoozed within the aristocratic crowd and haunted ritzy establishments that served wine in crystal goblets worth more than she earned in a month. He wouldn't sully the soles of his Italian leather shoes by entering the type of pubs Harley preferred. The kind that allowed balls out fun. Raunchy jokes. Sarcastic teasing. So, her partying buddy must have been Cerise. She must have hauled Cerise out for a jaunt on the wild side. Lord knew that woman didn't drink enough.

Bolts of pain throbbed within Harley's skull.

*Or maybe Cerise has the right of it. Rum hurts. Ow.*

Foreboding tendrils slithered at the fringes of her thoughts, fear mingled with them. Something felt wrong. Something happened that had nothing to do with tipping back a few too many glasses of rum. Something she ought to remember, but...

*What?*

When had she last–

Vivid green feline eyes surrounded by darkness floated through her memory. Wet claws gleamed, their sharp tips rimmed in torchlight.

*Werepuma.*

"Can you wake her?" A voice trickled through her consciousness. Male. Deep with a strangely soothing cadence. He was a few feet away. He sounded concerned, but Harley didn't recall hearing his voice before. She'd have remembered that warm timber.

*Where am I?*

She forced herself to lie still and pretend she wasn't awake. Could they be weres? Until a were turned into one of its primal forms—either a very large version of its animal counterpart or, the most dangerous form, a hybridization between man and beast—there was no way to tell the difference between were and human without blood tests. Hence, why the Church and the government funded so many blood drives and free immunization clinics to find the weres hidden within human society. She had test kits in her truck, but she had no idea where her Tahoe was or if she could get to it. Plus, she didn't think they'd allow her to go poking at them without a fight. On any other day, she'd be happy to give them a hell of a brawl.

Today? Not so much.

She sensed someone else close to her. It wasn't the man. A scent, cinnamon, mixed with other herbs that she couldn't quite place. Orange? And something that vaguely reminded her of the Italian seasoning mix Cerise added to her spaghetti sauce.

Light footsteps. Movement. Closer. The cinnamon swirled and shifted.

"You won't have to wait much longer," a woman said. Her voice reminded Harley of a breeze through evergreen boughs. Whispery. Soft.

"They know she's missing." Another male. His voice was as deep as the first, but it was rough, a boulder crunching against gravel. He was the farthest from her at about five to six feet away. "We need answers soon."

*Where's my pistol?*

Her hips felt weightless, naked without the belt that housed her grenades and her .45. Anger flicked within her. Harley didn't allow anyone to touch her weapons, not even Cerise. She tamped her rising anger down and remained still. It wasn't time, not yet. She needed a better idea of how many people were there.

"Fain's latest text indicates the Church hasn't raised an alarm about the pride," the first man said. He paced, light on his feet, his steps muffled by what she assumed was carpet, still it gave her a fix on where he was.

"They'll search for her," the second male voice said.

"They can't find her here," the woman said. "Even if they did, Celeste's wards would warn us. I can add some wards if it makes you guys more comfortable."

The second male shifted his position and issued a sound reminiscent of a growl.

"We can't assume," the first man's voice dropped to a near whisper. "Remember, they had Livia for however long. We've no way to know for certain what information they dragged out of her."

There was a ponderous silence.

*Who are these people?*

From the gist of their conversation and concern over the were-puma pride, it was unlikely they were weres. But why were they hiding her and from whom? And how had she gotten here wherever here was?

Assuming no one was doing a silent lurk thing, there were only three people positioned in a rough semicircle to her left with the gravelly voiced man being the furthest. Since cinnamon woman had walked three quarters of a circle around her, the area to her right was open. Harley tried to pierce through the fog that clouded her memories, rummaging for clues. Caves. She'd been mucking around some grimy, Godforsaken caves with Cerise and found bones. Everywhere bones.

"The bigger danger might be here," the second man said. "We all read her file. And she destroyed the pumas' tunnels and part of the forest along with it."

*What file? And where was Cerise?*

There was something she should remember.

*But what?*

"It probably saved her life," the first man said.

*Tunnel. Blood. Lots of blood. Whose?*

The woman said, "She's in no condition to blow anything up for a while."

"If she knows where the werepuma pride might have gone," the first man said, "then we need to talk to her. Now."

"I'm not saying shit to you," Harley said. The words scratched their way up her throat. Her tongue felt thick, clumsy. "Except last rites over your damned carcass, if I'm feeling benevolent."

"Told you she would awaken tonight," the woman said.

Harley opened her eyes. The light in the room, muted as it was, sent firecrackers of pain exploding in her head. She groaned, pressed her palm against her forehead, and clamped her eyes shut, welcoming the blessed dark.

"Don't get up yet," the woman said.

"Seems the only one close to requiring last rites," said the second man, "is you."

"Where's Cerise?" Harley only partially opened her eyes this time, using her lashes as shades.

"Don't mind him," the woman said, "he's not always this rude." The woman smiled, a flash of white teeth against smooth, suntanned skin. "I'm Cree, and the rude lump skulking behind me is Thayer."

Harley glanced past Cree's crazy wad of hair. Thayer blended into the shadows, at once a part of them, yet not. His thick arms crossed over his chest, he nodded but remained silent. She couldn't see his eyes through the swath of shadows but felt his gaze studying her.

The voice from the other side. "I'm Brahms. We already know who you are."

Slowly, to avoid jostling her aching brain, Harley turned her head toward his voice. He was about three inches taller than her; his deep brown skin contrasted with the stark white of his T-shirt. His straight black hair ended at his broad shoulders and his eyes were a rich brown. In another setting, she'd have said he was cute, handsome even. At the pub, she might have offered to buy him a drink. You could tell a lot about a man by what he drank.

They could have gathered her name and other information from her license and the registration in her Tahoe. But what files had they read on her and where had they gotten them? She might have believed Brahms and Thayer were allies of the Order, but not Cree. Harley guessed she walked the druidic path. Harley didn't mind the druid tending her, provided they didn't follow the darker paths, but the Order itself would never officially send or ally with one. Which meant none of them were with the Order. If information on the Order's existence had leaked, she needed to know from where so she could plug it.

But first things first.

"Great," Harley said. "Now that we're all buddy-buddy, where's my partner?"

Brahms and Cree shared a look that rankled Harley's patience. Their hesitation slashed across her nerves, and the last shred of the willpower that held her temper in check snapped.

*Diplomacy be damned.*

"Who the hell are you people? What the hell did you do with my damned weapons? And where. The. *Hell.* Is. Cerise?"

Brahms arched his eyebrows in surprise. "For being raised by the Church, you have a mouth that competes with the New York sewers."

Harley glowered at him. "It was a slayer stronghold, not a convent."

"What's the last thing you remember?" Brahms asked. How did he keep his voice so damned calm?

Her brow furrowed.

*How long have I been here?*

"You're in Tennessee," he prompted.

"I know where I am. Now, answer my questions." Harley desperately wanted to hit him. Heedless of the thin men's T-shirt that barely covered her thighs, she sat up and instantly regretted the swift motion. It felt as if her head was stuck in a giant vice with some maniacal madman wrenching on the lever.

"Easy now." Cree held her hand out, palm facing Harley.

Her stomach threatened to hurl its contents.

*I do not puke.*

At least she didn't in front of strangers. To take her mind off her roiling stomach, she swung her legs off the bed and concentrated on the issues facing her. Like who had undressed her? It had better have been Cree, or she'd have to blacken Brahms's eye in payment for the stolen views.

"You've been here a few days without food or drink," Cree said.

"A few days? How many is a few?" Harley gingerly touched her ribs and chest. They were tender, but not sore.

"The healing is compliments of Cree." Brahms came to the side of the bed to flank the druid. Did he think Harley was going to fall over and he'd conveniently catch her in his arms? To hell with that.

"Here." Cree poured iced water from a sweating glass pitcher into two cups.

Harley's eyes narrowed. Death didn't concern her. If they'd wanted to kill her, they would have done it when she'd been unconscious and unable to retaliate. Because they hadn't, they didn't intend to kill her. Not yet anyway. Brahms said that they wanted information. Plenty of drugs could aid them with that, drugs they could lace into food or drinks.

As if sensing Harley's suspicions, Cree lifted the first cup and took several swigs. Then, she set it down and motioned toward the full glass. "Go slow. The belly has an odd way of reacting when it's suddenly flooded."

Her belly was already threatening a stomach wide revolt, but the rest of her body craved water. Beads of condensation dripped down the glass in teasing streams.

*Shouldn't risk it.*

But her body overrode logic. Her throat was desert dry and her muscles weak from dehydration. She'd need strength, food, and water if she were to find a way out of this. A daunting prospect given her current condition.

*Roll the dice.*

Harley plucked up the cold glass and sipped. The beautifully chilled liquid soothed its way down her parched throat.

By the time she set the half-full glass back down to allow her stomach time to adjust, she felt better and her headache ebbed.

"Once you finish that," Cree nodded to the glass, "I'll fix us some crackers and cheese. You'll feel even better after some food."

Harley's stomach growled. "I'd prefer a big, greasy burger with the works, extra onions, and lots of mustard. Fries. Curly fries." Her stomach twisted, and she grimaced. "Or not."

"I like her," Cree said.

"She's trouble, just like you." Brahms cast a sideward glance at the druid.

Harley did a quick sweep of the room, searching for signs of her weapons or anything nearby that she could fashion into one. Other than the furnishings, a laptop near Thayer, the serving tray, and some bowls filled with fragrant water and herbs, the room was bare.

"Oh, I've yet to define trouble for you." Harley glanced at the two doors. One must lead out to the rest of the house. The other appeared to lead to a bathroom. Maybe the bathroom had a window big enough to wiggle out of. "Now, answer my damned questions. Where is my partner? Where is Cerise?" Was she also somewhere in this house, locked away? Were they keeping them separate on purpose? If so, they'd find out that their notion of strength in numbers was over-rated. She was a slayer. She'd knock the answers out of all three of them if she had to. After she got something to eat.

Cree angled toward Brahms.

A dark expression passed across his face and then vanished.

"First," Brahms said, "you tell us why you were meeting with Niko's pride and where we can find them."

*Niko's pride.*

Cerise had insisted upon the same theory. That the recent disappearances in the remote Tennessee area were the work of a werepuma pride the slayers had vanquished years ago. Had Cerise planted that same idea in Brahms's head? It'd be just like her to recruit more people to her cause.

"Niko," Harley corrected, "and what little remains of his followers are locked away in cages, where they belong."

She'd have preferred Niko's life ended in that last raid on his lair, like so many of her fellow slayers' had. Unfortunately, Ian had insisted on following Germaine's orders right down to the flourished loop of his cursive *T*. So, she and the slayers who'd survived the raid had brought Niko and a handful of his pride in chains to one of the most secure sanctuary churches in the area, where he remained to that day, living, breathing, eating, when many of her friends were gone. Rotting in the ground. Their headstones monuments to the price the slayers paid to protect those unable to protect themselves.

Brahms's eyebrows rose, his brown gaze studying her for a moment. "You weren't there to meet him?"

"Are you insane? What part of what I said was misunderstood?"

Brahms opened his mouth, but Thayer spoke, cutting his friend off, "But, there was a pride of werepuma there?"

Harley nodded and instantly regretted it as sharp pains poked through her brain. "Shit."

Cree slid the cold cup back into Harley's hand. "Drink." Then, she turned to the men and waggled her finger at them. "I'll not have the two of you pushing my patient. Rest is what she needs and what she will get."

"And we need answers," Brahms snapped, "or have you forgotten that?"

"This'll help." Thayer slid a laptop off the table beside him and brought it to Harley. He opened it and hit a button.

The room brightened with light from the screen.

Harley winced and turned her face away from the screen. "Can you lower the wattage on that?"

A few more taps and the screen dimmed to a reasonable level. Then, he turned the computer to face her. There, in full color, Niko prowled behind the thick metal bars of his prison, right where Harley had put him.

Niko and his pride had been under the were virus's influence for so many years that holding a human form was difficult. Therefore, they remained in their hybrid half human, half puma form, as there was no benefit to expending energy to hide their true nature within the confines of their cages.

Muscular and tall, Niko's furry ears nearly brushed the cell's ceiling. Even under the sanctuary's harsh lighting, his golden fur shone in tones of copper, gold, sunny yellows, and dark chocolate browns. He wrinkled his lips back to brandish wicked teeth so stout they could pierce a skull in a single snap of his jaws. Cold amber eyes stared at the camera, promising death.

She wondered if he could sense she was watching.

In the cells beside him, several other werepuma lounged on their cots or paced along with him.

"I told you he was caged." Harley looked away from the screen and swung toward Brahms, ignoring the lightning pain that shot through in her head. "How the hell did you get this footage?"

Brahms pointed to the screen. "Keep watching. Fast forward it."

Gritting her teeth, she hit the button and watched as the weres went through their various activities with the quickness of squirrels on speed. Lord forbid they ever get that fast in real life. No one would survive.

The female in the cell next to Niko leaned on the clear, thick barrier between them, her green gaze filled with a primal longing.

*Green eyes.*

"I don't think so," she muttered. While in human form, the werepuma kept their original human eye color, but once they changed into their hybrid or cat form, their eyes turned a tawny gold akin to that of natural pumas. Rarely did the color deviate much from one puma to another, and green was exceedingly rare. Not unheard of, but...

"Keep watching," Brahms said.

The numbers on the video's time stamp flashed by. A.m. turned into p.m. and then back again. She continued to watch. "I don't see how—"

*Wait.*

There.

*That expression. That movement.*

She'd seen it before. And the next movement and the next. Yet the date stamp changed, reflecting the next day and the changing hours and seconds.

"This footage is looped," she said. "Why?"

"We were hoping you'd tell us," Brahms said, "since it was your people who let them out."

*Cerise.*

Harley hadn't believed her.

*Because it's...it's...*

"Impossible," Harley thrust the laptop back to Thayer. "Why the hell would we let any of those creatures out, let alone Niko? Do you have any idea how many slayers he killed? How many kids his pride ripped to shreds before we were able to take him down? We'd be more likely to assassinate his furry ass, not let him loose."

"Yet someone has," Cree said, softly, "and not just him, others, too."

"What do you mean?" Harley rubbed her temples. Could it be true? She didn't want it to be. But she also didn't want rum to have so many calories, yet it did.

"And someone hunts us, one of yours." Cree's large, mossy green eyes searched Harley's. The woman was either worthy of the Best Actress Award or genuinely aggrieved.

"Do you recognize this?" Brahms shoved a paper in front of her, a photocopy of the slayer's cross, a cross made of two swords surrounded by a circle to signify the unbroken chain of protection, the wall that stood between lambs and the lions. Only it wasn't on a ring, as it ought to be, nor was it embossed. It was seared into skin.

"If you know I'm a slayer," Harley said, "then you already know what it is."

"Whose is it?" Brahms's voice was strained, his muscles tense as if he were ready to explode. She wouldn't mind tussling with him, but right now she didn't feel up to walking to the bathroom let alone dodging blows.

"No clue," Harley said. Every slayer received the cross in one form or another, their preference, after they successfully completed their final tests. Some chose a pendant, others chose rings, and others chose a bracelet. Hers was a chunky men's ring downsized to fit her hand. Harley didn't care for jewelry of any kind, so she kept it in her truck, hidden safely in one of her secret cubbies.

The way the cross was burned into the flesh, however, like a stamp or brand, led her to think it was a ring, a sturdy one like hers. Most women slayers chose daintier rings, but that didn't clear them as suspects. Slayers wouldn't have any trouble getting a hold of a chunky slayer's cross. And even if they weeded the list down to anyone with a ring, that was a lot of slayers. Plus, the slayer might have just been doing their job. It could even be an enemy who'd stolen a slayer's ring and was shifting blame for their crimes on the Order. Because the crosses had been a thing since the Order's inception, the ring could be very, very old, or even a freshly made counterfeit.

"Why would someone do that?" Brahms jabbed his forefinger at the photocopy.

"There are valid reasons for branding," Harley said. "Coupled with the proper rite, the slayer's cross can seal a corpse, rendering it impervious to reanimation from necromancers or possessions by the demonic. Seems to me whoever did this," she stuffed the paper into his hand, "was protecting the body."

He balled the paper in his fist and stalked closer. "There has to be—"

"Thayer," Cree turned to him, "take Brahms for a walk. He needs to work off some energy."

Thayer set the laptop on the nightstand and clamped a hand on Brahms's shoulder. "Allow Cree to work her magic."

For a second, Harley wasn't sure if Brahms would leave. She kind of hoped he wouldn't. She was in the mood for a dirty brawl, even if her body wasn't up for it. He stood there, towering above her, tense and looking ready to lunge. His anger remained a mystery that niggled at her curiosity, but not enough to entice her to play nice. He wasn't the one who'd fought the pride of were-puma in their wretched cave. He wasn't the injured one. He wasn't the one held captive. He wasn't the one who didn't know where their partner was. What right did he have to be angry with *her*?

A large part of his anger seemed to come from the photo. Why he'd have issues with a slayer, or anyone else, preventing a reanimation or possession was mind-boggling.

Brahms grunted, threw the wadded paper to the floor, turned on his heel, and left with Thayer.

Once they were out of the room, Harley looked at Cree, the most rational of the bunch. "Now. Where is my partner?"

Sorrow filled Cree's eyes, and she glanced away. "I'll get you some crackers and a bit of cheese. Then, I'll take you to Cerise."

Something in the way Cree held her shoulders, that sadness and the way she phrased her words sent a shiver of foreboding up Harley's spine.

*Cerise, you best be alive. Please.*

Brahms planted his hands on the cool kitchen counter and took a deep breath to steady his riled emotions. Anger wasn't the path to anything positive, let alone to getting answers out of a stubborn, beautiful woman. But it was imperative to find the person killing Cerberus agents and find where Niko's pride had slunk off to before anyone else died. Thayer had hacked into the Church's computer system, but none of the information they'd gathered was any help. All it'd done is confirm someone was setting the beasts free and the Church was covering it up. Cardinal Germaine was at the top of his short list of suspects because nothing happened in the Order without his approval.

"Why?" Brahms asked. "What would the Order gain by releasing a tide of vicious creatures that would just as easily kill their own slayers as they would anyone else? It makes no sense."

Thayer followed him into the kitchen. "Yet that's what they were doing. It might be someone trying to score more funds for the Order. The more people that're killed, the more invested the church and governments need to be."

"Or they risk blowing all their secrecy. Yeah. I can see that tactic being right up Germaine's alley. Still. Money seems a trite reward for the blood, chaos, and pain the monsters cause."

"Nations have gone to war, bombed entire cities for less."

"True." Brahms pulled his hair back and confined it within an elastic band. Then, there was the Slayer Harley. "She's not what I expected from a woman raised by a cardinal."

He'd read through her files right after the meeting with Fain and Celeste to get a grasp of who they were dealing with. Despite the years she'd spent with Cardinal Germaine in the strict Catholic upbringing of the Order, she hadn't seemed the least bit concerned or insulted by Cree's presence. If she would have been, she'd have said so. Fiery and bold with a mouth that needed a thorough scrubbing with bleach, she obviously didn't fear saying what was on her mind.

She wouldn't lie. Someone who'd face the Order's Tribunal to tell them in no uncertain terms why she'd seen fit to blow up a mausoleum and, accidentally, half a cemetery along with it, wasn't the type to lie. She wasn't pious, certainly thought outside the box, and her multitude of conflicts with the Tribunal comprised a thick portion of her file. The only thicker portion was her successful captures and kills, though they noted her tendency to favor killing instead of capturing needed to be addressed in future training sessions.

He doubted their opinion mattered much to Harley.

"I don't think raised is the right term," Thayer said. "Germaine comes off as more the absentee father figure to me. The slayers of the stronghold raised her. Germaine just dropped by when it was convenient."

"Accounts for her skills," Brahms said. And her legs. Long, muscular legs honed from relentless training. She stirred feelings he'd thought were dead. If they'd ever existed in him at all. The image of her perched on the side of the bed in nothing more than her bra, panties, and his T-shirt brought forth a sudden burst of heat and desire.

If she was this fiery outside of bed, what would she be like in it?

He was no priest. He'd seen his fair share of beautiful women and slept with a few of them, but none had elicited the strong and unwanted desire that flowed through him when he thought of Harley's sharp sea-blue eyes and the rise of her breasts beneath the thin fabric of his shirt.

He shook his head to dislodge her image from his mind. "Cree is being too easy on her."

"Best to talk out here." Thayer pushed through the kitchen door and strode out into the backyard. "She's got uncanny hearing."

"They all do," Brahms said.

As he stepped outside, the brisk night breeze washed over him in a welcome respite from the artificially controlled interior, set at seventy-five degrees, always. He preferred open windows and screen doors, letting the house breathe in tune with the outside. He and Cree had agreed to temporarily give up the natural rhythms of nature in exchange for the extra security of closed windows and locked doors.

Though the secluded safe house sat in the center of a forested fifty-acre parcel, the land immediately around the house was lawn, bare of trees and bushes that'd make convenient hiding spots for someone, or something, to sneak up on the occupants. Dual mesh and chain link fencing surrounded the clearing, allowing them to get a full view of the surrounding forest yet have a barrier of protection.

Not that the fencing would keep anything other than mundane animals out, but it would slow most beasts down.

The true protections were the wards snugged near the fence and throughout the property. They wouldn't keep weres out, but would repel dangers like demons, imps, and other fell beasts. Plus, regardless of what trespassed on the property, the wards would alert the agents within, giving them enough time to mount a defense or escape.

Besides magical protections, the safe house was also equipped with modern scrambling devices that prevented eavesdropping within the perimeter, blocked the tracking of cell phones, and, thankfully, the chips the Order used to track their slayers. Otherwise, all the slayers in the area would have come down on their heads, killing him and his friends, to save Harley.

Harley didn't need saving, but he was beginning to suspect she did need help.

Thayer sat on top of the picnic table and hoisted his feet onto the bench. He stared out into the forest's depths, where the perimeter lights failed to penetrate. Brahms often wondered what his friend saw in the shadows, but he'd never been nosey enough to ask.

"There was no use arguing with Harley," Thayer said. "She'd only get more hostile than she already is, and she was right. We know this answer. Not liking it won't change it."

Brahms took a seat next to Thayer and rested his elbows on his knees, comfortable in the dark, amid the forest. Out in the wilds, everything was simple. Kill or be killed. There were no politics, no hidden agendas, no lies. Staring into nature, one would find the frankest truth, everything died. Perhaps that's why so few people gazed into nature anymore. Instead, they contented themselves with the seemingly immortal world of pixels and code.

Brahms preferred what was real, tangible, over illusions, even comforting ones. He'd rather face Niko's entire pride on his own than attempt to untangle the wadded mess of intrigue that wrapped around the current situation and Harley.

Almost.

The gift he possessed, the spirit of the great grizzly, hadn't been granted to his family for generations. There'd been no need for it to resurface until now. The mighty grizzly awoke within him to fight the current rising darkness. The power to call upon and shift into the shape of the grizzly bear was an honor Brahms refused to disgrace with inaction. He had to fight this evil, to defend the innocent as the grizzly protected its young. For duty, for Cerberus, for everyone.

"Do you believe what she said about sealing the body?" Thayer asked.

"There was no lie in her voice. But I think whoever branded Livia and our people wasn't interested in protecting anyone but themselves."

"No spirit, no witness."

"That's what I'm thinking," Brahms said. "Warded away from their body, the spirits are more inclined to pass on instead of seeking aid or retribution for their murder."

"That would explain why our mediums have failed to contact them."

"Do you think Harley is a part of this?"

Thayer chuckled. "I think she's involved in a lot of things that would singe a nun's habit, but I don't think she's guilty of what we'd thought."

"So Celeste was right?"

Thayer's smile vanished and his face hardened.

"Hey." Brahms turned to him. "Don't take it out on me."

"I think," Thayer rose from the picnic table, "if anyone has a grudge against monsters, it is that slayer."

Thayer strode away, heading toward the far end of the clearing and paced along the fence as if patrolling. Brahms hadn't meant to poke at a sore spot. It just irritated him he'd been wrong. He'd committed the error of assumption, judging a person before he knew the details. She was muddying his thoughts when he needed them clear, leaving him even more irritated he'd left Livia there alone, that she'd lied, that she'd died.

Tonight, he had a litany of irritations, and the tiniest was the self-assured way Celeste hinted she already knew Harley's part in this mad conspiracy and that she wasn't about to share the information.

"Mages." As soon as the words left his mouth, his phone played Celeste's ring tone.

"Brahms," he said, as if he wasn't fully aware of who was calling.

"The pines are not willows," her sweet voice flowed through the mic and wrapped around him, easing his tension, "but they ask you prepare for a journey, nonetheless."

"You are neither shaman nor druid."

Celeste laughed. "Indeed, not. I am much worse."

Then, the line was cut.

"Always the truth, but never straight," Brahms found it difficult to be angry with her because her ways reminded him much of his grandfather's, and that brought solace to his heart. "Let's put your energy to work," he said, motioning for Thayer to follow him out of the fenced area and into the woods.

"Doing what?"

"Gathering dry pine branches." Brahms plugged in the security code to open the side gate. He preferred to burn willows in his spirit fires, or if they weren't handy, ash or rowan wood. But any wood would do, even pine. He liked that Celeste knew his ways and respected them, much like his grandfather had known and respected others. But thank the spirits the two had never met. If they had, he was sure they'd conspire and cause rampant chaos in the lives around them.

"And why do we want to do that?" Thayer followed him out, securing the gate behind him just in case.

Brahms wondered if they'd ever live in a world where they didn't have to worry about locks, wards, or thick walls for safety. But had that once upon a time ever existed? Not that he knew of, but he wished it, nonetheless.

"Celeste kindly informed me to prepare a spirit fire." A rite in which he'd draw upon the powers of the elements—earth, wind, fire, and water—to grant him the strength necessary to prevail during a difficult time or journey. Sometimes, the spirits granted answers or knowledge, as well. Sometimes, they didn't. That Celeste thought a fire was necessary meant the situation was about to deteriorate. Fast.

"She did?" Thayer's dark brow furrowed.

"Yes, in her own unique way."

Thayer grunted, and Brahms knew his friend would question no further. Regardless of the unresolved issues that bristled between them, Thayer would be among the last to question Celeste's visions.

# CHAPTER SIX

*It's a lie.*

Strength sapped out of Harley's legs. She dropped to her knees in front of the bed. Cerise's make-shift coffin. Harley's heart fissured, threatening to crack into a million pieces and scatter to the far ends of the world where she'd never find them.

*A vicious fiction.*

Death masks. Fabrications movie directors used to elicit cheap thrills out of their audiences were a lie, too. Harley knew. She'd seen plenty of death, little of it through peaceful or natural means. And not a single victim's face was ever locked in a state of horror or a scream from beyond the grave, no matter how terrifying their moment of death had been.

No. The truth was worse.

The dead wore the same lack of expression that now sullied Cerise's beautiful features. Utterly slack. All hints of personality stripped away. It left you to wonder if your memories of their smiles, mischievous winks, and delighted laughter had been a cruel joke of the imagination.

"I was supposed to die first, remember?" Harley barely recognized her own voice. With her brash actions, bold plans, and recklessness in battle, Cerise had always told her that Harley would see heaven, or hell, first.

And if life was any sort of fair, that would have been true. But it wasn't.

Someone had changed Cerise out of her bloodstained khakis and peach shirt and dressed her in a frilly pink shirt and cream pants. An outfit Cerise would have chosen for herself if she'd been given the chance. They'd cleaned the blood off Cerise's face and arms and bandaged the gouges on her side to hide them from view, granting her dignity after a violent death. They'd placed her on a neatly made bed with the top sheet folded in a crisp line below her still ribs.

From a distance, it looked as if she was asleep, exhausted after an intense battle. But up close, death could only be mistaken for sleep by those blessed with healthy doses of denial and wishful thinking. Harley had lost those gifts long ago and didn't want them back, for with them came blindness. Death.

*Emptiness.*

Cree set a firm hand on her shoulder and squeezed. "Brahms did what he could."

Surprise filtered through Harley's sorrow.

"He tried to save her," Cree said, "but it was too late. From what I saw and what he described she would have been beyond even my ability to heal."

Harley closed her eyes, trying to block the memory of Cerise's blood dripping onto her boots, pooling on the console of her truck and sliding down in a red river soaked up by the charcoal carpet.

"She is at rest with your God, where she is safe," Cree whispered. "Where she will not suffer the debasement of the were virus. It is not much comfort, but it is something."

Yes. Yes, it was. Cerise was no longer in pain. She lived now in a world without horror, without death, without monsters creeping in the dark, ready to rend flesh or steal the lives of precious loved ones. Where she was, there was no risk of her spirit degrading into that of a beast. If Cerise had been infected, she wouldn't have wanted to live the rest of her life locked in a cell. No. Cerise would have asked Harley to kill her, grant her spirit redemption, peace.

*Could I have?*

She'd done it for other slayers who'd asked for mercy and even some who hadn't asked. Each time, a mountain's worth of weight resisted the pull of her .45's trigger, yet she'd bulldozed through it to send them to St. Peter's gate while they were still human.

*Thou shalt not kill.*

But none of them had been her partner. Could she have gazed into Cerise's eyes and moved that mountain for her? She touched Cerise's lifeless cheek. Yes, she would have given Cerise's spirit its freedom, no matter what the cost to herself.

*I'm so going to hell.*

Cree released her shoulder and then relit one of the three jarred candles that had sputtered out. They'd done their best to make the room and Cerise's body as reverent as possible.

*For strangers.*

Would she and Cerise have done the same if their positions were reversed? With a pang of guilt, she realized they wouldn't have. They'd have walked away and left the mess for the cleaners to tend.

*What do the cleaners do with the dead?*

She didn't know. She'd never asked. She should have.

"Thank you," Harley said, "for what you did for Cerise and me."

"I'll take the thanks for your healing, but other than the change of clothes, Cerise's state is Brahms's design."

Harley's surprise must have showed. Cerise used to tell her she was abysmal at keeping a poker face.

"He's not a bad man," Cree said. "He wants what I believe you want. An end to the killing. But," she scooted a chair up to the bed and took a seat beside Harley, the multitude of pouches on her belt swayed against her hips, "he's frustrated. All of us are. We lose people by the day to these things and to the killer that hunts us. We search and pray and fight and all we've found is that the problem lies somewhere within the Church you serve."

"Cerise suspected that." Harley slipped her hand under Cerise's cold, flaccid hand. Why did the dead always feel so icy, even when the room was warm? Was it because when you touched someone's hand you expected to feel warmth that wasn't there? "She wanted to prove that the pride in the caves was Niko's. That someone within our Order released him and others, too. I..." Harley stared at Cerise's face, the swath of thick lashes upon eyelids that would never open again. "I didn't believe her."

Even with others echoing Cerise's suspicions and the looped video feed to support their theory, she found it difficult to believe. For thousands of years, the Church and their slayers protected the people from the vile creatures who killed without thought, without reason. Why would the Order suddenly want to harm the same people they swore to protect?

"It is painful," Cree said, "to think that which we believed in and put faith in would betray us."

Was that it? Did she not want to see because the Church, Germaine, had been there for her when no one else had been? Who'd believed her, taken her in when others thought she'd lost her mind?

Partially. It was also incomprehensible Germaine would allow the Order to stand aside as the innocent were slain. He took his calling seriously, watched over the Order like a momma bear. He would have known if something as evil as this was going on under his nose. Wouldn't he? If he discovered such treachery in their Order, she'd be the first one he'd call upon to stop it, right?

"Maybe," Harley said. "If it is someone in our Order, then it's a rogue who is exceedingly good at staying under our radar."

"Don't you owe it to Cerise to find out? To discover who set these beasts free and killed her?"

"Yeah. Yeah, I do. I just don't think she was looking in the right direction."

"Did you trust her?"

Harley nodded. A small, sad smile curled on her lips. "Though, she hated being right at the end."

"Then, why would you assume she was wrong?" Cree asked.

The truth in her simple words hit Harley as hard as an ice pick jammed into her heart. Yet she couldn't conceive of it. The slayers didn't turn their backs on their duty, let alone undermine it. They just, they didn't. Couldn't. Wouldn't.

*We are the Sworn.*

Cree gave her a strange look. It seemed the druid wanted to say more on the subject, but she refrained. Instead, she rose, straightened her bright, flowing skirt, and brought the topic back to Brahms.

"Brahms lost his partner today, too. Her name was Livia."

"What?" Harley studied the druid's smooth face. "The were-pumas killed her?"

"No, the one who hunts did. That brand he showed you, that was on Livia's body, as it has been on each of our people that this killer has slain."

*Well, aren't I a dunce?*

That was why he'd been so agitated. So reluctant to believe the slayers had a valid reason for using the brand.

"Where is he?" she asked.

Cree cocked her head, angling it toward the curtained window. "Outside by the fire. Readying himself for the journey before us."

"What journey?" The only trip Harley planned to take was straight to Chicago, straight to Germaine.

*After she buried Cerise.*

"You'll see." Cree headed toward the door. "Despite your initial impression, Harley, we are not the enemy. Tonight is for mourning. Tomorrow for acting. I'll bring you some tea before bed. It'll help you heal."

Harley turned her attention back to her partner's still form, staring at the face that was now so devoid of life she almost didn't recognize it. Maybe the face of death could be associated with a mask, but not one of horror, rather, one of vacancy.

*Cerise is not here.*

"Neither of us is digesting in werepuma bellies, so I guess you weren't completely wrong, which sucks shit nuggets. Could've used something new to tease you about when we meet again." Harley wiped a tear off her cheek. "Cree said tonight is for mourning. She's wrong. There are promises to keep. Lars is out there. I'll find him. The werepuma pride and the enemy are still out there. I'll kill them. All of them. Then, it will be time to mourn."

If Cerise was right this one final time, then the enemy was much closer than she realized. If it was a rogue slayer, Harley had no intention of bringing them back to Germaine for a Tribunal trial. Oh, no. They would face justice in its most brutal form. Her.

*Yeah. I'm definitely going to hell.*

Harley didn't care. There was a cost to everything, and if the price of stopping the madness was her soul, she'd pay it.

# CHAPTER SEVEN

The next morning, Harley awoke tucked in the foreign bed still clad in the borrowed t-shirt. She remembered drinking Cree's tea and nothing else. Not even dreams. Still. She didn't feel groggy.

She wiggled her way into a seated position. Even better, not a single twinge of pain. She ran her fingers down her side to examine her ribs, poking here and prodding there. They were tender, but there were no sharp pains, and her headache was blessedly gone. She wondered if the foul-tasting tea Cree prepared for her last night had anything to do with the improvement and the night of uninterrupted rest.

If so, forcing it down it had been worth the assault on her taste buds.

She looked up, as if she could see past the ceiling, past the roof, and up into heaven itself.

"Told you guys."

When she was little, Harley had seen some strange, unexplainable things her parents had scoffed or snickered at. Like most 'good' parents, they'd taken her aside to explain that primitive beliefs were silly fairytales people clung to out of fear, born of ignorance, to convince simple minds that what was false was true. To teach them to fear what didn't exist. They'd fallen back on the usual trite explanations. The kind that made them feel safe and thus, they'd figured, would do the same for her. The same old excuses that what she'd seen were tricks, illusions her imagination conjured because she was reading the wrong books or watching the wrong movies or hanging out with the wrong crowd. They'd taken her books, filtered the shows she was allowed to watch, and told her teachers she wasn't allowed to check out books with any sort of fairytale lore or magic in them. They picked her friends and, using their network of people from church, always caught her when she snuck out to be with her real friends. Then, they'd told her if she prayed hard enough, she'd see the truth and know she had nothing to be afraid of.

They'd laughed at the legends of weres, too. Said people couldn't possibly turn into beasts. But their words and comforts hadn't stopped those legends from slinking out of the shadows and ripping their throats out on a family camping trip.

She'd warned them. Told them she'd seen shadows prowling the woods. Told them she'd heard unnatural growls. Her parents hadn't believed her.

*As I didn't believe Cerise.*

That night, the mundane world had ended for Harley and another darker world began. At least Harley was alive and would soon rectify her mistake in not believing her partner's instincts. And unlike her parents, she'd know the satisfaction of vengeance. On the plus side, her parents had been killed outright, ripped to bloody ribbons, instead of left to continue the were virus. Becoming the very things that'd attacked them. And Harley didn't have to live her life hunting her own parents.

Some slayers did. Their toll was heavy.

She pushed the covers back and swung out of bed without a single protest from her head or muscles. Good.

*On today's menu, do I have to kick some asses to get out of here or are they going to play nice?*

Last night, Cree had echoed her sentiments about today, that it would be a day of action, as would each one that followed until she'd made good on her promises to Cerise. Harley didn't make idle threats. She also didn't make idle promises.

She'd been in too much pain, emotionally and physically, last night to do much more than maintain her control, such as it was.

*Today, the game's on.*

She found her freshly washed clothes and a new shirt piled on the table next to the bathroom door. Her belt lay coiled on top, minus her weapons. Her phone was beside the pile, plugged into the wall socket, and fully charged.

"Nothing if not thoughtful."

They weren't afraid of the Order locating her through her chip and they didn't seem concerned over her phone, which could also be tracked, albeit not as easily as Cerise's, which was filled with all the latest in stalkware. Because none of them appeared stupid and Thayer showed an aptitude for technology, she guessed they possessed a device that blocked signals. Yet each of them was wearing a cell phone last night. Selective blocking? Was that even possible? It wasn't Harley's area of expertise. She knew firearms and weapons, not electronics.

She picked up the shirt and held it out. It was the perfect size, black, not some obscene eye-searing color, with a subtle scent of lemon grass. Cree's doing, no doubt.

The siren scent of coffee, frying eggs, and bacon filtered into the room, along with the muted whispers of conversation. She leaned toward the door, hoping her growling stomach wouldn't give her eavesdropping away. Last night's dinner of crackers and cheese hadn't eased the hunger from three days without food.

*Going on four. Good God, I need a fat, juicy burger.*

Between the scrapes and sizzles of breakfast in the making, she couldn't hear much of what they were saying. She turned from the door and checked the time on her phone. It was 10:00 a.m. The green light on the corner of her phone blinked incessantly, demanding attention. She wasn't sure she wanted to see the messages in her flooded inboxes, but she plopped onto the bed and checked, anyway. Voicemails, texts, and emails from Germaine, Max, and Francis. She plumped the pillows, kicked back, and listened. Germaine and Fr. Francis's were as expected, a mix of worry edged with frustration. Max's just pissed her off.

A light knock on the door.

"Yeah," Harley said, as she fantasized about her knuckles impacting with Max's perfect teeth. It'd make such a beautiful crunch.

Cree entered, and the scent of cinnamon swirled through the room. "Killing your phone won't make you feel better."

"Men," Harley muttered. "Why, exactly, did I think I could have a normal relationship?"

Cree's face broke into a wide grin, and her green eyes sparkled. "Ah. The elusive normal. There's no such thing. There's only what is and what isn't."

"What Max is is a dick. There's a werepuma pride licking peoples' rib cages clean, a murderer out there using the slayer's cross to make some kind of sick statement, and Cerise is dead. And Max? Max is pissy because I didn't show up for dinner and my absence embarrassed him in front of his precious little friends at the 'let's swing a metal stick and put the little white ball in the hole' club." Harley tossed the phone onto the rumpled bed. "He thinks I'm avoiding him or actively trying to undermine him instead of, you know, almost cuddling with the worms myself."

"Max is your boyfriend?"

Harley snorted. Was he? "He's not even worried." It stung, but not as much as she expected. What did that say about her, about Max? Was she as cold-hearted and closed in relationships as Cerise had said?

"Some men hide tender hearts behind tough exteriors." Cree glanced behind her toward the muted voices that came from the kitchen.

"He's an arrogant ass."

"Aren't they all?" Cree chuckled and then turned to leave. "Breakfast is ready. You wouldn't want to miss out on Thayer's omelets."

As delicious as the scent of eggs and bacon were, the going on four days without a shower feeling bugged her out. Harley couldn't wait to scour the remnants of the werepuma cave off her skin.

"I'll join you in twenty."

IT WAS CLOSER to thirty minutes by the time Harley showered, dressed, and entered the kitchen. Admittedly, she'd tinkered more with her hair using the products Cree had set out for her than she normally did. But that was because...because she'd just avoided death. Yeah. That was reason enough to have nice hair.

*Liar.*

Cree and Brahms sat at the table opposite of each other, glasses filled with orange juice and a pitcher of the same in the center of the table. Thayer shook the frying pan on the burner, and though he didn't turn to acknowledge her presence, she had a feeling he knew she was there.

Brahms's brown gaze tracked her as she moved through the room. It was disconcerting. He'd swept his hair back into a ponytail that accentuated his face. Did she like it? Or did she like his hair loose? Hm. Why choose? Both looked–

*I really need to get away from these people.*

He motioned to the chair between him and Cree. "Feeling better?"

She'd feel a lot less better sitting next to Brahms, but there were only four chairs, and each of the two available was beside him. Had he planned that? Either way, she wasn't about to give him the satisfaction of thinking he made her gut feel as if it were full of nasty fairies. Which he did, but that was beside the point. What he didn't know, he couldn't gloat about.

"Yeah." Harley slid into the seat with as much casual grace as she could manage. She was close enough to him to smell the hint of wood smoke that lingered beneath soap and shampoo in a distracting combination. "How was your bonfire?"

Brahms shifted his interest from her to the lovely, fat glistened bacon on his plate. "More than I expected."

He was going to be vague. Great. The day was halfway over, and she was no closer to actionable answers than she'd been when she'd went to bed. "We all have questions, so let's get them over with. Then, after breakfast, I'll gather my stuff and get out of here."

"What about Cerise?" Brahms asked.

"I'll take her–her body with me." Harley pulled a glass of orange juice toward her. Cerise. In the back of her truck, shrouded in a tarp. She deserved better. "Bury her in consecrated soil."

Cree frowned. Her brow wrinkled. She, Brahms, and Thayer shared a conspiratorial glance.

"You've yet to answer the questions we asked last night." Brahms leaned back in his chair.

She knew she ought to be gentle with him. No matter how much his presence simultaneously intrigued and irked her, they'd both lost a partner. Even though he appeared calm, he had to be hurting as much as she was. She also owed him for saving her life. And he'd tended to Cerise's body with dignity, instead of taking the easy way and finding a place to store her as-is or leaving her body in the woods to decompose.

*Or calling a group of cleaners to make everything go away. As if I'd never existed.*

Okay, so she owed him a few favors, but he was making it difficult, being all cute and pushy at the same damn time. She reined in her temper and continued in a calmer note, "I don't have the answers you want."

Thayer slid an omelet onto a plate and set it in front of her. "The mind thinks better with food."

Herb-scented steam zinged up her nose; her mouth watered. Whatever it might or might not do to her brain cells, it sure activated her taste buds.

"What questions do you have?" Cree asked.

"Let's start with, who the hell are you people and how did you gain access to the Church's network?" She dug into her omelet. Max wasn't there, so she didn't have to pretend to be all ladylike. Normal. What the hell had possessed her to try to be normal, anyway?

"That's two questions." Thayer snapped the knobs on the stove to off.

"Neither of you are being helpful." Cree twisted in her seat to face Harley. "We work for the Cerberus Foundation. It's a private organization dedicated to much the same cause as the slayers—"

Brahms interrupted, "Finding and eliminating threats, be they beast or man."

"Or men in beast's clothing," Thayer joined them, somehow fitting his large body into the chair.

"Only, we don't keep them alive in cages or cells." A challenge glimmered in Brahms's gaze. "We kill them."

"Why do the slayers cage the beasts?" Thayer asked.

Though none of them had pinged her instincts hard enough for Harley to say she didn't trust them, that didn't mean she was ready to tell them everything. Still, the question was innocuous. She saw no harm in answering that one and in exchange that'd open them up to answer more of hers. Besides, they seemed fully capable of hacking into the Church's computer system to track down the answer themselves, eventually.

"Can't say I agree with the Church's protocol on that myself," Harley said to Brahms and then glanced at Thayer. "They're for the white coats, eerrr scientists, who're developing a vaccine against the were virus and evaluating each creature for weaknesses to create more effective weapons and tactics. The more effective we are, the safer the world, you know?"

"Lore tells us most of what we need to know," Brahms said.

Harley resisted the urge to brag about all the advances they'd made in weaponry and how effective Fern's new gadgets were in the field, like her Vamp Buster grenades and whatever Fern laced her machine gun ammo with. And many other creations, including some damned spiffy vehicles Harley couldn't wait to try out.

But there were many things Cerberus didn't need to know. She settled for a brief, "But not all."

"Have they made any progress on the vaccine?" Brahms asked.

She opened her mouth to say yes, but slowly shut it. Had they? She'd seen them in their white lab coats staring into their microscopes, plugging away at their computers, and mixing weird fluids together, yet she couldn't recall ever reading the reports that came out of their labs. Come to think of it, she didn't recall seeing any to read. Nor heard any news of success, though she'd heard plenty of tragedy, white coats who'd accidentally infected themselves or had been bitten by their test subjects. A few who'd been killed or driven insane when they'd failed to take the proper precautions against insidious monsters such as fae or demons, who could twist a person's mind and perceptions to the breaking point.

They didn't take enough precautions. It was easy for them, she supposed, to view the beasts as lesser when they were trapped behind bars and reliant on humans for their food and basic needs. Taking pity on them was an all too fatal mistake.

"I don't know," she answered Brahms, "never asked."

"You should have," Thayer said.

"Yeah, thanks for the twenty-twenty. Now, how did you break into our network?"

Brahms answered, "Cerberus isn't as old as the Church, but we're not without resources."

"Not going to tell me. Got it." She assumed they had hackers, damn good ones, to get through the security the Vatican's computer gurus fastidiously monitored. When she returned, she'd report it so they could hunt down the weasels and plug their dirty holes. "Other slayers should have come for me by now. Why haven't they found me?"

"We jammed the signal on your chip," Brahms said. "Though, I suggest you remove it."

"What? Why would I do that?" No slayer in the history of slayers had ever removed their chip. Not since the chips had been invented, anyway, and she wasn't keen on being the first.

"It's difficult to investigate someone," he said, "if they're always aware of where you are and where you're heading."

"What makes you think I'd investigate my Order?"

"Honor. Justice." He planted his elbows on the table and leaned toward her. Too close. She wanted to scoot back to create some distance between them, but she refused to allow him to see how he affected her. "Because you know Cerise shouldn't have died. Because she knew something was wrong or the two of you wouldn't have been out there."

He'd named every reason why Harley intended to investigate. It annoyed her he not only knew but he could blurt it out without the slightest hint of self-satisfaction. Maybe strangling him wasn't completely out of the question. "There's a hell of a lot more evidence needed other than suspicions and wild theories before I'd think my Order would turn its back on beliefs we've held for centuries and oaths each of us took."

"We'll find it."

"What do you mean, we?" She narrowed her eyes.

"We're coming with you," Brahms said as casually as he'd say it was a sunny morning.

"Not a chance in hell." If there were rats scurrying about her Order, she'd be the one exterminating them. She neither wanted nor needed their help. "Give me your number and after I figure a few things out, I'll tell you what I can."

Brahms shrugged. "Have it your way. It'll raise a lot of suspicion when we drop you off in the middle of town with a dead body at your feet."

"You're not keeping my truck." She'd custom rigged her Tahoe to her specifications, from the burly tires to the tricked-out suspension, to the monster motor and, of course, the paint. Blue. What had Fern called it? Mariana Blue. A custom color Fern developed and named after the Mariana trench. Fern was more than a tad obsessed with megalodons. Harley wouldn't have put Fern through repainting it, but Chevy hadn't been kind enough to think of offering a full spectrum of colors for that year and model of Tahoe. The jerks.

Not only was the truck itself valuable to Harley, but it also contained several stashes of goodies hidden in the nooks Fern had installed for her. When she found the pride that killed Cerise, she wanted every single knife, bullet, firearm, and explosive she'd collected at her disposal.

"It's in the forest," Brahms said. "Or more likely, your church's cleaning crew has already retrieved it. Either way, it's not here."

"What? You left my truck out there? By itself? Tell me you locked it." If anyone stole it or good God, if her weaponry fell into inexperienced hands innocent folk could be maimed or killed. There were weapons in there developed specifically and only for her. If anyone else attempted to use them, it'd be a disaster for them.

"Talented as I may be," Brahms said, "I can't drive two vehicles at once, and neither you nor Cerise was in any condition to drive. So, unless you want to walk back..."

Harley glowered at him. "Fine."

She'd have to tolerate them for a few more hours until they reached St. Ambrose. She'd been through worse. The cleaners probably dropped her truck off at St. Ambrose, entrusting it to Francis's care. After ensuring Cerise's body was safely in Fr. Francis's hands, she'd take her truck and pay a surprise visit to the sanctuary where Niko and his pride were held. As much as she hated to admit it, there were too many similarities between the pride that had killed Cerise and Niko's. Enough to warrant an investigation.

*A very quiet one.*

The only question that remained was would she do it from inside the Church or from the outside?

Francis was used to her taking off without giving him an itinerary, so that part would be easy. Dealing with Germaine would be an entirely different matter. In his messages, he'd insisted she return to Chicago to meet with him immediately. She'd also have to fill out a lengthy report on the pride and Cerise's death before they'd release her into the field again. If there was a rogue slayer or group of slayers, they'd see that report and realize she knew enough to puzzle out their vicious deception. At that point, they'd have to know she'd stop them. If they were smart, they'd go to ground like scared little rabbits, which would make hunting them difficult. With access to the network, they'd be able to track her every move, yet until she figured out who they were, she had no way to track them. No.

Working from the inside would give betrayers far too many advantages.

By working from the outside, she could keep the advantage she currently had, the element of the unknown. No one knew where she was or even if she was alive. They might have concluded that the pride killed her, too, which would suit her well because they wouldn't expect the dead to come looking for them. Yeah, she liked that idea. The next best thing to meeting the enemy with disproportionate force was springing a special surprise party for them.

Unfortunately, that also meant that Brahms was right. The tracking chip would have to go. She couldn't risk anyone in the Order figuring out that she was alive until she was damned ready to make whoever had betrayed them snort a few bullets.

*And what of Max?*

Harley glanced at Brahms.

He and Max were as opposite as heaven and hell. Max was polite, coifed, and oozed about the city like a charming ameba. Brahms was forward, calm, and more at home in the forests and wild areas than glitzy city life. Max's body was carefully sculpted in the gym under the tutelage of a personal trainer. Brahms probably hadn't set sneaker in a gym in his life. He had the physique of a warrior, honed in battle and tested by adversity. Max could talk circles around most people mingling truth with lies until neither existed independent of the other. In courtroom battles, he was a formidable opponent.

*But can he handle reality? My reality?*

Harley frowned and pushed the last two pieces of bacon around on her plate. Max wouldn't hold his bladder against even a mediocre monster, let alone anything like a were.

But Brahms. She bet he'd give them a hell of a battle.

"You protected us from the were, didn't you?" Harley asked.

Was that also why his partner had died? Had his partner been taken as he'd been fighting to save her?

"Wasn't a ghost," Brahms said.

"Alone?" Harley asked. He hadn't mentioned his dead partner, and she didn't want to get Cree in trouble if it had been some sort of secret they wanted to withhold from her.

"Yeah. Why?"

"That was either very brave, or very dumb."

"He tends to blur those lines," Thayer said.

"Funny." Brahms's lips curled up in a slight smile. Then, he glanced back to Harley. "Would you rather have died?"

"Point," Harley ceded. "Thanks, for everything."

"Doing what's right requires sacrifice," he said.

The room fell into an uncomfortable silence laced with sorrow.

Harley occupied herself by plucking up one of the crispy bacon strips.

"To gain trust," Cree's dark gaze locked on Brahms, "you need to give trust."

Brahms seemed to struggle with the comment. The silence lingered. Then, he shoved his plate away and stared at the table.

"I was only there to do some scouting," Brahms said, "to see if the rumors of a werepuma pride were true. If I could substantiate them, we'd return with multiple agents to destroy the pride before they moved on. I left my partner here, alone."

"I thought this place was safe," Harley said. "What happened?"

"It is safe. With the hunter tracking our people, I didn't want her wandering around without me. I made her promise not to leave the property. She apparently got tired of waiting."

"I don't know," Harley said. "If my partner was out there alone with weres, I wouldn't stay here, either. Can't blame her for wanting to find you and help. We're not all as damselly as you guys think."

"If she'd done that," Brahms said, "it'd be easier to take. I could understand wanting to help. But she broke her promise because she was hungry. She left the safety of the house to get pizza."

"Pizza? Now, that was–" Harley stopped herself shy of uttering "stupid." After years of Cerise drilling it into her head some truths were best left unsaid, some of it had sunk in.

*Hope you're proud up there, you little brainwasher.*

"They found her body yesterday," Brahms said. "That brand I showed you was burned into her skin."

Harley hesitated. The questions she wanted to ask would be difficult for him, and they didn't need asking right now. "On the way to St. Ambrose, you can tell me more. That someone would use our sacred crest to mark his victims pisses me off. If there's a way I can find this bastard, I will."

Brahms studied her for a moment and then nodded. "And there are other things we'll discuss."

Harley didn't like the tone of his voice, but she owed him, and she owed Cerise. If her own comrades were in question, it wasn't such a bad idea to get outsiders involved and keep the knowledge of her investigation solely between them. Besides, accepting their help didn't mean she had to tell them everything about the Order. She could feed them harmless details and keep the more sensitive data to herself.

"There's a little something I need to take care of before we go." Harley rose and looked at Cree.

The druid nodded. "I can take it out."

"Good. Digging it out with my fingernails wasn't appealing." Harley took a deep, steadying breath. The step she was about to take was huge, and once done, there was no going back. The chip couldn't connect to the network here to give updates to the Order, but it was still functioning and recording. If the Order turned out to be innocent and she returned here to replace the chip, the instant it reconnected to the network, it would log the time she'd removed it from her body. She'd owe Germaine a hell of an explanation and apology, after which he may or may not kick her out of the Order, the only family she'd known since her parents' slaughter. But ignoring the coincidences, ignoring Cerise's beliefs, was not something she could do again.

*For Cerise.*

As she steeled her spine and headed to the bedroom, she couldn't help but wonder if Cerise's brother, Lars, had run into the same issue. Perhaps he'd even run into Cerberus, too, and that was why his and his partner's chips had stopped reporting. Maybe, just maybe, Lars was alive, and she could bring a Disney ending to at least one of her promises.

*But if one organization can learn to jam our signals, couldn't others? Others who weren't quite as benevolent.*

~

"Think we can trust her?" Thayer whisked the plates off the table and dumped them into the sink.

"We could trust her less on her own." Brahms pondered the complication that was Harley. She was even prettier cleaned up and in full temperamental sprite mode, which made her more dangerous than he'd prefer in a way that had nothing to do with their duty. "I don't think she's involved with the murders or Germaine's schemes."

"But?"

"I don't trust her to not steamroll toward an enemy that's best approached in stealth. She's too—"

"Full frontal." Thayer said. "Are we going to tell her where Niko's pride is?"

"She doesn't even believe the pride is Niko's. Until she can accept that, and us, she's not going to believe a vision from 'bonfire' smoke."

Brahms's phone rang with Celeste's ringtone, again. Celeste contacted him now and then, usually to impart a quick bit of data, but this was unusual. Was Celeste's frequent contact because of Harley, Thayer, or the pride? Or all three? Thayer stiffened and turned toward the sink, as if refusing to listen, but he'd be paying attention to each word.

"Hello, Celeste," Brahms said.

"Is everything there all right?" she asked. "Thayer wasn't answering his phone."

Brahms translated what she really wanted to know to Thayer. "Celeste wants to know why you're not answering your phone."

"It's not supposed to be a tether." Thayer's shoulders tensed. He squeezed the dish soap bottle and squirted a bit too much soap into the rushing water. "It's in my room. Charging."

"I see," Celeste said. "Please tell him that is dangerous. Had this been an emergency, I might not have reached you in time."

"Not sure it'll help, but I will."

"Thank you. Don't act strange, but someone has crossed my wards at the house."

"That's impossible." Brahms forced himself to stay seated, to not turn toward the window and tip off anyone who might be watching. "The alarms would have alerted us as soon as they crossed."

"They would have, if they hadn't been disabled."

"The secondary alarm would have tripped unless..." Brahms didn't want to know where the conversation was heading. On the outside, Celeste looked innocent, an angel gracing the Earth, but she could scheme like the devil when she felt inclined. "They were disabled on your end."

"Yes."

"Celeste, what did you do?"

Thayer dropped the dishtowel on the counter and turned, watching intently.

"Please act normal. You must believe me. This has to play out as it is meant. It's unlikely Cree or Harley will realize he's there, but you and Thayer will sense him once he's closer. Allow him to watch, but do not interfere."

"Why? Who is it?"

"Someone whose time on this mortal plane is drawing to an end, but does not, cannot, end this day." There was the faintest hint of anger in her voice, but he realized it wasn't aimed at him. Celeste didn't get angry often, and when she did, people died. That tiny tremor in her words gave away what she wanted to keep secret. She didn't like letting this person live any more than he would.

"The only way someone could find this place and know what it is," he said, "is if they got the information from Livia."

Thayer crossed his arms over his chest, eyes narrowing.

"I am so very sorry to ask this of you, Brahms," she said.

With those soft-spoken words, she planted a sucker punch to his gut. He fisted his hand on the table, trying to contain the building rage. The hunter, the murderer of their people, of Livia, was out there within his reach. How could she expect him to do nothing?

"I need you to explain this," Brahms whispered. It was that or shout, and that would alert the enemy outside, and Cree and Harley. Cree he might be able to stop. Harley not a chance.

"He must live if we are to win."

"He is a murderer," Brahms said. "He's on our turf now. There're three of us. We can catch him here. Stop him here."

"And in so doing you'd set into motion a chain of events that allows evil to triumph."

"And murder isn't evil? How many more innocents will he kill if we don't end him here? Now."

"Less than if we do," Celeste said. "Can you reveal every detail you learn in your vision quests?"

Brahms's jaw tightened. Some knowledge gleaned from the sacred ways wasn't allowed to be vocalized. Some visions were gifts. If those gifts were revealed to others, it could anger the spirits and cause a backlash, physically, emotionally, or spiritually. Celeste was no shaman, but her ways were as old and sacred as any. It would be shameful for him to disrespect her path.

"No," he admitted.

"Then, trust I have no other choice but to ask this of you," Celeste said.

"You are pushing the trust card too far, Celeste," Thayer said loud enough for the mage to hear him.

The silence on the other end of the phone overflowed with pain. It stretched on so long Brahms thought she'd already disconnected. Abrupt arrivals and departures were but a few of her trademark tactics.

"I wish you knew what trust was," she said. The barely controlled waver in her voice made Brahms wish she'd just hung up. "The world is teetering. Each of us must do what we can to keep it from plunging into the darkness. I hate this, Brahms. I hate all of it."

There was a brief pause as she struggled with her emotions. "I wish it were different. That I possessed the power to change it. But I do not. Do as you must but know this–if that man dies this day, the repercussions will be dire and the effect more devastating than you can fathom. And Brahms, please refrain from shifting in front of Harley. She is not in a state to understand or forgive. In losing her trust, we will lose the slayers. Without them, there is no hope for anyone."

Then, the line went dead, and she was gone in typical Celeste style. He wanted to be mad at her. To use anger to justify what he wanted to do. Needed to do. But her quiet valiance in the midst of heartache swept the fury away.

"She can't expect us to let this man, this monster, go free," Thayer said.

"She can and does." Brahms set the phone on the table and stared at it. With the anger gone, his head was clear, and he could look beyond their immediate concerns into the potential future. "Ripples. For every action there's a reaction that creates multiple reactions, like a stone thrown into a pond."

"Inaction has its own consequences."

"Can you see how the ripples of what we choose to do here affect the future?"

"No, but—"

"I can't, either. So, there's only one question we have to answer. Has Celeste ever led us astray?"

"She asks too much."

"The past doesn't dictate the future." Brahms pocketed his phone and pushed away from the table. "You'll have to let it go, eventually."

"What is going on?" Cree stood on the threshold between the kitchen and the hallway that led to the bedrooms, holding a bloodied towel in her hands.

"Nothing." Thayer stalked past her and disappeared down the hall.

"Brahms?"

"How's your patient?" He switched the subject. Further arguing with Cree, or anyone else, would erode his willpower, which was focused on keeping himself from hunting the hunter and killing him.

"Better than expected." She tilted her head, watching him quietly. He hadn't fooled her, but Cree would drop it now that she realized she wouldn't get answers.

"I'll tend to Cerise," Brahms said. "Have everyone get packed and ready to go. We have to leave."

*Before my willpower snaps.*

And before the hunter could do any more harm to those under his protection. Celeste said he was there to watch, and she was usually right. Still, he wasn't willing to take chances. He walked past Cree, pretending he didn't notice her questioning gaze, and entered the serene room they'd set up for Harley's partner. It didn't seem right to extinguish the candles before removing Cerise's body, so he let them burn. The darkness had consumed too much already.

"Taken too soon." He stood beside the bed, dug into his pocket, and carefully pulled out the lacy silver cross Cerise had given him to pass on to Harley. "You said I'd know the right time to give it to her, but I don't. I thought she'd have her lowest low today, knowing you were dead. Knowing her order is betraying everything they hold dear. Instead, she just seems more determined. Stubborn, as you said." He rubbed his thumb over the intricate looped designs bordering the stronger inner cross. Her blood lodged in the crevasses, dried and dull. "I'll clean it before I give it to her."

He coiled the rope chain in his hand, set the cross on top, and tucked it back into his pocket. It'd be easier if he could hand it over to Harley before they left, but Cerise's last request had been for him to wait until Harley needed inspiration. Problem was, he couldn't imagine Harley needing much of that from anyone. He'd given his word though and so he would hold it even if the cross burned holes in his pocket.

He ran his fingers over the fold on the soft cotton sheet that covered Cerise's corpse and slid the sheet up, draping it over her face. Then, he wrapped the sheet around her, tucked the ends under her feet and head, and carried her body outside.

It hit him the instant he stepped out onto the porch. The

hunter, the murderer, was watching. The lurking presence slithered down his spine in icy tendrils. The source emanated from the bushes to his right, where Livia's killer hid behind the dense foliage. So close that if Brahms changed his form to that of the grizzly, he could overtake the man within seconds. Decapitate him a scant second after that. A far more merciful death than he'd given Livia.

Deep inside him, the bear's spirit reacted. It stirred and gathered, demanding the change, demanding to be unleashed. If he allowed the grizzly control, there'd be no returning to his human form until he'd eliminated the threat. Brahms wanted to kill this man as much as the grizzly did. He wanted to feel the hot blood of the enemy dripping down his claws and watch it as it soaked into the forest floor, feeding the roots. He wanted to know that the man who'd killed his partner and other friends in the Cerberus Foundation would never take the life of anyone else ever again. But he couldn't risk being responsible for the deaths that'd follow.

And Celeste was right. Their trust with Harley was tentative, at best. Unlike Cerberus agents, who'd work with any good-natured being, slayers didn't work with anyone other than slayers. Harley would see him as one of the things she hated most in this world, a were. Even though he wasn't.

The grizzly balked, for the bear was a protective spirit and didn't take kindly to being thwarted from its sacred duty. Energy bulged in his heart and pumped through his veins. A huffed growl rose in his throat. He clamped his lips shut and forced it down. Their enemy already knew too much. He didn't need to give the killer more knowledge of who or what they were.

*In time*, he thought to the grizzly's spirit, *we will take our vengeance.*

He tromped down the steps. The wood creaked under his and Cerise's combined weight. The birds had fallen into silence as they, too, sensed the monster prowling in the woods. A breeze rustled the leaves, a discordant, harsh sound in the foreboding quiet that raked across his taut nerves with all the grace of nails on a chalkboard. The sharp scent of the killer swirled with it, tantalizing the bear within Brahms.

*Celeste wouldn't ask this of us if it weren't necessary. Remember his scent, for we will hunt him soon.*

Brahms believed it more than the bear did. Still, the grizzly drew back into its lair within him. It didn't slumber as it did most of the time. It hunkered, waited, ready to rise should Brahms change his mind.

He stepped onto the gravel driveway and to his car. The trunk was open, awaiting Cerise. It wasn't the ideal way to transport the honored dead. But if the police pulled them over, explaining why he had a body in his back seat would be problematic. Thayer had already lined the trunk with a tarp and removed their heavier equipment so it wouldn't damage Cerise. Angling her in feet first, he lowered her into the trunk and then tightened the sheet, tucking her in for her final ride. He put his hand on the trunk lid and stared at Cerise's impromptu shroud.

Death was becoming an all too common, and unwelcome, occurrence.

Every day, reports flowed across Cerberus's communications systems of deaths or very near misses from across the United States and the few countries where Cerberus kept loose ties. He'd overheard Celeste months ago, during his last visit to headquarters, and he wished he hadn't. Her words haunted him. Celeste's accuracy with divination was renowned, and he never wished her to lose her gift or her track record, but he dearly hoped she was wrong.

For if the creatures really were–

Creaks on the stairs behind him. They weren't Cree's or Thayer's footsteps, so they had to be Harley's. He turned.

Cree trailed after the slayer, but held back, leaning against the porch post, watching from a respectful distance.

Brahms motioned to Cerise's body. "We have no options. I can't risk us getting—"

"I know." Harley stood at the edge of the bumper. Sorrow filled her eyes, but there were no tears. Then, quick as a November storm, her blue eyes hardened into sheets of ice. "She deserved better."

She looked even more beautiful when she was angry. Dangerous. Beautiful.

*What is wrong with me?*

"We'll find the weres who did this." Brahms wanted to tell her he already knew where the pride was lurking, but she wasn't ready to hear, to believe, how he'd come across the information. He had a feeling she soon would.

"Yeah." Her fingers slid across the sheet, caressing Cerise's cheek. "The chip is out."

Right back to business. Brahms frowned and wondered if bottling her grief would cause more problems for Harley than allowing herself time to mourn.

"It was a wise decision." He stepped away from the car and motioned to the trunk. He didn't want to be the one to lock her dead partner in there.

She hesitated a moment and then carefully shut the trunk lid. "Our Order is not the bad guy here."

"If Cerise was wrong, if we are wrong," he motioned between himself and Cree, but also kept the trunk in the loop of his motion to include Cerise, "they can replace your chip and there's no harm done. But if we're right—"

"You're not." Her words didn't carry as much confidence as they had before. That boded well. She was entertaining the idea there might be something dark slithering through her Order, that was progress and hope. No amount of proof could break through a closed mind that wouldn't consider the possibility that they might be wrong.

*Now we need to find that proof.*

"But if we are," he said, "then your best weapons might be stealth and unity with us. We all want the same thing."

Her lips tugged down in a frown, and for a drawn moment, she stared at him, assessing. Weighing. As if judging the value of his words and, more important, if he could be trusted. Caught within that blue gaze, the wind stilled, and time slowed to an unbearable crawl.

Finally, she whirled on her heel and stalked toward the house, clamoring up the stairs. "I'll be ready in a few." She disappeared into the house and let the door slam shut behind her.

Cree chuckled. "Nicely played."

"That was good, right?" He stared at dark rooms beyond the screen door, but they were as hidden from him as the knowledge of what women really meant by what they said or did. Of all the creatures who roamed the Earth, they were the most baffling.

She pushed away from the post. "Depends on your definition of good."

Brahms wanted to ask if Harley's behavior meant she trusted him even a little more than before. But one look at the impish glow in Cree's eyes and he knew she'd never give him a straight answer.

There was one thing he was certain of–something was about to change. The grizzly within him sensed it and wasn't amused.

## CHAPTER
# EIGHT

Delighted, Ian sank into the leather driver's seat of his car and flipped through the photos on his phone. There, in full hi-res, was the evidence he needed to thrust a wedge between Cardinal Germaine and Harley. Picture after picture of her consorting with the enemy, joking with that foul druid, helping that beast, Thayer, carry a bag of something out to the car, and thoughtful chats, as thoughtful as Harley got anyway, with Brahms.

One by one, he texted them to Germaine.

He'd already edited out the portion with Harley arguing with Brahms, of course, because it'd give the cardinal a glimmer of hope his favorite slayer was acting on behalf of the Church or they could redeem her from the enemy's influence. Then, he'd arranged the order he sent the pictures to reflect a congruous period as if nothing had been removed so the cardinal would see a progression of comradery until the four had packed into their cars and left their not so safe house.

His eyes narrowed on the photo of Brahms stuffing what he assumed to be Cerise's body into the trunk. There was something about him, an energy. An invisible and yet indelible thing that churned Ian's stomach and placed Brahms on a scale of loathing above even the druid. And Lord knew, he crossed himself, he brewed a mighty hate for her kind.

"Blasphemers."

Druids. The mere thought of it made him want to shower and sluice its filth from his mind.

"Dear Lord, grant me patience."

Holding the phone steady, he flipped through the pictures until he found one of Cree.

"I have other obligations. Priorities. Once those are done," he zoomed in on her face, "I'll come for you and cleanse you of your sins."

# CHAPTER NINE

Harley adjusted herself in the passenger's seat of Brahms's car so she could see him better. They'd been on the road for a couple of ours and she hadn't killed him yet. Something to be proud of. And yet disturbing. She'd found herself enjoying his company and the drive, even though she wasn't the one in the driver's seat. Where she always was. She was glad Cree and Thayer were following in Cree's car, so she had Brahms all to herself.

Unlike her Tahoe, Brahms's car was neat and clean. No fast-food bags or candy wrappers littered the floor. And it smelled like him. A forest locked in glass.

"I just don't get it," she said, antsy to move the case forward. "Why would the Cerberus Foundation work with creatures who are so untrustworthy?"

His lips quirked up in a smile. "And humans are trustworthy?"

"More than a were or fae or demon or, yeah, any of them."

"Really?" He turned the corner. St. Ambrose's cemetery lined the street to the left. Behind the iron fencing, old headstones flecked with moss rose from well-tended lawn. Small family tombs near the back, peeking between tastefully pruned bushes. "Let's pretend for a moment that's true. Let's also pretend Cerise was right. How are you going to call upon slayers that you know you can trust without the Order finding out?"

"Problem easily solved. If I had my phone."

"We already went over this. They could use your phone to track you. They can also turn the mic on and listen to our conversations."

Although Thayer and Brahms reasons were valid and the Order was capable of either, understanding the why behind Brahms snatching her phone and being all giddy about it were two entirely different things that didn't coexist. Besides, she needed to call Max to hand him his ass in a basket, and officially break it off. Because she was sweet and thoughtful that way. She didn't appreciate his assumption she'd just blown off their date or the prissy attitude that oozed from his messages. Her partner had died, and she'd almost died along with her. And Max was leaving her angry messages about missing a fancy-schmancy dinner party? That pissed her off beyond all pissdom.

*But why am I not hurt?*

She ought to have been. Shouldn't she? Even knowing Max wasn't her type, wasn't it within her girlfriend rights to expect the guy she'd been dating for the better part of a year to be concerned when she didn't show for a date instead of angry? Maybe even expect him to squeal tires over here to break down the door to see if she was all right? And when he did neither, shouldn't she feel heartbroken? Probably. But she wasn't.

Maybe it was her. Maybe she was as emotionally distant as people thought. Not that she didn't feel stuff. She felt a lot of things. Like anger. But anger didn't count. That was easy. Irritation didn't count either. Excitement on the edge of battle. Yeah. Yeah, that counted. But that four-letter cringe word, love? Was she even capable of that? She'd loved Cerise like a best friend, like a sister. Like a partner. So, maybe she was.

*And now I'm alone. Again.*

She'd experienced crushes when she was a girl, some had been intense. As she grew, as she learned, as she fought, the fewer and less intense those crushes became until she stopped really caring. Sure. She liked to have fun with her dates. Get intimate with them on a physical level. Until now, she'd thought that her ability to feel more than sexual interest had disappeared altogether. Maybe people like her who'd seen the brutality, the evil she'd seen, who walked down the dark, twisted paths of nightmares, who shed enough blood to satisfy Ba'al, strayed too far into the void to know love or any relationship beyond the boundaries of professional killers. Maybe people like her weren't meant to have a family.

*Curse of the Slayer, coming soon to a theater near you.*

But she liked Brahms, which might be part of the problem. He was thoughtful. Nice. Earthy. Strong. She couldn't find fault with him, and that irritated her.

*Irritating. Yeah. Found a flaw. Ha.*

Brahms had potential. She'd bet he'd never make her don some glittering, uncomfortably tight gown so he could haul her to a ritzy restaurant, where she'd have to endure hours of inane conversation. Brahms's friends, and from what she could gather, Cree and Thayer were friends, spoke her language, the tongue of monsters. He also scored bonus points for his fighting prowess, something Max utterly lacked.

*Easy, now. You didn't win him on the Dating Game. Who says he's even interested?*

Maybe he was, maybe he wasn't. She could enjoy the view either way and make a better effort to get along with him. In any other circumstance, it'd be easy. Except she wondered about his past, what he liked and his plans for the future, and if it would include her after they discovered the truth about the Order and Niko. She didn't need those kinds of thoughts infesting her head, particularly about a man whom she wasn't sure she could trust.

Brahms's warm voice broke through her thoughts. "You're getting quiet on me."

He pulled into the driveway of St. Ambrose's rectory. Thankfully, he'd unwittingly taken the spot in front of the garage door, where Francis kept his car. Her Tahoe should, she hoped, be behind the other rolling white door.

"What am I going to tell him?" she asked. She stared at the rectory windows. It was a single-story building, about a decade newer than the old wooden church it served. The church, with its white paint and bell tower with a real bell, not some modernized digital recording, had stood on that spot for a century. Maybe longer.

It appeared small from the outside. But there was far more to it than met the eye.

The sanctuary beneath it sprawled out beyond the church's walls. In some places, it infringed on the cemetery. It was okay. The sanctuary's metal ceiling began quite a bit deeper than six feet under.

"The truth." Brahms unbuckled as Cree pulled her car to a stop alongside the curb.

"Easier said than done." She grabbed her garbage from lunch, slid out of the car, and led them around the rectory to the back door. "We always come in this way. Protocol. Come on in."

She slung the unlocked back door open and strode into the kitchen, dunking her fast-food bag into the trash can.

*Home.*

She never would have thought she'd be happy to hear the incessant hum of the old refrigerator. How many times had she petitioned Francis to get rid of that rattling pile of junk? Or rip up the decrepit seventies floor tiles? Blech. The jarring, clashing colors made her eyes hemorrhage. But it was home.

*In all its blaring glory.*

Brahms carried Cerise's shrouded body in, his light steps and fluid grace unaffected by the additional weight. "Where would you like me to put her?"

"Second bedroom on the left." Harley pointed to the narrow hallway with the well-trod pea green carpet that led to her and Cerise's rooms. "The one with the lacy curtains and bed that's actually made." Never again would Cerise tighten the sheets and fold the extra blankets into those crisp squares that Harley itched to rumple.

Pain and loss squeezed her heart until she thought it would pop right there in her chest, splattering in chunks and goo over her ribs.

*This isn't the time. It's a body. It's not Cerise.*

Cerise's soul, that which made her Cerise and not an empty, unanimated husk, had passed on. Safe and at peace. Was Lars up there with her? Harley hoped so. That way, Cerise could again play the goof with her brother. Then, she wouldn't be lonely up there. After all, who else besides Lars would tease her if Harley wasn't around?

*Can't have you bored in heaven, can we?*

After Cree and Thayer entered, Harley locked the door. Between the four of them, she doubted they were in any real danger, but some habits shouldn't be broken. Most successful attacks occurred when the victim believed they were safe.

Complacency was an insidious trap.

Thayer stalked silently to the window, cracked the curtain, and peered out at the street. "Much traffic on this street?"

Cree checked the coffeepot and frowned when she found it was empty.

"Not really," Harley said. "Unless it's Sunday." She yanked the fridge door open, grabbed the plastic coffee container, and slid it across the counter to Cree. "Francis might have some numbers written somewhere. Other sanctuary churches, maybe some slayers. He's into the whole getting back to papyrus days thing. Wouldn't be surprised if he started writing with a quill and ink."

"Any food in there?" Thayer asked.

"We ate a late lunch, what, a little over two hours ago?" She shut the fridge door.

"Don't let that face fool you," Cree poured water into the coffeemaker's reservoir, "he's more pig than man."

Thayer gave her a scowl that didn't appear the slightest bit intimidating then returned his attention to Harley. "You don't remember any phone numbers?"

"Seriously?" Harley raised her eyebrows. "When's the last time you memorized a phone number?"

"Last week." He shrugged. "The new agents'."

Cree groaned. "Ignore him. He's an affront to nature."

"So where is Father Francis?" Brahms returned, walked past her, opened the refrigerator, and peered inside. "Bacon, lettuce, mayo. I'm thinking BLTs."

She looked between Brahms and Thayer. "What is it with you two and food?"

"We're growing boys," Thayer said.

"Boys?" Brahms shook his head. "Speak for yourself."

"Boys have more common sense," Cree turned the coffee pot on to percolate, "and better manners than either of you."

"Harley?" Francis rushed down the hall that led from his study. His sandy hair disheveled, trousers wrinkled, and in his stocking feet, he looked as if he'd tumbled right out of bed. He cast a bleary glance at the others, probably assuming they were also slayers, and then went straight to Harley. She decided to let him keep his assumption. Trying to explain why she'd brought Cerberus agents to a sanctuary would be problematic. Though she didn't think he'd tattle, the less he knew of what she was doing, the better and safer for both of them.

"In the flesh," she said. "Did we wake you from a nap or something?" She wondered if he already knew about Cerise. Unlike other sanctuary priests they'd worked with, she and Cerise had a close rapport with Francis. More so than handler and handles. Friends.

Francis blushed, and then he lifted her arms to examine her. "Are you all right? They said, they thought..."

"I'm fine, thanks in no small part to Brahms," she nodded to Brahms, who'd shut the fridge and taken a seat at the table, "Cree and Thayer. They kind of saved my ass." Since she hadn't specifically labeled them slayers, she wasn't technically lying. She was just letting him continue in blissful ignorance. It was the humane thing to do.

"Kind of?" Brahms raised an eyebrow.

"I can't thank you enough," Francis said. "Harley and Cerise, they're rather like, well, like family." Francis glanced at each of them and continued to look around, searching. "Speaking of, where's Cerise?"

Harley cleared her throat, buying time to collect her emotions. Keeping the sorrow and pain under control was difficult, but doable when she didn't have to talk about it. Saying Cerise was dead, having to explain how and why could smash right through the wall she was building to keep the grief at bay.

"We tried to save her, too," Brahms said, "but her wounds were too grievous, even for Cree's considerable talents."

Harley offered him a tiny, grateful smile. She supposed she could forgive him for commandeering her phone.

Francis's hands slipped off Harley's arms. He dropped into a chair and rested his elbows on his knees, his shoulders slumped forward. "That's what Ian said. I'd prayed he was lying and the two of you had gone off to find Lars. I thought you'd found him, and your chips experienced the same anomaly. You know how adamant Cerise is–was that Lars is alive. There was no reason all of you couldn't be..." His voice trailed off as if he'd lost the energy to speak.

Harley frowned.

*Now, why would Francis think Ian would lie?*

She'd never liked Ian, personally, and still held a grudge from when he'd ordered fellow slayers to intervene in her fight with Niko, capturing him instead of allowing her to kill that filthy cat. She couldn't pinpoint exactly what it was about Ian that bothered her, aside from his obsession with keeping the beasts they fought alive. But he was one of Germaine's most trusted slayers, so she'd shrugged the dislike off as a simple matter of different strokes. He being on the keep them alive side and she being on the kill them and call it good side. She wanted to ask Francis what had happened between him and Ian, but not in front of the Cerberus agents. Working with them was one thing, being attracted to one was skirting some dangerous ground, trusting them with sensitive Order information was outright silly. "I promised Cerise I'd find Lars, and I will."

"I like to think you're...you're..." Francis threaded his fingers together.

"Invincible?" Harley asked.

Francis nodded. "After Ian left, I checked your signals myself. I couldn't conceive...wouldn't believe that..."

"We could die?" It was a naïve, but sweet thought, one she didn't feel compelled to call him out on. Most sanctuary priests were jaded men. Others were trainers who'd retired from the slayer strongholds, who knew the dangers of the job too well to form attachments to the slayers in their charge. Francis was different. Harley admired him because he was neither of those things. He was a scholar at heart, meant more for monastic life than watching over a sanctuary church.

As much as she enjoyed working with him, she hoped he received that transfer he'd been asking for soon. She'd hate to watch him transform into one of the dour, cold-hearted jerks. She had some pull with Germaine. Once this was done and his anger with her over removing her chip had passed, she'd put in a word for Francis. Hell, if it wasn't for the fact the Church had to operate under the guise of a functioning parish, she and Cerise would have been able to run the place themselves.

"I set the computer to alert me when your signal returned." Francis glanced toward his study. "I suppose it didn't work. Never understood that system, anyway. Unless..." His inquisitive gaze homed in on her.

"You're friends with the sanctuary priest at St. Mary's, right?" Harley switched the subject before he could voice his suspicions, and she was forced to lie. If Cerberus was right and there were rats in her Order, the less Francis knew, the safer he was.

"We went to seminary together but—"

"I need you to call him to see if everything is running smoothly. Tell him to check his systems and make sure there're no anomalies."

"Anomalies like..." Francis watched her with a questioning gaze.

Thayer answered, "Looped footage, glitches with their time-stamps. Any breaches in their security, even if it appears slight."

Cree set five mugs on the counter and poured the freshly perked coffee.

"But why would there be—"

"It's important." Harley cut Francis off. If Niko and his pride were loose, every second could mean the difference between innocents living or dying or being infected with the were virus.

Cree set a mug of black coffee on the table by Francis.

He took the mug and studied her. "Thank you." He sucked in a swig of coffee then stood. "I'll call now." He glanced at his watch.

"Martin should be available." He shambled down the hall and then turned. "Oh, they brought your truck back. It's in the garage."

"They didn't touch my stash, did they?"

"I wouldn't count on it. They were out there for a while." Francis disappeared into his study and shut the door.

"He's not friendly with visitors," Thayer said.

Cree chuckled. "And you are?"

"Francis is," Harley searched for a way to explain him without making him seem socially inept, which he wasn't. He was just, "Reclusive. Germaine made a mistake assigning him here."

The Cerberus agents shared a look, and Thayer cleared his throat.

Harley grabbed the half-and-half out of the fridge. "Germaine isn't involved in this." He couldn't be. If he were, it'd rock the Order to its core. Possibly even give their critics enough ammo to shut them down entirely. If that happened, who would be there to stop the creatures from reveling in unfettered bloodshed? She was certain many of her fellow slayers, including herself, would continue in their calling to protect, but without the info structure and financial support of the Church, how long could they function? How effective would they be?

"Trust in the wrong person at the wrong time can be lethal," Brahms said.

Harley fought the instinct to shove a fist in Brahms's face, which would serve the secondary purpose of splattering blood on the white grout that would be impossible to remove. Hence, Francis would finally have to replace the floor. Instead, she mentally ran through a litany of Brahms's positive attributes and ended on the one flaw she'd found...irritating. And he was that, in spades.

"Germaine wouldn't betray us." There. Nice, simple, and

somewhat diplomatic. Sorta. Certainly more so than busting his nose.

"While we're on the subject," Thayer cocked his head toward the hall that led to Francis's study, "are you sure we can trust him?"

"Francis? Yeah." Harley grabbed her mug of steaming coffee and wished she could douse it with half a bottle of Bailey's Irish Cream. "You? I'm not so sure of."

After doctoring her coffee with creamer, Harley escaped to the garage, leaving Thayer to make the BLTs and Cree to keep watch over him. It appeared the suspicion she felt for the Cerberus agents was mutual because Brahms insisted on following her out to the garage, probably to make sure she didn't take off or contact Germaine. She'd do the same thing if the situation were reversed, so she couldn't blame him, much.

Lucky for him, the lovely view of her Tahoe, washed, waxed, and gleaming in the florescent garage lights, lifted her spirit. The cleaners had even buffed out the scratches on her custom brush guard. She'd designed it for the slayers' rugged lifestyle, and Fern had constructed it from the same alloy they used to make the bars on the creatures' cages. Aside from the special acid the white coats developed to melt the metal, it was nearly indestructible. Coupled with the impact-absorbing frame Fern had added, the brush guard was strong enough to take a direct hit from almost any monster without risk of damaging the radiator or the truck frame, which effectively turned her vehicle into a weapon in its own right. With some creatures, trolls for instance, it took a hit from a fast-moving, burly vehicle to knock them out. A tank would be best, but Fern had yet to develop one that could pass as a normal vehicle.

That reminded her, she hadn't called Fern to check up on the new ideas she'd emailed over last month. She reached for her phone, hand hovering over her pocket as she remembered it wasn't there. Francis would have Fern's number. She'd have to snag a phone list from him before heading out. It wasn't wise to contact anyone in the Order for any reason, but Thayer said he'd give her a burner phone so the Order's computer system wouldn't recognize her number, and she was certain if there were traitors in their midst, Fern wasn't among them.

"Mommy's home." She unlocked the Tahoe with the fob and opened the driver's side door, releasing a waft of new car smell. Inside, the cleaners had eradicated every sign that Cerise had bled out in there. The charcoal carpet was fluffy clean, the console and leather seats freshly polished.

*Creepy.*

She climbed onto the bucket seat and dug around, reaching down into the crevasse between the seat and center console, where her cell phone and other debris, like French fries, invariably fell.

"What are you looking for?" Brahms asked.

"Cerise's cross. Last time I saw her, she was holding it over the console." She snagged the flashlight out of the console box and checked closer. No cross. No fries. No anything. "The cleaners probably took it. Damn them. The least they could have done is left it here with Francis." When this was over, she'd have to call them and get it back, assuming they hadn't destroyed it. After replacing the flashlight, she flipped the lever to pop the hood. "What kind of name is Brahms, anyway?"

"Classical."

"I know that." Harley scooted out of the truck then grabbed her stained denim jumpsuit from the hook on the wall and slid herself into it. It smelled comforting, old oil and grease.

"Johannes Brahms, the classical composer." He pulled out the rolling stool from under the workbench and took a seat. "My parents were fond of orchestra, particularly Johannes's work. They wanted a son who could dazzle their friends with pianos and violins." He waggled his fingers, pretending to play the keyboard.

"You don't seem the fiddling sort." She opened the back of the Tahoe, pulled the false sides, and scrutinized the contents of her hidden boxes. Thank God the cleaners had left her stash alone. She wouldn't want to ream them out again. It'd make getting Cerise's cross back nearly impossible.

"I said violin not fiddle."

"And the difference is?" She could see him through the Tahoe's front window, sitting there, completely at home in a tool scattered, greasy work area. Yet he hadn't pulled the whole "I'm a man, you're a woman. let me take over on the truck" thing. She had to admit, the combination of manliness and respect was very attractive.

"Not much from a technical perspective." His dark gaze caught hers. "Same instrument, different setups. Regardless, I'm musically inept across the instrument spectrum, and according to multiple instructors, I'm also hopelessly tone deaf."

"Can you shoot your pistol and hit the target?" Harley asked.

"Yes."

"I'd take that talent over the fiddle any day."

"Yeah." He'd pulled the tie out of his hair, so it hung loose in a glossy black sheet that grazed across his broad shoulders.

To distract herself from him, she tore her gaze away and dug around in the compartments, doing a quick inventory of her ammo, guns, and various toys of destruction. "Do you see them much, your parents?"

"Every day," his voice lowered, laced with sorrow, "in my nightmares."

She risked a glance up. His face was taut with anger. "They were that bad?"

Having lost her parents to werewolves at such a young age,

she'd never considered having awful parents was worse than no parents.

"They were great. Their deaths weren't." He stood and prowled in front of the Tahoe. His moves reminded her of a lumbering bear.

"What happened?" Since she'd accounted for her ammo and weapons, she couldn't find a valid reason to continue searching the compartments. She snapped them shut and rolled the carpet back down, securing it with the Velcro edges.

"The fae."

"The fae killed them? That's bold." Harley didn't trust the fae, even though some mystics in the Church proposed they were a harmless race, an idiotic stance that furthered her belief the monks smoked too much weed. The fae were masters of glamour and stellar actors, much like politicians. In fact, there were quite a few fae lurking in the various arms of world governments from small towns right up to the national level. And Hollywood? Infested with fae. Though they weren't above killing, they preferred to ruin lives instead of take them. When they resorted to murder, they usually constructed the scene to look like an accident with no ties to themselves. Or murder by proxy, like Manson, who rallied his cronies into killing for him.

"They were agents with Cerberus, back when Fain's grandfather was in charge. They discovered a fae cult preying on the young and weak-minded." He fell into an uneasy silence and quickened his pacing. "Stealing their money, debasing them."

She went to the front of the Tahoe and sat on top of the brush guard, giving him time to think. The fae led many fringe cults. Not all, but enough for concern. When they oozed their charm, they could lure staggering amounts of people with the most insane and unbelievable lies—for instance, finding a new life in the tail of a comet if the followers committed one tiny act of suicide as it passed by, or that drinking Kool-Aid laced with cyanide was a good idea—everyone was doing it, don't you know?

"They infiltrated the cult," he continued. "What they discovered was unimaginable. What they were doing to those kids."

Something in his energy changed, shifted. She frowned. The rippling energy seemed familiar, as if she ought to recognize and slap a name on it. Yet it eluded her.

"The fae figured out who they worked for," he continued, "and killed them before Cerberus had a chance to send backup."

"What did Fain's grandfather do?"

He stopped and turned toward her. Something simmered in his brown eyes.

*What is it?*

"Cerberus never adopted the catch and release policy on monsters." He growled.

"Hey." She hopped off the brush guard. "Watch it." She poked a finger at his chest. It was thick, harder than she'd expected. What did the man do? Bench semis?

Brahms grabbed her wrist, his hold gentle, considering the power she sensed surging through him, right below the surface. "You asked."

"Ahem." Francis stood on the stairs. "Everything all right in here?"

Brahms released her wrist and turned away from them, wandering to the workbench. She'd liked the fleeting contact with Brahms, even with the weird energy she'd felt from him and then Francis had rudely interrupted.

"Yeah," she said. "Did you get a hold of your friend?"

He shuffled down the stairs, with Cree and Thayer following behind him. "No, and I don't suspect I ever will."

"What do you mean?" She hated it when he spoke in riddles. Why couldn't everyone speak normal, clear English with frank statements instead of dancing around issues?

"Martin wasn't there." Worry tightened Francis's face. "The temporary priest said he was visiting his sister."

"What's concerning about that?"

"Martin doesn't have a sister."

"That doesn't bode well." Thayer said.

Harley favored him with her best shut-the-hell-up look then turned to Francis. "We'll find out where he's really at," she said, even though her gut told her they wouldn't. "Did the temp have anything to say about the security?"

"He um..." Francis twisted his hands, "didn't respond to the codes. It was as if he didn't know them."

"Well, shit." Now *that* truly didn't bode well.

"Codes?" Cree asked.

"The Order uses code terms," Harley said, "so we can recognize right away if someone belongs or doesn't. It ensures information, items, and other vital assets aren't passed to unauthorized persons. They're changed every so often, just in case."

"Hmm," Thayer said. "An archaic but effective security measure."

Francis said, "The Church wouldn't have placed a non-initiated sanctuary priest in charge of a sanctuary church, even if temporarily."

"And," Harley added, "they wouldn't move a sanctuary location without the area slayers knowing. That leaves one glaring conclusion."

"Which means?" Brahms asked, his voice no longer quite as growly as it had been.

"Something is very wrong in Kansas, Toto." And she'd figure out just how bad it was. Then fix it. With bullets, if need be.

# CHAPTER TEN

Harley spent the next hour in the garage with Thayer, combining her mechanical skills with his computer wizardry to remove the tracking system on her Tahoe without tripping the monitoring system. It'd taken some doing, but now the Order would believe her truck was tucked away in St. Ambrose's garage while she was out driving it anywhere she pleased.

"There." Thayer shut the hood. "Even if they find out you took the truck, they can't track, follow, or listen in on you."

"You didn't add anything," she said, "so you guys could find me, did you?"

Thayer's laughter boomed through the garage. "No. But you'd really have no way to find out."

Oh, yes. Yes, she would. But that would involve getting to Fern. Which would give away one of the Church's most secret operations. "Not funny."

The rectory door opened, and Cree stopped on the threshold. "It's time."

Harley went to her workbench and twiddled with a set of

greasy wrenches. She didn't want to go. Didn't want to see clods of dirt falling on Cerise's casket.

*It's not her. She's free. It's just a husk. Nothing more.*

True as she believed that to be, it did nothing to mend her fracturing heart. She caught the scent of forest, earth, and a gentle hand squeezed her shoulder.

*Brahms.*

"You're not alone," he said. "We'll be there."

She blotted an errant tear with her sleeve cuff. "Cerise always did make friends fast. She'd be happy to have you guys there."

They left the garage and followed the winding drive through the cemetery. Night had fallen, and a thin mist hazed the ground, pooling around tree roots and headstones alike.

"She liked to walk out here," Harley said. "Reading the headstones and musing how, where, and why they'd died." It was another morbid habit, much like her tendency to collect the IDs of the fallen. Habits Harley would miss.

"Her way of honoring the dead," Cree said.

Thayer said, "And now, she'll have answers."

"Yeah," Harley said, "she's probably pestering them at this very moment to see how close she'd been to the truth."

They rounded the final curve. Francis had chosen the perfect spot. Secluded in the rear of the cemetery where no one from the road could see them and tucked within a clearing ringed by mighty oaks. A cozy spot that Harley could imagine Cerise sitting against a tree trunk reading a book on a warm afternoon. Yes. There, Cerise's body would have peace.

The grave was already dug with the dirt piled discreetly to the side.

"I was expecting to help," Harley said as she brought Francis into a tight hug. He trembled, struggling to keep his tears from shedding.

"Thank Brahms," Francis said.

She glanced to Brahms. Sure enough, dirt smudged his shoes and the lower portion of his jeans. "Thank you."

He nodded and came up alongside her as Francis left to stand at the head of the grave. Brahms remained beside her offering silent support as Francis presided over a reverent ceremony. Francis added personal flair to the funeral rite, tailoring it just for Cerise. He even slipped in some Latin and Spanish, Cerise's favorite languages. It was poetic. The moonlight glistening off Francis's tear-streaked face. The eerie mists and still night.

*You'd have loved this, even if you made Francis cry.*

After the ceremony concluded, Brahms handed each of them a shovel, and together they buried Cerise's body in the consecrated soil.

After they'd placed the last shovel of dirt on her grave, Harley stood back. All that remained of Cerise on this earth was an oblong pile of dirt surrounded by grass. "It looks so bare."

Francis squeezed her hand. "I'll have a headstone for her by the end of the week. I promise. And she'll have flowers. All her favorites."

Harley gave him a slanted look. "Just how are you going to do that without the Order finding out?"

He winked. "I have my ways."

He'd never broken his word before, and she didn't suspect he would on this. That was what worried her. "Don't take any risks. If you're killed, too, I swear I'll hunt your soul down and we'll have words."

"I'm safe here," Francis said. "It's you who's in danger."

"Yeah, but I was raised for trouble." She wasn't so sure he could defend himself, even here at the sanctuary if the worst situation happened. "I can handle it."

"You better." He touched her cheek with a trembling hand. "I can't lose you both."

SHORTLY AFTER RETURNING to the rectory, Thayer and Cree had made a hasty and mysterious departure. They hadn't even said goodbye to Harley or Francis. It didn't seem like them. Not that she knew them well enough to say for sure.

She hunted Brahms down, finding him out on the porch leaning against a post and staring out into the night.

"Where did they go?" she asked.

"To prepare," he said. He looked up at the stars. She'd bet he could name and point out every constellation.

"For what?"

"Did you know Ursa Major is the third largest constellation?"

"No, but it's a bear so, it kind of makes sense." She crossed her arms and sighed. "You're not going to tell me anything, are you?"

"Not yet."

"Whatever. I'm hungry." She stalked back into the house, letting the door slam behind her. He'd have to fend for food himself because she wasn't about to make him anything. Not when he was being so stubborn.

Brahms seemed intent on sticking with her, at least until she figured out who'd been killing Cerberus agents, or else he'd have left with his fellow agents. She got that. She'd want answers, too. He also seemed intent on helping with the werepuma pride. She understood that, too. No one who valued life would want a pride running loose in the world.

Though she understood his involvement and was grateful for Cerberus's help, there were some things she needed to do on her own. He might be angry when he found out, but he'd get over it. Particularly if she found information that would give them a direction to either the murderer or werepumas.

Alone in the kitchen, Harley opened the pantry, surprised to see Francis had purchased fresh avocados and thrown away the over ripe ones that Cerise purchased before...before...

*Mourning is for later. Get with it.*

Francis claimed he was allergic to avocados, but Harley suspected he'd said that to spare Cerise's feelings and to politely discourage her from asking if he wanted any of the atrocious green goop she made with them. Harley eyed the strange fruits, then the coffeemaker, then the wine and brandy Frances had kindly left out on the counter. Within the cabinet was her usual nightcap of choice, Captain Morgan's Black Spiced Rum. On the rocks. Neat. Straight up. Didn't matter as long as it wasn't mixed. That would be a true atrocity. Blasphemy even. As much as she'd like to indulge, she needed a clear head for tonight. She couldn't risk any sloppy work because of the numbing effects of rum. Coffee would suit her plans well, but she never drank caffeine after 3:00 p.m. Frances would be suspicious if he saw her downing a cup this late.

"Fine, you win," Harley whispered. She snatched an avocado, wrinkling her nose at the rough texture of its skin. She plunked it onto the cutting board and then pulled out Cerise's vanilla protein powder. The container itself was biodegradable, which had been a selling point for Cerise. "This better not make me vomit."

Though, if it did, Cerise would laugh her ass off up there in the great beyond. Which meant, no matter how horrid this tasted, Harley would have to choke it down and keep it down as a point of pride.

She poured coconut milk to the halfway mark on the bullet blender and then added a scoop of the protein powder. She removed two sealed bags filled with vile green powders from the pantry and resisted a shudder.

*Algae and seaweed. Gross.*

Harley added a teaspoon of each. For iron, Cerise used to say, to which Harley would argue that a nice, fat cheese burger had plenty of iron and didn't look like some Star Trek inspired Klingon concoction from Quark's bar. She got a knife and set the avocado on the cutting board.

"Getting in an extra helping of vegetables?" Brahms asked. He leaned on the doorframe, casually holding a tumbler of brandy he hadn't sipped since Francis gave it to him.

"Avocados aren't vegetables," she sliced it in half and peeled it the way she'd seen Cerise do countless times, "they're fruits, berries."

"Green berries. Appetizing."

She dropped the pulp into the blender and grimaced. "Yeah. All sorts of yum."

"Then why are you eating it?"

"Drinking it. I think." Sometimes, Cerise's protein concoction was thin enough to drink like a shake. Other times it turned out more like pudding. Since that was Harley's first time making it, she wasn't sure how hers would turn out. Maybe Cerise never did either. "I need something to drink. Not in the mood for alcohol, and coffee will keep me up all night. Cerise swore by this so." She shrugged. It was sort of the truth.

Before Harley could stop him, Brahms grabbed the protein carton, his gaze scanned the back panel where the ingredients were listed. "Ashwagandha, sea buckthorn, maca. This won't help you sleep, either."

Great. Why was she not surprised Brahms knew his herbs? Her knowledge was limited to the herbs that hurt or killed the beasts she hunted. Cerise had been the health nut and knew what that combination was for. All Harley could remember was her saying it helped boost energy, something she'd need tonight.

"It's almost made so I have to drink it now. Waste not, want not." She drowned out any retort he'd planned by firing up the blender.

Within seconds, it whirled the ingredients into the familiar green substance Cerise had been so fond of. She unscrewed the top and tilted the plastic container. Yup. Shake consistency. Her wariness must have shown.

Brahms chuckled. "Drink it down, champ." He pushed off the doorframe and disappeared into the living room.

She glanced out the window toward the cemetery in the direction of Cerise's fresh grave. "If this poisons me before I've fulfilled my promises, I will not be happy." She lifted the container of thick liquid toward the window in a toast. "Cheers."

She slurped it down, fast as she could, then wiped her lips. Out in the graveyard the mists thickened. Staring out there felt different. More connected now that Cerise's body lay out there beyond her sight. Harley had always respected the cemetery, but now it felt almost like a lost friend's house.

She sighed, turned away from the window, and headed into the living room with Brahms and Francis. Table lamps shed warm light throughout the room. Both the coffee bean colored couch and the old, caramel chair faced the windows. Though the drapes were drawn tight, the seating arrangement was more adventitious to them during an attack than having their backs to the enemy.

"How was it?" Brahms asked. He looked perfectly at home nestled in the corner of the puffy couch. He and Francis were getting entirely too cozy. There they were kicking back like old friends chatting about the great ball game of nineteen-forty-two or something. Well, if they weren't talking about her, it didn't matter what they talked about.

"Not bad." Her lips skewed to the side in thought. She didn't want to admit the concoction that looked like it'd been mixed by a Ferengi and that she'd resisted for years was tastier than her traditional McDonald's vanilla shake. "Better than I'd thought."

"She'd be glad," Francis said, "you'd tried something new." He sat in the chair, idly twisting his wine glass.

Harley scoffed. "I try new things. I bought two new guns last month. And who plays field guinea pig for Fern's new toys, huh? Me. And let me tell you, brilliant as she is, some of those buggers don't work the way she envisioned."

Fern was one of Harley's favorite people in the Order. They were fellow weapons enthusiasts only from two different spectrums. Fern couldn't handle weapons to save her perky ass, but she was damned amazing with designing and creating them. Harley tossed her ideas but couldn't make the mechanics of them work for squat herself. But she could sure use them when Fern completed whatever magic she wielded in her workshop.

Francis grinned and tried to hide it behind his glass of wine, but she saw it. "My mistake. Cerise would be happy that you tried a new *food*."

Harley opened her mouth then snapped it shut. She wasn't so irreverent as to argue with a priest when he was right.

"Picky, is she?" Brahms asked the priest.

"Heavens, yes. You should have—"

Harley interrupted him, "I'm going to bed." She narrowed her eyes at Brahms. "You should, too. We have an early morning." And the sooner he went to bed, the sooner she could leave.

"We do." Though Brahms tried to make it seem like he was agreeing with her, her gut told her he might be on to her plan. Or at the least he wasn't completely buying her I'm-tired-and-innocently-going-to-bed-act.

"Good night, Harley," Father Francis said. "Oh, the list of phone numbers you asked for is in your room. Try not to lose it."

"No gossiping." She whirled on her heel and strode away.

~

After Harley walked out, Brahms said, "Talking history isn't gossiping, is it, Father?"

Brahms set his brandy on the end table's coaster. He'd only taken two sips, enough to be polite and keep his hands occupied, but until they found Livia's killer and put that rabid werepuma, Niko, and his pride down, he didn't want his head muddled with drink. Besides, his judgement was already slipping where Harley was concerned, and he didn't need it tumbling completely off the cliff. Why had Celeste insisted that he stay with Harley? Why not Thayer or, better yet, Cree?

*Yeah, and where would my mind be then?*

Back up here, wondering if Harley was all right. Worried she'd do something brash or get to the swamps before Cerberus had their agents in place. No. Celeste was right. If he'd gone with Thayer, he'd be distracted, and a distracted warrior was a liability. As much as he wanted to protect Harley, she needed vengeance for Cerise's death, and that she'd never forgive them if they denied her that. Staying there, he could monitor her and ensure she got to the right area at the right time. Plus, it gave him the opportunity to butt his nose in her business. Harley and Father Francis were close. The friendly pokes at each other reminded him of his relationship with a few Cerberus agents. If anyone could tell him things about Harley that weren't in her official files, it would be the priest.

Besides, Brahms had a feeling there wouldn't be sleep for him, or Harley, that night. He'd known her for only a few days, most of which she'd been unconscious, but she was acting off. Enough so that he wondered what she had planned that she wasn't telling them. His first guess was a nighttime excursion without him.

*We'll see who's the better sneak.*

"No," the priest cupped his hands around his goblet. "No, I suppose it isn't."

"What's her history?" He nodded to the hallway that led to Harley's bedroom. He doubted she was asleep.

Father Francis's eyes narrowed. "Most slayers know."

"Hearsay maybe," Brahms said. Harley hadn't seen fit to dispel the priest's assumption her guests were fellow slayers, and Brahms didn't see the point in doing so now. "You and I both know stories get twisted with each retelling."

Mollified, the priest nodded. "I'm glad you realize that. There are some in the Order who feel she's had it easy because of her relationship with Cardinal Germaine, when in fact, it's been quite the opposite."

Brahms leaned forward, resting his elbows on his knees. "How so?"

"Don't get me wrong, the cardinal is a good man, and he undeniably has a soft spot for Harley. Perhaps that same affection is why he pushes her so hard."

"To do what?" The only records they could pull up on her showed she'd been placed in one of the Order's strongholds at a very young age, too young, in his opinion. The cardinal should have found someone to foster her in a stable environment, with an actual family, not shoved her in a stronghold filled with warriors and not the warmest ones on the planet, either.

"To be the best. It wasn't against her will, mind you. From what she's told me and from watching her now, her job is what she lives for and the Order what she breathes for. It worries me, to be honest."

"I never heard that she competes with other slayers," Brahms said, furthering the illusion he was, indeed, part of the Order. What the priest had said didn't fit Brahms' picture of Harley. She seemed open to teamwork if she wasn't forced into it, but they'd just met, so perhaps he was missing something.

"No, no, if anything, she is protective of all of you. She only competes with herself." The priest frowned into his wine and then continued in a lower voice, as if realizing something himself for the first time. "Though, I suppose, she is competitive. With the creatures she hunts. It makes sense in a sad sort of way. You see, Harley came to us as a shattered young girl, the sole survivor of a werewolf attack that killed her parents. Harley saw it all. Imagine the impact of witnessing such violence on a young, impressionable mind."

"Did she ever come to terms with that?" Brahms voiced it the best he could. He hoped Father Francis would figure out he meant no insult to Harley because how could a child ever reconcile such a nightmare?

"In her own way, I suppose. She uses her strength, training, and even some of her humor as a shield. Though I wonder if that shield protects a healed woman or one whose soul still bleeds."

"What do you mean?" The idea of Harley experiencing such great pain was more discomfiting than he'd admit.

*Yeah, definitely sliding into unknown territory here.*

"She hates weres to the point of being reckless. Not that anyone in the Order would ever accuse her of being overly cautious about anything," the priest chuckled, "as I'm sure you know. But even Cerise worried about Harley's focus on eradicating weres, often without regard to her own safety."

"It makes sense. That she would hate them, after what happened." Brahms's belly tightened, not a good sign. If she hated weres that much, what would she think of him if or when she found out what he was? Few people understood the differences between weres and shifters. One was born of a virus, a mutation that wiped away the human side, creating a monster. His kind, the shifters, possessed a divine gift, the ability to house within them the spirit of a powerful totem. And though they changed into the animal when the need arose, it was more of a shift in their physical nature not in who they were. They maintained their identity throughout the experience and afterward. Would Harley recognize the difference? If she didn't, then maybe he didn't have to worry about falling in love with her. If he didn't stop his tumbling heart, she would do it for him. He should have found that comforting. He didn't. Instead, he mentally ran through various scenarios about how he could tell her. Ways he could explain what he was that wouldn't end with her storming out of his life or attempting to kill him.

"I'm not sure," Francis said, "what possessed the cardinal to bring Harley into the Order versus any of the other survivors of such atrocities, but I'm glad he did. If I had to guess at his reasoning, I'd say her spirit caught his attention. The cardinal favors fighters. Even in the days when she'd cry herself to sleep at night, she'd still wake the next morning and put that pain into her training, turning it into an asset. She never played with dolls or had sleepovers with girlfriends. She studied, practiced. The only normal things she did for a child her age was watch movies and read. Though part of me wonders if that, too, wasn't just another way to glean information or come to some sort of understanding."

"You care for her," Brahms said, "more than you do the Order."

"Of course." Suspicious again, the priest stiffened. "Why?"

"Then, I can trust you with this." Brahms took another sip of brandy and then put it down on the battered side table. He didn't want to lie to the priest, but he also didn't know how Father Francis would react if he discovered that he, Thayer, and Cree were with Cerberus, not the Order. If the priest took offense, or worse, thought that they were a danger to Harley, he might alert the wrong people and turn an already dangerous situation into a deadly FUBAR situation.

Though he could have left the priest none the wiser, he needed to know. Knowing would keep the priest safer. Harley had suffered enough loss in her life. She didn't need to lose another friend. It was also possible that if Father Francis believed him, they'd have another safe house to run to in case things went sideways, which they invariably did. Choosing his words carefully to keep the priest's assumption he was a slayer intact, Brahms related the recent events and their suspicions to Father Francis.

Whatever Father Francis lacked in courage he made up for in intellect. His gaze sharpened, and Brahms could see him mixing and matching pieces of the puzzle until he came to a conclusion.

"Niko," Father Francis said. "This is worse than I'd imagined."

"A pride of werepuma is never good."

"If this is Niko, I'm surprised he hasn't made an appearance here."

"Why would he come to a sanctuary? I'd think he'd want to get as far from the influence of the slayers as possible."

"Harley," the priest said it as if her name explained everything.

"What about her would make him come back here?" He prodded.

"As you know, she headed the task force that eventually brought him down."

Brahms hadn't known, but he didn't let it show, as it was apparently common knowledge within the Order.

"Given her past with weres," Francis said, "it surprised me when the cardinal chose her for that mission. In hindsight, though, perhaps her background was the why. He knew she wouldn't rest, that she'd do everything within her power to find and stop Niko, no matter what toll it took on anything or anyone. He must have figured Harley was their best chance of success."

"So, Niko would want revenge because she destroyed his pride."

"And then some. What isn't well-known is the last moments of that battle." The priest's eyes took on a faraway look, as if he were conjuring the events in his memory. "Harley's team had Niko and a handful of his pride cornered while the other teams hunted and destroyed the stragglers. The slayers had taken heavy casualties, killed by the pumas, and some, unfortunately, had to be dispatched by their fellow slayers after they'd been infected. According to Cerise, Harley was in a fury unlike any she'd seen or has seen since."

A brief flash of sorrow crossed Father Francis's face, and Brahms knew it'd take him a while to think of Cerise in past tense.

"Harley went straight for Niko," the priest said, "his mate interfered. Harley killed her, sending Niko into a rage. After that, there was no keeping the two of them apart. They were so equally matched that by the time the rest of her team had killed or incapacitated the others, she and Niko were still going at it. They probably would have continued until one of them was dead. Lord knows Harley wanted to kill him."

"Then, why's he alive?" If there was one thing he was sure of with Harley, it was her stubbornness. He couldn't fathom much of anything stopping her from killing something she wanted dead.

"Ian, who'd been leading a different team, arrived and stepped in. He ordered a few slayers to pull Harley off. Then, he and a few others incapacitated Niko. His excuse was that the white coats would want to study Niko, to see what it was about him that caused the others to follow him. His secondary excuse was that if they lost Harley, the cardinal would never forgive him."

"Do you believe either of those excuses?"

"The last, yes. Any slayer that stood by while Harley was in mortal danger would face the cardinal's full fury. Which is considerable. The first excuse though? At the time, yes, I believed it. Now? I'm not so certain. What I do know is that if Niko is loose, he's waiting for Harley. He knows once she finds out he's free, she'll move God's green Earth to find him."

"Maybe that's why she and Cerise were lured to that cave. For Niko to have his revenge."

"No. That wasn't Niko." Father Francis shook his head. "I'm sure of it. Harley killed his mate. He'd want to destroy her personally. If he'd been there, Harley would have recognized him immediately."

"So then why lure her there?"

The priest twisted the goblet in his hands. "To get rid of Cerise. Or..."

After a few moments passed, Brahms asked, "Or what?"

"Or Niko didn't know. Maybe the pride has fissures we weren't aware of back then. Or they're new strains. Another male vying for dominance of the pride, perhaps. If he accomplished something Niko couldn't, like kill Harley, it'd give him a great deal of clout."

"Maybe." Brahms doubted it. Niko was too sly and too alpha to allow even the tiniest threat to his leadership.

"Please, stay with her. Don't let her trust anyone in the Church," the priest whispered, "even other slayers other than yourself. She'll want to because they're...you're her family. The Order is all she's known since Germaine pulled out of that nightmare."

The priest fell into silence, nibbling on the inside of his lip as he mulled.

Brahms's gut told him Harley wouldn't let him get much, if any, sleep tonight, so he was in no rush. He waited until Father Francis was ready to continue.

"If this is true," Francis folded his hands on his lap, "it has to reach to the highest authority. If so, then the person she's most apt to trust is the one least worthy of it."

## CHAPTER
# ELEVEN

Sneaking out of St. Ambrose without alerting Brahms had been easier than Harley expected.

She glanced at the review mirror of her Tahoe. A few headlights glowed on the highway behind her. Normal late-night traffic. No one followed her closely or consistently. No one had taken the same turns or round-about route. She frowned and concentrated on the road ahead.

It was disappointing. She'd kinda expected to get caught.

After she'd left Brahms and Francis to their friendly chat, she'd stuffed a few items in her bag, grabbed her laptop, and the printout of phone numbers and emails that Francis had left in her room after she'd told him she'd lost her phone in the caves, a tiny white lie that would save him sleepless nights. And perhaps save his skin if the Order came knocking at his door, loaded with questions. He would be safer if he couldn't answer them.

And so would she.

Then, she'd waited until she'd heard both of them go to bed. Waited even longer until she was sure they were asleep, and then she'd quietly escaped through the window.

Brahms was so in tune with his surroundings Harley had expected him to be waiting outside. She'd imagined him insisting on coming with her. But he'd been nowhere in sight.

Not that she wanted him with her on this self-assigned mission.

*Just keep on lying.*

An accomplice would be nice. The Tahoe felt so quiet without Cerise's chatter or humming. Hell, Harley would have settled for Cerise's singing. Wrong lyrics and all. Without anything other than her own thoughts buzzing around in her head unwelcome thoughts of deceptions took hold. Lies. Death.

Brahms. And his damned eyes. The strength he kept carefully contained.

But it was too late to ask him to join her now. Even if she called and rousted him from bed, and assuming he'd agree to drive out to meet her, he'd arrive too late, and their window of opportunity would have slammed shut with the dawn.

She'd consider dragging him into her schemes next time. It'd give her someone to pick on while they waited. Or at least to keep the memory of Cerise's slack, expressionless face out of her head for a while.

A few turns later, still with no tail in sight, she pulled off onto the winding, wooded driveway of St. Mary's. She flicked off her headlights and crept the Tahoe along the asphalt until the trees thinned enough where she could see the outlines of St. Mary's church and rectory while remaining hidden herself.

Harley pulled to the side to nestle the Tahoe along the shoulder of a slight curve that marked the end of the driveway and the beginning of the parking lot. If she went any further, she'd risk someone spotting the gleam of the truck's metal through the trees.

She cut the engine and stretched her legs, settling in to watch. Wait.

Lights burned within three of the rectory's windows. Was someone still awake or was it the new priest's habit to keep some lights on at night. Wouldn't be a bad habit, considering what lurked under the floor of his church.

Harley tugged out her binoculars and focused on one window, then the other, then the other, trying to get a glimpse of the priest or anyone else within. But her view was hampered by curtains that were sheer enough to let out light yet thick enough to obscure the interior.

*Damn it.*

Harley knew most slayers within her region and a fair amount within the United States as a whole. While she didn't know as many sanctuary priests, she knew enough. Chances were, if the priest assigned to St. Mary's was in the Order, she'd recognize them, if she could get a decent glimpse. That'd give her some idea of what sort of situation she was dealing with.

Francis's word was beyond questioning. But St. Mary's priest could have been playing dumb when answering Francis's questions. Or the poor priest had no clue what lay hidden next door to their rectory.

Both scenarios sucked and each opened its own basket of snakes. It'd just be nice to know what species of trouble she was heading into.

If Francis's friend, Fr. Martin, would have been there, she would have opted for the straightforward approach and talked with him first to gain access to his sanctuary. It was the respectful thing to do. Safer, too. She had no driving desire to fight her fellow slayers over a misunderstanding.

But with a temporary priest there, one who was neither sanctuary priest nor slayer, she had to opt for the sneaky approach instead. There was no way of knowing whose side this priest was on, or if he even realized there were sides. Most priests had no clue what the Church did in the shadows. Many of them didn't even believe in the monsters the Order fought. Hell, she'd met some who didn't believe demons existed, even though they preached the truth from the same bible that was rife with them.

Maybe an ignorant priest was worse than a betrayer.

If the priest at St. Mary's was conspiring with the rats within her Order, they might be on alert. Francis' call would surely have aroused their suspicions. They might even have called for backup.

But until she had proof to the contrary, she had to assume the St. Mary's priest was innocent.

Unable to see within the rectory, she set the binoculars on the center console and assessed the exterior for signs of trouble or potential ambush sites. She didn't like surprises unless they involved chocolate.

A warm, yellow-orange light illuminated the rectory porch. It produced few shadows, yet was strong enough Harley could make out the two empty chairs, a small table with an unlit candle in a hurricane glass holder, and the two clay pots that flanked the porch stairs, overflowing with flowers and dangling vines that spilled over the sides of the stairs. Nothing bigger than a fairy could hide over there.

Two bright floodlights flanked the garage casting harsh shadows behind the decorative bushes and trees. Thankfully, the garage was farthest from the church, so the bright lights wouldn't be much of an issue for her to dodge them and avoid being seen. If anything skulked in those deep shadows, it'd have to cross an expanse of open lawn before it got close enough to her to attack. That'd give her plenty of time for defense.

There were no cars in the parking lot for anything to hide behind, in, or under.

Knowing the creatures that stalked in the dark, Harley had always found it strange how packed a church's parking lot could be during the day and how utterly empty it was at night. The very time that defenseless people should gather there. Only a few creatures were inherently afraid of hallowed ground–devils, demons, the cursed, and such, but most churches covertly added other protections that parishioners never suspected were there, yet would ward off murderous beasts, nonetheless. So, few people knew how to protect themselves or their homes from such threats. If what Cerberus said was true, that there'd been a sharp rise in marauding creatures and attacks on people and pets, church parking lots would be full all the time. They'd be the few safe havens available until modern people learned the skills their forefathers had known by rote.

St. Mary's church itself was a burly structure of stone with high, arched stained glass windows. LED accent lights poked from the garden beds around it, spotlighting the rough texture of the stones. Only short flowers and ground cover plants were in the beds, leaving nowhere for anything of significant size to hide.

Double, rough-hewn wooden doors were shadowed within the entry's arch. She snagged the binoculars and trained them on the top of the arch where a human sized creature could easily hide, if it were able to crawl up stone or fly. She didn't see any tell-tale signs that anything was there, but that didn't mean it wasn't. She'd have to get closer to find out.

Setting the binoculars down again, Harley leaned back and waited. She checked her mirrors now and then to see if anything was trying to sneak up on her. Or if Brahms had tailed her after all. But there was nothing except for empty asphalt and trees.

She felt a little guilty for tricking Brahms and leaving him behind. She'd agreed to work with Cerberus, and that meant him, and here she'd gone and disappeared.

*Like his partner, Livia.*

Not quite. She fully intended to come back alive, though, she'd bet when Livia had walked out that safehouse door she hadn't expected to die. She'd have expected to come back to the house, pizza in tow, to relax, and stuff her face. Still, Brahms wouldn't know where Harley was at. What would he think if he woke in the middle of the night and found her gone, too? Then again, why would he seek her out this late, anyway?

*One could imagine.*

Still, she wished she'd possessed the forethought to leave him a note.

*Not like that helped Livia in the end.*

But she wasn't Livia. Harley didn't heal things, she killed them. She was a warrior. If someone tried to kidnap her, they'd initiate their own execution.

Besides, if the killer was part of the Order, would they dare to approach her? Preying on Cerberus agents was one thing, but other slayers? No. If they started plucking off slayers, Germaine wouldn't rest until the rogue slayer was put down, fast.

Maybe it was best she'd left Brahms behind. Trust wasn't exactly Harley's strong suit. Brahms had done nothing that caused her to think he was being dishonest. He was refreshingly open and schmooze free. But that didn't mean he should be privy to the Order's secrets. Sanctuary locations were known only to those in the Order, and even then, it was usually on a need to know basis. That precaution had kept the monsters where they belonged and provided shelter for the slayers during the few times in history when monsters had hunted them.

*Can't kill what you can't find.*

Brahms didn't know what sort of creatures lurked below the marble floor of St. Ambrose. He didn't know under those glossy tiles were several inches of metal alloy and the latest in sound dampening technology. He hadn't been in the church itself or the sacristy, nor near the hidden stairs that led downward into the heart of the sanctuary; hadn't seen Francis's face grow taut and drain of color whenever he glanced at the door.

So, he didn't need to know what lurked below St. Mary's, either.

*Niko.*

Many others, as well, but her prime concern was the were-puma and what remained of his pride. Proving he was here, imprisoned in a nearly indestructible cage, would go quite a way in proving to Brahms, and the rest of Cerberus, that her Order wasn't behind the rise in attacks as they claimed. That Germaine wasn't the slimy liar they made him out to be. Once she established that, she could bring in more slayers, and working together with Cerberus, find and stop the real culprit.

The first light winked out. Harley did a quick check of her weapons. The second light snuffed out, and a few minutes after that, the last light went out, too.

Being cautious, she waited. Listened. Watched.

She checked the clock. Ten minutes passed with no sign of movement in or around the church. Good enough. It was time to act. She'd disengaged her interior lights so they wouldn't automatically fire when she opened the doors. Few beasts were afraid of light. Most of them, including humans, were attracted to it, like wee moths.

*Where there's light, there's prey.*

Making darkness both friend and foe.

Harley slipped out of the Tahoe and into the night. She stepped to the side, into the woods. They smelled clean and crisp.

*Like Brahms. Ugh.*

If she didn't return before he woke up, she'd have to make a hell of an apology.

She slid through the shadows, ducking smoothly under low-hanging limbs as she crossed through the small swath of trees between the drive and the church. Her footsteps silent on the soft bed of leaves and hummus. She kept low, within the protection of the trees, until she'd reached the edge nearest the entryway.

Harley glanced at the rectory, checking the windows and doors. Lights off, no one visible in the windows, no sounds.

It was late, and if the temporary priest didn't realize what sort of church he lived in, she had no reason to suspect he'd be on guard. On the slight off chance that Francis had misinterpreted the situation, she decided to take precautions, anyway. Besides, even if something wonky had happened to Fr. Martin, the real priest and Francis's seminary friend, the St. Mary's slayers might be lurking about. Given the current situation, she wasn't about to trust them, either. Not yet. Not until she saw Niko firmly behind bars where she'd left him.

*And if he's not?*

Then, there was a mound of shit to wade through to find the truth.

She focused on the archway. Even that close, she couldn't quite see the top of the arch or if anything hid within that deep, dark shadow. Only one way to find out. She wasn't exactly in any rush, but she wanted to be back at St. Ambrose before Brahms woke because, well, she wasn't all that great at apologies. If she came clean with him over a heaping plate of breakfast and told him about her nocturnal jaunt, he might be a little less pissed than if he woke to find she was gone.

Francis wouldn't be too pleased with her, either. But he'd be easier to handle. And considering how Livia had died, Francis wouldn't be hurt she'd taken off alone. Brahms might be. A detail she'd failed to think about when she'd planned this whole thing.

*Damn it.*

She assessed the entry. Moonlight illuminated the yard and shone off the short blades of grass. There was no cover between the woods and the door. Nowhere for anything to hide, including herself. She'd be exposed until she reached the archway that protected the wooden door from the weather. If only she possessed the power to pool herself on the ground, like shades, and slink around, then she'd have it made. Bereft of any supernatural talents, she'd have to do it the old-fashioned way.

Harley darted out of the tree line and jogged toward the doorway, keeping as low to the ground as she could. Her gaze constantly swept the yard, church, and rectory. Nothing moved. No sounds that weren't ordinary nocturnal sounds. She ran up the stairs, taking the steps two at a time until she was safely within the stone archway. She glanced upward.

Just stone, no hunkering beasts hanging from the ceiling.

God, she hated when they did shit like that. Creepy as hell.

She tried the door on the off chance it was unlocked. It wasn't. Churches had once been open twenty-four-seven to provide a place to pray or shelter. Unfortunately, priests had been forced to lock their doors when thieves started pillaging holy ground for any sort of valuables they could hawk. Not to mention the people who broke into churches to vandalize them. Sad testaments to the world's tumbling morals and degrading faith that Germaine often lamented.

Leaning against the cool stone wall, she dug into her pocket to retrieve her picks and studied the yard again.

A light ping shimmied across her senses.

Something. Someone was out there. She felt them watching her. But what or who? Father Martin's slayers? If so, why hadn't they attacked her? If she caught someone skulking around St. Ambrose, she'd hit them like a barreling Mack truck. Although, more slayers were like Cerise than her, so maybe they were watching to see what she did. Her actions would give them a fair idea of what she was after, answering questions a real bad guy might not answer once caught, not truthfully, anyway.

If it was Father Martin's slayers, they'd inevitably confront her before she got to the sanctuary. What would she tell them? She preferred the truth. However, there was a miniscule chance Brahms was right and the Order was involved in releasing those beasts on the unsuspecting world. Could she trust the St. Mary's slayers with the truth? If she did, it wouldn't be just her life on the line. They'd wrongly figure that Francis was involved, and after some investigation, they'd find out about Brahms, Cree, and Thayer. The Cerberus agents could take care of themselves, Francis not so much.

She'd have to lie to protect him. Either way, she'd decide once they made their move because their actions would tell her just as much as hers would tell them.

Crouching in front of the door, she went to work on the lock. The hair on the back of her head rose. Yeah, someone was definitely being a peep.

*And if it's not Father Martin's slayers?*

Then she hoped to God it was whoever had started this murderous mess. She was all for quick, bloody resolutions.

The lock tumbled and released.

She pushed the door open and scooted in, keeping close to the floor until she was safely beyond the threshold. After another quick glance toward the woods, she *shicked* the door shut and debated whether she should lock it behind her. If the watcher was her fellow slayers, they'd already have keys so locking it would only hamper her efforts for a fast escape. If it was something else, she'd have to face it or them eventually, so it may as well be on hallowed ground where she'd have a bit of an advantage.

Leaving the door unlocked, she made her way back to the sacristy as unobtrusively as she could. She doubted anyone was in there, but caution was called for.

The last time she'd been to St. Mary's was when they'd brought Niko and his furry friends to their pretty new cat boxes. Still, she didn't expect any surprises or changes in protocol. Akin to the Church that started it, the Order stayed the same throughout the years, taking change slowly, if at all. Since the Order's slayers came from across the globe, they liked to keep things uniform to avoid confusion. So, like most other sanctuary churches, the entry to the sanctuary itself was hidden behind an enormous cedar closet. Built of heavy, solid wood and attached to the wall, floor, and ceiling, no one in their right mind would attempt to move it.

She opened the closet door, parted the priestly vestments, and stepped into the incense and cedar laden closet. Then, she pushed on one of the rear panels, revealing a glowing, electronic keypad.

*Well. Shit.*

When she'd planned this excursion, she hadn't thought this far ahead. She knew her code, Cerise's, Francis's, and Germaine's–assuming he hadn't changed his recently. The system kept a running log of who entered and exited and when. If she used any of the codes, the Order would know it was her and thus know exactly where she was, or had been, if she got in and out of there fast enough. Cerise was dead. Francis would never venture somewhere like this on his own. Germaine was up in Chicago.

*Who'd bother to look?*

If she didn't touch, change, or remove anything, chances were that no one would check the log unless Niko ran his filthy mouth. If she played him right, he'd have no way of knowing she wasn't there on official Order business, so he'd have no reason to get chatty with anyone who didn't ask.

Regardless, she had to get into the sanctuary, and there was no way to do that other than to enter a valid code.

*Whose?*

If the situation went wildly awry, she didn't want to get anyone else in trouble. If anyone were to be put in danger because of her actions, it'd be her. She plugged in her own code. The LED flashed green. The wood clad metal door whisked inward to reveal a wide staircase with muted yellow lighting.

She took a step forward and descended into the chilly sanctuary, each step taking her closer to answers she might not want to know.

IAN WATCHED the darkened church from the comfort of his car and pondered his next move. If he killed Harley without the cardinal's permission, there'd be hell to pay, both literally and figuratively. However, he could set the scene to appear she died while under attack by one of the creatures. Hmm. Weres, maybe. Yes. That would be an apt end to her. Poetic even. A slayer initiated into their ranks by a werewolf pack's violence and later killed by the same. Yes. He liked that a lot.

But even if she died at their claws, there'd be a digital trail that would lead straight to him. Even if he erased it, the timing for the attack was off, and Cardinal Germaine was likely to suspect someone in his ranks, most likely him, of setting up Harley's demise. He liked to think he kept his disdain of Harley well disguised, but the cardinal saw too much too often.

No. As much as he disliked waiting for approval, it was in his best interest to rein in his desires.

Unable to make his move, he was about to start the car and leave, when his phone rang.

"Speaking of the devil." He plucked the phone out of the console and answered, "How are you this night, cardinal?"

"I received your texts. Now, I want to hear what you've found."

So much for pleasantries.

A furious tapping came through the line, a pencil mercilessly thwapped against paper, something the cardinal did when he was most agitated.

"You're not going to enjoy hearing it," Ian warned. They said pictures were worth a thousand words, but the cardinal always expected explanations, which was prudent. After all, images also lied. Then again, so did people.

Such delicious dilemmas.

"I'm growing impatient, Ian."

Drawing a breath, Ian laid out what he knew of Harley's movements for the cardinal, twisting the truth just enough to shed the worst light he could on Harley. He started with finding Harley in the company of Cerberus agents, in their safe house, no less, to bringing those same agents onto the sacred and most secret grounds of a sanctuary church to burying Cerise without filing a formal report. He added in a few dashes of salt to the wound, some real, some not, but if Cardinal Germaine believed it, then it hardly mattered. Harley was a threat to his noble goals, and if it took less than honest stories to prod the cardinal into action, he was sure the angels would forgive him. It was all for the greater good.

When he finished, there was a long, drawn silence.

"Your Eminence?" Ian asked, wondering if the cardinal's cell had dropped the call. It had better not have. He didn't feel inclined to repeat the entire story over again.

"Why is her signal not transmitting?" The cardinal's voice was tight with anger.

"Assuming that it wasn't damaged—"

"Our system shows no sign of that."

"Then I'd have to guess she has—" He cleared his throat. This next bit of information would surely throw the cardinal off the edge, and the cardinal's fury wasn't an easy thing to face, even if it wasn't directed at you. "That she has removed it."

Silence. Deep and utter silence threaded with anger. This time, Ian didn't dare break it. He tugged on the charger cord and waited, watching the flittering leaves of the trees glimmer in the moonlight.

Finally, the cardinal spoke, "You know what to do."

*Yes.*

Ian contained his excitement and said, "Are you sure?" with

the greatest amount of concern he could summon on Harley's behalf, which wasn't all that much.

"She's left us no other option." Then, the line went dead.

As dead as Harley was about to be.

Ian grinned and tossed his phone back into the console, his body humming with excitement. He'd waited for this night a very, very long time. He was going to bask in the glory of it and remember dear Harley's dying screams for months to come.

# CHAPTER TWELVE

*This can't be.*

With feet that felt as heavy as two sledgehammers, Harley forced herself to take another step into the sanctuary beneath St. Mary's. Her stomach felt gutted. Like a deer.

*What happened here?*

Instead of the customary brightly lit interior sanctuaries were known for, St. Mary's sanctuary was dim and rife with shadows. The backup lights bathed the hallway in amber, casting an eerie orange sheen over the metal alloy bars.

Order protocol demanded that if anything went wrong, no matter how slight, at a sanctuary, that the slayers in adjoining turfs were to be alerted. Immediately. Harley's turf was the next one south. She ought to have been notified that St. Mary's had been compromised. If they couldn't get a hold of her, they were supposed to leave a message with the sanctuary priest. Even in his distracted state, Francis wouldn't have forgotten to tell her if a notification of that magnitude had rolled in.

The auxiliary power system hummed. Something she shouldn't have been able to hear over the growls, snarls, or screeches of the creatures housed there. But other than the burr of power, the sanctuary was silent. Nothing banged on the walls, no claws scratched over bars. There were no animalistic huffs. No keens of yearning as the males and females of each species smelled one another but couldn't touch.

Down the hall, as far as she could see, the barred doors that once securely held their dangerous tenants gaped open at haphazard angles, yet none appeared broken. Whatever had happened there happened fast, and no one had stayed around to clean the chaos.

*But what and why?*

Evacuations were almost non-existent in modern times. Built to withstand the most brutal of storms and completely sealable to withstand extensive floods, the Order didn't abandon their sanctuaries due to weather or much of anything else. Diseases and illnesses were treated within the confines of the sanctuary to avoid spreading it to other populations. If creatures attempted to riot, the local slayers swiftly destroyed them, and if that somehow failed, they'd pump the central air system with noxious fumes, killing almost everything in the sanctuary within minutes. In the case of smaller creatures, mere seconds. The extensive fire systems could douse any sort of blaze, so even the threat of fire wouldn't require an evacuation. The Order was so adept at keeping their sanctuaries secret, their security and firepower so daunting that the raids, which had once been prevalent, to both break their cohorts out of the sanctuary and kill slayers had ceased decades ago.

Why, then, had they evacuated that sanctuary?

St. Mary's sanctuary was bigger than St. Ambrose's, boasting several hallways that spoked off the main hall, each lined with cells on either side. It was also one of the few sanctuaries in the area capable of housing the wispies, slayer slang for insubstantial beings, such as apparitions, shades, air elementals, revenants, and their misty ilk.

*Where were they?*

Harley crept down the hall, glancing into each cell. They were empty. Every single one.

Had they cleared the sanctuary to make room for more beasts? She frowned. Were they expecting a major influx of creatures? It'd make some sense, especially if the rate of attacks and sightings were on the rise. But why hadn't Germaine told her? He usually requested her help to oversee any major moves, particularly when the sanctuary was this close to her home turf, and especially if that move involved Niko.

"They should have let me kill that bastard." Her words echoed down the empty hall.

The Order would occasionally purge a sanctuary, sometimes sending creatures to other sanctuaries for holding and other times killing them. When that happened, they notified slayers within the entire state so they could prepare their sanctuary for new creatures or help contain them during the move or put them down. There'd been not a single peep about purging this or any sanctuary within Harley's range.

*The white coats?*

Not likely. Even if the white coats put in a massive order for beasts to experiment on, she'd never seen them clear out an entire section, let alone an entire sanctuary. They were picky folk, pulling a bit of this and a bit of that from different sanctuaries across the country, leaving sporadic open cells in each one.

Whatever had happened, it'd flown under her radar and that ticked her off.

The quiet was creeping her out. But wait. There. A soft buzz threaded through the incessant hum of the backup power. Computer fans. Of course. The office. The slayers would have kept a record of what they removed from the sanctuary and why. She ought to be able to find where they'd taken them by sifting through the files. She hesitated at an intersection of halls and listened. Yup, the office was down there.

Since no one and nothing was around, she stopped being stealthy and opted for fast, marching down the empty hall to the office. That door, too, was ajar.

She pushed it open with her fingertips and peeked inside. Everything seemed in order, nothing in disarray. If the regular lights had been on, she wouldn't think anything was amiss. With a light tap, she woke the computer, plopped into the office chair, then rolled up to the desk.

A few seconds after entering her code to gain access to the system, she navigated to the file category where the slayers would have recorded the event that had emptied their cells only to find nothing. No records of any move, let alone one of such a great magnitude. No requests filed from the white coats. No evacuation orders. Nothing to show why the sanctuary ceased operations.

According to the files, the sanctuary was fully operational, the creatures were snug in their cells, and everything was normal.

When it wasn't.

Either the local slayers had grievously neglected their duty and failed to file the right paperwork, or something had prevented them from doing so. Perhaps permanently.

"Who?" A few keystrokes later and she was staring at the names listed on the entry log. "Why hello, Ian."

She crossed her arms over her chest and glowered at the screen. Ian's name was the last on the list. He wasn't assigned to St. Mary's. He wasn't local. Though he did do lots of things for Germaine, including inspection duty. No one liked the inspections, but they were a necessary evil to keep track of who was keeping what where. It also helped them track creature lifespans. Maybe he'd been there for an inspection?

Had Ian found something so amiss during that inspection

he'd petitioned to shut this sanctuary down? If so, why hadn't she been involved, and why was there no paperwork? Germaine loved his redundancies. He'd have insisted on extensive files for something like that.

She checked the date of the sanctuary's last login, which was Ian's code dated a week before Cerise had dragged her into those Godforsaken caves. So, she'd been around for Germaine and Ian to contact. It wasn't as if she'd been missing or anything, like now, so why the secrecy?

It irked her Germaine trusted Ian with such an important move but not seen fit to bring her in on the action. She'd have loved to help move Niko, if for no other reason than to hope he resorted to violence, and she was forced to kill his ass. Germaine knew damned well that Niko was held here and knew she had a vested interest in that furry bugger. Why the hell would he not only leave her out of it, but leave her completely in the dark?

Unless...

What if Brahms was right about everything?

No. Germaine wouldn't do that. He loved his flock. He'd never put them in danger, never put her in danger, and he had to know if Niko ever tasted freedom, she'd be one of his first targets and he'd be hers.

"Ian." She pushed herself up and away from the desk with such force that the chair clattered against the wall. That made more sense. As Germaine's little go-to boy, Ian had access to every sanctuary in the world, to any information he wanted. He possessed the clout to get in and out of any sanctuary and any system whenever he felt like it. If anyone in the Order was apathetic enough to commit such an atrocity as loosing bloodthirsty beasts upon the unsuspecting public, it was Ian.

Francis's comment about thinking Ian was lying about Cerise's fate floated through her head. She hadn't had time to ask him what he'd meant, but it'd been clear Francis neither liked nor trusted him.

"And he was in *my* sanctuary." She slammed past the chair. It skittered into the hall where it hit the wall and tipped onto the floor with a clamor of metal on metal. "If he messed with anything–"

A low grating sound came from her right, farther down the hall. She froze and listened. *Creak. Scrape.* Stone against stone. She knew that sound and it was nothing good.

*Thud. Thud.* The floor quivered under her feet.

She turned toward the racket.

A hulking mass stomped out of the shadows, the top of its head whisking only inches away from the twelve-foot ceiling. Its arms and legs built of bulky, oblong rocks held together with swirling, misty magic that pulsed between lime and forest green. Its chest was several thick slabs of stone protected by several more for its back. Glowing green emanated within hollows drilled into the dark, hewn stone face that served as its eyes and its gash of a maw.

Stone golem. Great. And she'd woken it up.

They were grumpy in the best of times, but infinitely worse when first activated. A favored creation of powerful mages, golems relentlessly protected the area or item the mage ordered into their charge. They were a loyal and effective means of security. If only their mages would be kind enough to dismantle the golems or pass them on to another master before they died, she wouldn't take issue with them. Unfortunately, mages were prone to sudden deaths, magical mishaps, backfiring spells, rival families, and enemy factions, which left golems without a master to instruct and control them. When that happened, the golems ran amok, viewing anything and everything that moved as a threat that needed squashing.

Though she was faster and could outrun it, golems were

sleepless and single-minded. Once activated, there was no guessing where it'd rampage or how many people it'd hurt after she escaped. There was no choice other than to destroy it before it left the church grounds. A task that'd take considerable doing even if Cerise were there to back her up.

*And here I am, by my lonesome.*

Yeah, she should have brought Brahms. "Twenty-twenty hindsight is a bitch."

Curling its burly arms like a weightlifter peacocking for the women, the golem leaned forward and roared, washing the hallway in its strange green light.

Harley shuffled backward toward the main hall. If she could keep it moving slowly, it'd limit the amount of damage the monstrosity could do to the church. She was going to be in enough trouble with Germaine as it was. She didn't need to add destruction of a sanctuary church to her growing list of offences.

The golem hunched its shoulders, shifted its considerable weight from left to right, and then charged, its heavy feet banging against the metal floor.

*So much for damage control.*

She whirled and ran. She had nothing on her that could take the thing down. Even the grenades she packed on her hips would barely scathe it unless she slam dunked one into its mouth and then bolted the damned thing shut so it couldn't spit it out. Chances of it sitting placidly still while she did that were slim. She had the perfect solution if she could make it to her truck without getting pummeled to death.

She skittered around the corner and ran smack into another warm body. Hard. Definitely male.

*Ian coming back to inspect his handiwork?*

She bounced off him and before she could hazard an upward glance, a stone fist thrust toward her. She ducked and rolled.

White sparks flew around her as the stone impacted with the metal bars.

*This night keeps getting better and better. Maybe fancy restaurants and inane conversations with Max's friends aren't a bad way to spend the evening after all.*

# CHAPTER THIRTEEN

Snuggled under his thick, warm blankets, Francis stirred in his bed.

What was that?

He strained to listen. The ancient refrigerator clunked, whirled, and hummed. Was it the fridge's rattling that jostled him out of his dreams? Perhaps he ought to spend the money and replace it, like Harley said. It'd certainly bring peace to the rectory on two fronts, less noise and less hounding by Harley. The hit to the church's budget would be worth it.

He didn't hear anything other than the fridge, which never woke him before. Had he imagined the noise, a lingering sound from a forgotten dream?

Confused, he roused himself enough to peer out of his mound of blankets and check the time glowing in neon blue from his alarm clock. The early wee morning hours. Not even Harley would be up at this ungodly time.

He groaned, dropped back into the mattress, rolled over, and tucked the covers in around him.

It must be that second glass of wine he drank before bed that was disturbing his sleep. He slept fine when he drank one glass. Two did something weird to his sleep pattern, but he hadn't cared. He'd only wanted to erase the hard knowledge of Cerise's death, murder, if what Brahms said had merit. He'd gone against his better judgement and downed a second glass, hoping he'd forget Cerise's waxy expression, and the hollow sound of dirt hitting her pine coffin.

She'd deserved better.

A full slayer's funeral with all the trimmings and ceremony. Her fellow slayers gathered at her graveside. Yet even that had been taken from her.

Precious Cerise. So different from Harley, yet such an integral part of both of their lives. Cerise's serenity and thoughtful ways kept Harley on as even of a keel as was possible, considering Harley's nature.

But Cerise was in heaven now, her soul safe, guarded by the angels. That knowledge eased some of his sorrow. She was far from the trials Harley had yet to face. No, his grief wasn't for the dead. It was for him. For Harley. For those who must persevere through the loss of their dear friend. His heart broke for Harley. She'd lost more than a partner, she'd lost a friend, a sister, a confidant. Yet no matter how devastating her loss, Harley wouldn't mourn until she'd brought justice to those responsible for Cerise's death. It was in her nature to fight first and deal with the aftermath later. If at all.

Francis was both proud of Harley's dedication and worried one day the dams she built around her emotions would break and she'd be swept away by their chaos or her pent emotions would leak out in other unexpected but no less dangerous ways. Mourning was a natural and necessary process. Without that purging of sorrow, Harley could make mistakes she might not otherwise make if she'd allowed herself to process and clear her emotions.

When a slayer was in the field, mistakes often proved fatal.

What would happen to Harley now? Who would stand beside her and keep her steady? To keep her from spiraling from righteous vengeance to death? If what Brahms had told him about betrayal within the Order was true, and Lord forbid the cardinal was in on it, would she get another partner? Would the Order fall?

He prayed not.

As much as violence wasn't his way, he realized its necessity. If guardians like Harley didn't exist, the wolves would be free to ravage the lambs, which included him. His book knowledge was vast. Fighting skills? He rated his as slightly below mousy. And he passed out at the sight of blood.

Besides, seeing those beasts behind bars was enough to give him nightmares. Seeing them loose in the world?

He shuddered, pulled his knees closer to his chest, and curled into a fetal position.

Phah. Surely, his worries were for nothing. His mind was over-dramatizing. The Order had existed since the dawn of the Church, and it'd exist until the snuffing of time, when God called an end to this world.

A light scrape.

It wasn't the scuff of a shoe over carpet, no. It was a scratching noise, as if something were trying to get in or out of something. He listened. There, again, it came from the wall. Mice? He'd thought Harley killed all of them already. She couldn't tolerate the idea of mice in the house. They reminded her entirely too much of rats. She used everything in the mouse killing arsenal to get rid of them and keep them out. Her yearly ritual of sealing the house tight would put any handyman's work to shame.

He flopped to his other side and tried to ignore the strange, dragging scratches so he could drift back to sleep. He had no desire to tear through the walls to extract a mouse, nor did he want to leave his cozy bed to set traps. Once he told Harley about it in the morning, she wouldn't be amused. She'd move into action. The entire house would be lined with traps and poison within minutes.

He closed his eyes, pulled the blankets tighter, and yawned.

A gentle scrape on metal. Jiggling. A turn.

The saliva in Francis's mouth evaporated. The doorknob. Mice can't turn a doorknob.

*Creeeeaaaak.*

*The door.*

Harley refused to allow anyone to oil the hinges in the house so the creaks could function as a cheap alarm system, alerting the occupant when someone entered their room.

But who was it? Besides himself, only Harley and Brahms were in the house, and he didn't think either of them would be interested in sneaking into his room. If Harley needed to talk to him, she'd just bang on the door until he answered it.

Maybe, in his distracted state, he'd accidentally left the door ajar, and the breeze swung it open. It wouldn't be the first time he'd forgotten to shut or lock a door, and it wasn't likely to be his last. Heck, if it weren't for Harley's rabid insistence on security, he wouldn't bother to lock the entry doors.

A movement by the foot of the bed, soft as a whisper.

Cold.

An unnatural chill spread across his body and gripped his heart. Francis shivered. He wished he'd listened to Harley and kept a weapon under his pillow. At the time she suggested it, he'd thought she'd been being overprotective and a little paranoid to think he'd need to defend himself in his own bedroom. Who broke into a priest's house?

Without a weapon and knowing only the most rudimentary of self-defense, the only way he'd get himself safely out of this was to escape and get to Harley and then let her and Brahms hunt the intruder.

He released his hold on the blankets and rolled to the side. A freezing breeze swiped past him. Something smashed onto the bed, right where he'd been a second before. He hit the hardwood floor with a yelp. Harley was a notoriously light sleeper, she'd probably heard the impact, but he erred on the safe side.

"Harley," he yelled as loud as he could then offered a quick prayer that he'd hear her rumbling down the hall, barrels blazing, any second.

He just had to survive until she got there.

Francis disentangled himself from the twisted wad of sheets and blankets and pushed them away. The door wasn't that far, and it was open. He could make it there and possibly even out into the hall. Then, he looked up at who, or what, attacked him.

Arctic cold shot through his veins.

There, squatting upon the bed he'd just vacated, was a creature straight out of nightmare and myth. Its mottled corpse blue skin was slick with an unhealthy sheen that reflected the moonlight in a dull, unearthly glow. Curved yellow claws clung to the mattress, puncturing the material in pocked dents. Its thin shoulders slumped below a too-thin neck. But its face. Oh, Lord, its face. Its skin stretched tight against rigid cheekbones, then dipped low, plunging into shadowed, hollow cheeks. Its lips a deep, bloodless gash across its face. And the teeth. Oh, God, its teeth. Sharp and yellow. Oozing with mucus.

It watched him with eyes burning with unholy hunger.

*Vampire.*

Everything he'd learned about vampires in his training dissipated. His sensibilities fled. His mind scrambled for purchase but found none. Out of desperation, he mimicked the priests in the horror films Harley was so fond of. He reached under his nightshirt and held his cross in front of him like a shield. "Get back, in the name of God, you abomination."

Its foul, wormy lips peeled back in an amused grin.

His heart plummeted to his toes. *Virus.* Vampires were different from, yet similar to, weres in that they were infected with a virus that mutated their bodies and caused sensitivity to certain things like light. No cross, no hallowed ground, would save him because no virus heeded the holy power of God.

*Harley, where are you?*

It moved so fast Francis barely registered it. One blink it was on the bed, the next it was on top of him, its drool threading onto his chest. The rancid odor of decay, of death, assaulted his nose.

Francis opened his mouth to scream, but nothing came out.

IAN SKEWED his lips to the side and watched the exterior of St. Ambrose's rectory from the comfort of his car. He grabbed his drive-through coffee and sipped it, wanting the warm liquid to banish his growing disappointment.

Destroying Harley was turning out to be entirely too easy.

With the marvels of modern technology, he'd remotely accessed the security system with his laptop, he'd unlocked and opened every cell in St. Ambrose's sanctuary with one push of a button. Then he'd opened the main door to release the creatures in a sudden wave. He'd waited until the creatures had burst through the church doors and crashed through the stained-glass windows, making quite a wreck of the exterior.

Ian had expected Harley to react to the noise. Expected that she'd storm out of the rectory to find a horde of beasts surging toward her. Beasts she'd caged, beasts who'd enjoy toying with her, and ripping her to shreds. He'd been so looking forward to seeing her fight for her life, for Francis's life. Alone. She'd have ultimately failed because no single slayer could withstand that many creatures at one time. He'd thought that she'd either die fighting or forced into a hasty retreat.

But disappointingly, she'd never exited the rectory. The lights remained off with just the regular porch lights illuminating the grounds.

It seemed like no one inside had awakened to the ruckus he'd caused, and he didn't have all night to sit there and wait for her. He had to leave before either law enforcement or the creatures themselves caught him. Just because he'd broken them out of their cages didn't mean they'd curb their murderous impulses to thank him for their freedom.

"Come on out, Harley." He pushed another button to release acid into the sanctuary that would melt the bars and cages, leaving them as nothing more than a curiosity for law enforcement and the fire investigator. Then he pressed another button and released an accelerant through the church's sprinkler system. Chemically, it was so akin to gasoline even the best of fire investigators would rule in favor of arson.

As the first licks of flame flickered in the broken windows, Ian glanced to the rectory again. Still no Harley. He drummed his fingers on the steering wheel. Had the vampires gotten the best of her? He'd watched them sneak in and figured she'd make quick work of them before rushing outside to tackle the remaining creatures. But still no lights clicked on in the rectory. No Harley came racing out the door with bullets and grenades flying.

*A shame.*

He'd expected better of the Order's golden child.

His time was running out, and it seemed hers already had, or soon would. Not even the slayers or sanctuary priests knew the same accelerant that ran through the sanctuaries also ran through the rectories.

Harley soon would. Too late.

He hit a series of buttons to release the accelerant into the rectory. Within seconds, the building went up in a violent whoosh of flames.

Sirens sounded in the distance. Someone must have called the disturbance in already.

He cast a last look at the rectory and pulled away from the curb. He'd imagined Harley's death to be more dramatic. Bloody. Screamy.

But she'd died with less than a whimper.

Ian rolled down his windows to enjoy the smoke-tinged night breeze. Ah, well. It seemed Harley had lost her fight when she'd lost Cerise. Pity, that. He relaxed into his seat and smoothly eased his car onto the expressway. He'd be miles away before the firefighters put out the blazes he'd started.

His phone rang, disturbing his peace. The cardinal again. Probably wanting to know if the deed was done.

"It's taken care of," Ian said, forcing a smooth tone.

"Did you bother," the cardinal's voice was entirely too quiet for Ian's comfort, "to ensure Harley was there?"

"She was there earlier, and I didn't see her leave. Where would she go?"

"To St. Mary's."

"How?" He'd went to get a coffee from town after Harley had doused the light in her room. He'd left his post for only a short time and would have forgone the caffeine if he'd thought she planned to leave in the middle of the night. What would possess her to leave, anyway? Shouldn't she be mourning her dead partner?

"Why don't you tell me? You were supposed to watch her and take care of this issue."

"I can get to St. Mary's in—"

"No. I've already sent someone else to take care of it. Someone closer. By the time you get there she'll be gone. Again."

"That means she knows Niko is free," Ian whispered, giddy about the turn of events. No wonder she hadn't lived up to his expectations. She hadn't even been there. Fr. Francis would have been, though, and with any luck, the Cerberus agent was also in the rectory he'd just turned to ash.

This new twist would be so much more amusing. Harley was a challenge. A prey befitting of him. No. Not prey. Predator versus predator. Yes. Excitement radiated through him, and he feared he'd laugh with the cardinal still on the line.

The cardinal might send another of his faithful to take Harley out but whoever that was wouldn't best her. Now she realized she had enemies in the Order, and surely, she'd figured it out by now. The other slayer would fail, must fail, because killing Harley and her Cerberus friends was Ian's job, not theirs.

"I am extremely disappointed in you, Slayer Ian."

"Your Eminence, I can still be of—"

"Use? Yes. Indeed, you can. I need you to contact our faithful slayers and order them to cease their current missions immediately. They are to release the beasts, as planned, taking care of any other issues as they see fit."

A spiritual war was no different from any other; whoever wasn't your ally was an enemy, and enemies of the faithful died.

"All of them, your Eminence?" Another twist that would add another layer of difficulty to his pursuit of Harley. The beasts they released didn't hold any love for those who freed them. They'd attack Ian and the faithful slayers just as readily as they'd attack anyone else. While he appreciated the added challenge, the timing was wrong. It was wiser to wait, but perhaps he was misguided. The angels spoke to him, yes, but God Himself spoke to the cardinal, and who'd know better what time to enact the plan than he who was led by the Creator Himself? Ian felt instantly chastised. Who was he to disagree with the will of God?

"From all the sanctuaries in every nation," the cardinal said.

"Yes, your Eminence. Immediately." After he'd fulfilled this latest duty, he'd pray and scourge himself. Blood and pain would win forgiveness for his insolent thoughts. Once he was again in angelic good graces, he would begin releasing the beasts. Not all the sanctuaries would need to burn, just a select few to add dashes of fact and reality to the story Cardinal Germaine would use to help herd the flock back on the acceptable path and point their righteous anger and fingers in the correct direction.

# CHAPTER FOURTEEN

"Move." Brahms grabbed Harley's arm and yanked her out of the way a nanosecond before the stone golem's trunk of a leg smashed into the bars where she'd fallen. He pulled her tight against his chest and turned to shield her from the worst of the flying sparks. Ignoring the flecks of hot pain that skittered across his back, he pushed Harley forward trying to propel both of them toward the exit. "Come on."

But she wasn't cooperating. She whirled toward him, cocked her fist back, and he thought she was going to deck him. Surprise, followed closely by relief, flooded her face and she lowered her arm.

"Holy shit," she said. "Don't go sneaking around like that. I thought you were–never mind." Her eyes narrowed, slightly. "Wait. What are you doing here?"

Her reaction pleased him. She might not trust him, not fully, but the fact she hadn't clocked him was progress. Brahms decided not to fight or rationalize why his attraction to the feisty, irreverent, foul-mouthed woman continued to grow. A reason existed for everything, even if the seekers of those reasons never discovered them. He'd have to adapt to these new feelings and accept them, much as one accepted the existence of mosquitos.

"You're not as good of a liar as you think you are," he said.

"Stalker." She flashed him a grin.

Then they dashed down the hall toward the stairwell.

"This corridor is a dead end," she pointed to her left. Then she pointed to the right. "That one loops around to the corridor behind us, I think. You can use them to keep out of its reach for a while."

"You think?" She wasn't seriously planning to stay down here with a rampaging golem, was she? Sure, they both had pistols, but no sane person shot at a stone golem and only a suicidal one would fire on it in such close quarters. They were surrounded by metal. The bullets would ricochet like a barrage of lethal crazy balls. If they had a mage like Celeste, she could sever the magical ties that bound the entity to the rocks, and the golem would collapse, a limp puppet with no strings. Because they lacked a mage, they needed to crush the stone, but neither of them had a weapon capable of that powerful of a blunt blow. With no viable means to destroy it, their only reasonable option was to get to the exit and seal the doors then come back later with the proper weapons or a mage. He knew little about the metal the Order used for their sanctuaries, but they were overly cautious with everything else, so he had no reason to doubt that the metal would hold the golem here, as it obviously had in the past.

"Yeah, pretty sure," she said.

The golem lumbered around the corner and released an ear-pummeling roar. His open maw flooded the hall with an alien green light.

"Why did you have to piss him off?" Brahms asked. He suspected provoking people and things was an innate part of Harley's nature. Working with her would prove interesting in a demented way.

"I have that effect." Her eyes glowed with mischief. "But trust me, I have a plan."

Did he trust her? Surprisingly, he did. When had that happened? "All right, what is it?"

She gave him an impish smile then turned and darted toward the exit. "Keep it busy."

*Keep it busy?*

Brahms shook his head as Harley ran up the stairs, taking them three at a time. He groaned. "Hey, play fetch with the puppy, would you?"

Behind him, stone crunched against metal. The floor shook. The golem picked up speed, and it was no playful fluffy puppy. Not even the grizzly could withstand a tussle with a stone golem. Besides, Brahms wouldn't shift even if the bear's spirit could thwart it. Not now, not when he'd made some headway earning Harley's trust. When the time was right, when he'd helped her through the betrayal of her Order, once everything calmed down, then he'd find a way to tell her what he was so that she'd understand he wasn't one of the weres she hated. To show her that he and grizzly's spirit coexisted naturally and weren't a threat to her or anyone other than their enemies. And even with enemies, Brahms had witnessed grizzly show mercy and compassion when a were never would.

"Guess I'm the ball." He pivoted, hopping up and down to snag the golem's attention. "Come on, boy. Let's go for a run."

It stomped closer. He waited until it was within a few feet, and then he took off down the hallway to the right, with the golem clomping and scraping behind him.

*This better not be a dead end.*

~

HARLEY POPPED the back of the Tahoe open, opened the secret panel off the side, and dug into the hidden weapons box. She felt a twinge of guilt about leaving Brahms with the golem, but there were some things a gal had to do on her own, like rummaging through her weapons stash. Besides, he was plenty capable of keeping out of its strike range for a while.

She frowned.

Weird. It'd been an instinctual assumption he could tend the situation until she returned. Without a second of hesitation, she'd treated him like a partner and hadn't realized it. She wasn't sure how she felt about that. Having grown up within the Order, her only partners had been fellow slayers hand-chosen by Germaine. He'd even picked her sparing partners. She hadn't meshed with a few of them and had proceeded with her own patented form of vetting a partner until they'd adamantly requested transfers. Still, they'd been slayers and followed the same basic rules, mostly. Stranger than trusting in Brahms's talent was that she wasn't inclined to put him through her vetting process.

Come to think of it, she hadn't bothered to put Cerise through it, either. In both cases, the partnership just seemed right. It clicked.

*Or I'm going soft, damn it.*

Regardless, she could trust him more than her own Order at the moment, so it worked as a temporary thing. As for the future, well, who the hell knew?

"Where is it?" She tossed a metal ammo box to the side and felt around. She hoped the clamoring and roars of the golem didn't wake the temporary priest inside the rectory. Sanctuaries were soundproof, but she'd left the door open, and she'd clearly heard its roar inside the worship area. Maybe the priest was one of those white noise types who couldn't sleep without a fan or something running in the background. If so, that'd block some of the commotion until they lured the golem out of the church itself. Then, nothing would block that thing's roars.

She glanced back at the buildings.

The rectory remained dark, but that was no guarantee the priest wouldn't jolt awake soon or that he wasn't, even now, wise enough to leave the lights off as he peeked out the windows. She couldn't use a flashlight in case he took a gander out his window in search of the cause of the racket. As long as he didn't see anything that blatantly said, *Skulking human about,* he might shrug off the noise to raccoons and shuffle back to bed. But if he saw someone lurking in the woods flashing a light hither and yon, he'd call the police.

Under normal circumstances, the Order would have her back and she could proceed with confidence, knowing any dealings with law enforcement would be brief, end amicably, and there'd be no record of the event or her presence on scene. Tonight, she was working without the Order's blessing, and she didn't know how Germaine would react if he knew she was there investigating the Order without his knowledge or consent. At the very least, he'd be pissy she hadn't followed his orders. If he discovered she was alive and well, yet hadn't checked in and worse, had removed her chip, that Italian temper of his would make Mount Vesuvius's fiery eruption on Pompeii look like a backyard party sparkler. Most people knew Germaine as a kind and generous man, and he was, but when he popped it was a scary sight.

When Germaine worked himself into a fit of anger, he was impossible to predict. He might send a squad of slayers to bring her in, forcibly if necessary, or he might help her out with a bit of blackmail thrown in, or he might let her stew in a jail for a while until she reevaluated her priorities. She couldn't afford even a few hours dealing with the police, let alone days in a cell as Germaine decided how he wanted to handle her little excursion.

Niko was out there, somewhere, and she'd bet her pretty .50

caliber he was doing what he did best–slaughtering weak, innocent folk and infecting the strong ones with the were virus to grow his pride.

Much like her, he favored the use of superior force.

She'd hunt Niko's furry ass either way but knowing her Order was culpable for his release made finding and killing him a moral priority. Then, maybe, possibly, when she handed his tanned hide over to Germaine, he'd realize she'd done as she must, and it wasn't solely a personal thing. He'd be proud.

Her hand closed over a rectangular block. Plastic crinkled beneath her fingers. "A-ha."

She rustled around near where she'd found the block and located the detonator and wire that she'd tucked next to it. She shut and locked the truck with her fob then ran back toward the church, prepping the C-4 as she went.

If the priest wasn't already awake, he soon would be, and so would his neighbors for miles around. She'd have to destroy the beastie and haul ass out of there before a swarm of cops descended.

Leaving the door to the church open, she ran down the aisle flanked by rows of tenderly polished red oak pews. She trailed her fingertips over one as she passed. Soon, the golem would stomp them into splinters. Precious as they were, pews were replaceable. The people the golem would harm or kill were not.

"In the pursuit of right, many sacrifices must fall." She entered the sacristy, hesitated at the top of the stairs, and listened.

Brahms yelled something that sounded like a juicy cuss.

She chuckled.

"Sorry to break up your party," she called down, "but it's time to bring rock head up here for his nap."

"Easy for you to say."

Crouching on the top stair, she watched for them.

Brahms rounded the corner and ran toward the exit. His

muscles bulged beneath the fabric of his jeans, and his arms glistened with sweat.

*Nice.*

He reached the landing as the golem smashed around the corner. He tilted his head and tapped his fingers on the railing. "What's that smile for?"

"Nothing." She gave him her best look of angelic innocence and stood.

"You owe me for this."

"Yeah, well, Germaine is going to kill me when he gets the bill for the damage we're about to cause, so I might not be around to pay your bill." She cringed at the thought of what the stone golem would do to the church. It was going to reduce everything in its path to kindling and mangled metal, respectively. There was a reason most mages opted for lighter golems to do their bidding: stick, wood, and aluminum golems. She'd even seen one made entirely out of Mountain Dew cans. Heavier golems, like stone and iron, were sturdier and difficult to defeat, but also damaged their surroundings, including the very items they were supposed to protect.

"What do you have behind your back?" Brahms asked, his dark eyes narrowed. If he thought she was plotting something nefarious, he was right.

"A present for our friend." She left it at that, doubting he'd appreciate the merit of her idea or even go along with it. Besides, what he didn't know would ultimately help him.

"You really want me to bring this creature up there?"

"No, but we need to get it outside," she tilted her head toward the exit, "so unless you have a teleportation spell in your pocket..."

He rubbed his temples but didn't refuse.

Harley took it as agreement and said, "I'll meet you out there."

Brahms muttered under his breath. She couldn't quite make out the words, and she didn't care. He looked annoyed, and he was awfully cute when he was annoyed. His dark eyes sparked and flashed, orbs of black fire. It was a sight worth crossing words with him for. Maybe she ought to tick him off more often.

"Behind you." She pointed toward the golem. It clomped past the end of the hall and closed in.

Brahms glanced back.

She turned and ran, hiding the C-4 in front of her in case he spotted her before she got outside. Once the golem was out of the sanctuary area, there'd be no way to contain it and no time to argue about her choice of tactics. She crossed the threshold, stepped to the side, and pressed her back flat against the church's cool, bumpy stone exterior. No lights in the rectory yet. She scanned the wood line.

*Where are St. Mary's slayers?*

No slayer slept with noise in the background. If they were here, they'd have heard all the commotion and confronted her and Brahms. Which meant they couldn't be around. Were they out on assignment? Had they been re-assigned before they released the creatures to keep this foul secret? Or taken a horridly timed vacation?

*Or are they dead?*

If Ian could release those creatures, committing mass murder by default, he wouldn't be above killing a few slayers.

*Yeah, well. Wait until he meets up with me.*

She'd find him, and he'd pay for this. For every drop of blood these beasts shed, he'd pay.

*And for Cerise.*

The computer skills necessary to infiltrate the Church's system without getting caught were beyond her, but Thayer could do it. She'd talk him into some hacking spy work. Though she didn't know Thayer a lot, she'd bet he'd have no compunctions tracking Ian's slime trail. Particularly knowing Ian was in the area when Livia had disappeared. That alone didn't make him guilty but coupled with his code being the last entered into an emptied sanctuary certainly put him high on the suspect list.

And he had a slayer's cross ring. A chunky one. She'd be willing to bet it matched the brand on Livia's body.

Wood smashed, crunched. Ugh. The demise of the pews. At least she didn't need to risk blowing her cover to peek into the church to chart the golem's progress. She could hear it just fine. Floor tiles cracked and snapped, but the stout metal beneath that comprised the sanctuary ceiling would hold the golem's considerable weight so the structure itself wouldn't be compromised.

The golem's angry roar reverberated through the night.

Light clicked on in the rectory window.

*Shit. Hurry, Brahms.*

She silently willed the priest to be smart enough to stay safely inside where the golem couldn't see him. The situation was volatile enough without adding another potential target. Particularly one who'd probably never seen anything like their bumbling golem buddy. If the priest panicked and ran, the golem might ignore Brahms and go for the priest instead. Having to explain the damage to a church was one thing. Having to explain the death of a priest was an entirely different matter that she didn't want to deal with.

Besides, she'd never lost a priest on her watch, and she wasn't into starting new trends.

Brahms didn't bother with the stairs. He leapt from the threshold and landed on the grassy back yard with lithe grace. He glanced around, looking for her. When he spotted her by the doorway, he gave her a questioning look.

She supposed now was the time to clue him in to her plan. It's not as if they'd have another choice at this point. She grinned, held the C-4 in front of her, and waggled it.

"Don't you dare," he said, raising a finger toward her.

The golem smashed out of the doorway. Its broad shoulders

rammed into the arch's stones and jarred them from the mortar. A small rockslide tumbled down the stairs. It stomped down the steps, chipping and cracking the cement and then trampling the tender grass.

Damned mages. Always causing trouble. Never thinking of consequences. She wished there was a way to trace the golem's magic so she could locate and throttle them. She knew it was possible and some mages liked to leave energy signatures, as if they were an artist signing a painting, but it took a mage to know a mage and the order didn't work with mages.

The golem fixated on Brahms, hunkered its bulk down, it readied for a charge. Its stone feet dug at the ground, its feet swiped at the ground, flinging dirt and bits of grass behind it.

Taking advantage of its lowered height, Harley took a running leap onto its broad back. She released her breath as she hit into the solid stone.

The golem howled in rage and arched backward and forward in a wild attempt to buck her off. She'd never ridden a bull before, never seen the point in it, but she imagined it must be a lot like this, only closer to the ground and on a warm, fleshy animal, not hard, unforgiving stone.

She slipped her fingers into the gritty, cragged surface of its back, barely able to keep her grip. Her fingers dipped into the swirling green. Magical currents tingled across her hand and up her arm. Wrapping her knees around its sides, she held tight. Then she molded C-4 into the widest fissure in its back stone until it was secure and couldn't be jostled free by its movement. She kicked herself away and off the enraged golem, tucked, hit the ground on her leading shoulder and rolled across the grass, keeping the C-4 wire firmly in hand.

"You're crazy." Brahms jogged to her and offered a hand up.

She took it and stood.

"You should run. Truck is back there." She nodded toward the wood line where she'd hidden her Tahoe.

After he'd taken a few strides, she returned her attention to the golem, glad she'd opted for the longer wire instead of the short one.

"Hey, rock-head," she yelled, luring it farther from the church to mitigate some of the damage. When the golem blew it'd send chunks of rock everywhere and she wanted to avoid smashing any of the stained-glass windows.

It roared and clamored after her.

The rectory porch and garage lights snapped on and brightened the yard.

*Shit awful timing, Padre.*

The golem turned its head, assessing if the new threat was more worthy of its attention than she was.

It was now or never. She couldn't take the chance the golem would charge the rectory and the priest within it. If some stained glass broke, it was a small price to pay for the priest's life. She detonated the C-4 and ran, churning her legs as fast as she could, until she caught with Brahms at the edge of the trees.

"Get down." She thrust her hand out, planting it in the middle of his back.

They tumbled into the woods together, each scrambling to get behind a tree before the golem exploded.

A resounding boom broke through the night. Pieces of rock pelted the brush and trees, as well as the exterior of the church, but she didn't hear any shattering glass.

*Phew.*

One less thing for Germaine to rant about.

"I'll give you a lift to your car." Harley bolted to her feet and headed toward her truck. If the priest hadn't already called the cops, he would once he grappled with the reality of what he'd just seen, and if he didn't, a neighbor would.

"Must you blow up everything?" Brahms asked.

She shrugged. "Only when it's necessary."

"Define necessary."

She glanced at him and laughed. "It differs with the situation."

He groaned and split off, going to the passenger's side of the Tahoe.

Out of habit, Harley locked the doors as soon as they were both inside.

"I don't suppose one of your mages could trace binding magic once the object is destroyed, can they?" she asked.

"Yeah. A few of them can. Problem is, we'd need at least part of what's left of the golem and that isn't going to happen. Bits of him are scattered over the entire yard and the woods."

Harley twisted the key in the ignition and the truck started with a beautiful purr. "Admit it–"

A loud whoosh, shattering glass. Harsh percussion swayed the trees and rocked the Tahoe. A burst of leaves tumbled past the windows and down the driveway.

"What the fuck was that?" Harley twisted in her seat and stared through the orange-tinged woods. A wild, uncontrolled fire rose from the church, engulfing it in a writhing mass of blue and orange. Sanctuary churches each had a version of a self-destruct button the Order could activate under the direst of circumstances. In her years as a slayer, she'd never heard of it used in a real-life situation, only in small examples for training. The sudden violence was disturbing to the core. If they'd lingered in the church just a few minutes more, they'd be dead. As in, no body left dead. Just a pile of ashes dead. There was no hope of escape from a fire that quick and consuming.

"What did you touch?" she asked.

"You asked me to keep the golem busy. That's what I did. I ran and taunted. I kept it to the corridors and didn't touch anything."

If he and the golem had stayed within the hallways, there was no conceivable way either could have accidentally, through some miraculous feat of Murphy, activated the destruction sequence. That meant someone else had. Someone with access to their security system, someone in the Order, someone who knew she was there and knew she knew what they'd done.

She cranked the wheel to the side and whipped the Tahoe around. "Where's your car?"

"Farther up the drive." He turned around in the seat, gazing out the back window. "Uh. Harley? Tell me that isn't the rectory."

She glanced into the rearview mirror and braked hard enough to jolt them both against the seat belts. Flames billowed out the rectory's windows and licked over the roof. "Fuck. What the fuck?"

"The fire must have spread from the church."

"Yes, it could have spread, but not overtaken the rectory like that. Not that fast. Not naturally." Dread clutched her heart. It was the same fire she'd seen in training. Fast. Uncontrollable. Meant to thoroughly destroy everything in its path. The same as the church.

She released the brake and stomped on the gas.

*But it couldn't be. They wouldn't. Would they?*

A few days ago, hell, even one day ago, she'd have stated with clear, honest confidence her Order would never endanger the public or their people outside of the dangers inherent in the slayer job description. Now? She had to face the possibility corruption threaded through her Order and some betrayers might be her friends.

*How did this happen?*

"What do you mean?" Brahms slapped his hands on the dash to stabilize himself as she took the curve of the drive a little too fast.

If she couldn't even trust her own Order, could she really trust him? And even if she trusted Brahms, what of Cerberus?

After the second curve, she spotted his car parked off to the side. The sneak.

She pulled off the drive and slammed on the brakes, spewing rocks and dirt as the tires came to a sudden halt.

"Well, someone didn't want us leaving," Brahms said.

"What?" She leaned forward and pressed against the steering wheel to see what he was talking about. "Damn."

The two back tires were flat, slashed across the sides, and it was likely the front were flat, as well. Yeah. Whoever was behind this attack on the sanctuary knew she was there but didn't know her well enough to recognize what kind of vehicle she drove.

That crossed Ian off the list for this particular atrocity.

"Give me a sec." He hopped out, leaving the door open. Sirens shrieked. The cavalry was on its way.

*Too late to save the priest.*

They'd be able to contain the fire, though, after a good rowdy water brawl. That would save the neighbors and their homes. That was something. Not enough. But something.

Brahms threw a few bags into the back seat and jumped in. "Go."

She peeled out of the drive and floored it, heading in the opposite direction of town, where she assumed most of the emergency responders would come from.

It wasn't until the wailing sirens faded into silence that her shoulders relaxed, and she blew out a tense breath, forcing herself to breathe steady, slow breaths. She needed to plan and couldn't plan if tension taxed her brain.

"You're thinking the fire in the rectory wasn't accidental?" Brahms asked. It was the first time he'd spoken since they'd found his deflated car. She appreciated that. She hadn't fully wrapped her head around what had happened, and she wasn't sure she wanted to. Knowledge couldn't be unknown, and there was no denying the facts once you recognized them.

She couldn't trust her Order, wasn't sure about Cerberus, but Brahms. Yeah, she trusted Brahms. Cree and Thayer, maybe. In varying degrees.

"Accelerant." She rubbed the back of her neck to work out the kinks. "We have it piped into the sanctuaries just in case there's an outbreak that we can't control. We'd rather melt the place into a puddle than have those beasts running free."

"That I understand, but the rectory?"

She drew a breath, hating what she had to say. Not wanting to admit it to herself or Brahms, but to do otherwise was a lie. She was tired of lies. "Rectories, strongholds, and other places meant for residence, not holding cells, aren't supposed to have it. There's no reason for it other than..." She swallowed the rest, unable to speak it aloud. She didn't want to go there, couldn't go there. Admitting the next logical step was akin to admitting someone in the Order, someone with a lot of power who watched over everything, was a vile, murderous thug. A liar. A traitor. The only person with the power to insert something so dangerous, so insidious as accelerant in a rectory was...

*Germaine. No. Not Germaine. It can't be Germaine. Someone slid it in under his radar.*

Brahms continued for her, "To get rid of witnesses or people who might get in their way. People capable of fighting back."

She hated it. Wanted to deck him for saying it. Instead, she tightened her grip on the steering wheel. The truth wouldn't stop being the truth just because she didn't like it. Or because it hurt. Or because it threw everyone she knew, everyone she'd counted as a friend, as family, into suspicion.

She'd have to roll with this blow as she'd rolled with others life had given her.

"I have to warn Francis," she said. "Tell him to take an

impromptu vacay somewhere far, far away without letting anyone know where, even me." She checked the time. It was the wee morning hours and Francis would be burrowed under his blankets, sound asleep, but she punched in his number, anyway. She'd rather wake him and deal with a grumpy priest than wait and have something to happen to him. Something she couldn't fix. The phone went directly to voice mail. She didn't leave a message in case anyone accessed his account.

"He always answers." She gripped the wheel even tighter. "He must be dead asleep."

But even she didn't believe herself.

# CHAPTER FIFTEEN

Deciding neither of them was mentally alert enough to make the drive back to St. Ambrose without falling asleep at the wheel, Harley pulled into a rinky-dink roadside motel with a blinking vacancy sign. The siding was a dingy off-white, and the entire place had a "Don't look too close" vibe.

Exactly what they needed.

She stifled a yawn and slanted the Tahoe across two parking spots in front of the office. The lot was empty except for a puny compact car, a dusty sedan, and one minivan. God, she hoped none of them had loud kids. It'd be dawn in a few hours. She was running a severe sleep deficit, and the last few days hadn't exactly been full of leisure and cookies.

"I'll get the rooms." Brahms pulled his black hair behind his head and secured it in an elastic band. She decided she liked his hair down, yet she wasn't tired enough to let her guard slip and clue him in she'd not only noticed his hair but also had an opinion on it.

"I won't object. If someone has to wake up a grumpy

innkeeper, it may as well be you." She toyed with discarded straw wrapper to keep her hands occupied and away from the offending elastic band.

"If I didn't know better, I'd think you wanted me to get into trouble."

A jumble of images featuring Brahms rushed through her head. None of them decent, all of them lewd and some of them included oils.

"Depends on the type of trouble." The words tumbled out of her mouth before her mental filter realized they'd even formed.

He hesitated with his hand on the door, studying her. She could see the gears of his quick mind working behind his eyes, trying to determine the real meaning behind her words. What had she meant by them, anyway? She hadn't meant to flirt.

Had she?

When she chose not to elaborate, he shut the door without so much as a quip and headed toward the office.

Harley leaned back in her bucket seat and admired the way his backside pressed against his jeans. The only thing that'd make the picture perfect was the removal of that damned elastic band that confined his hair. He was attractive either way, but when his hair was free, he was nearly irresistible, and the urge to run her fingers through the glossy black strands was overwhelming in an annoying way.

*Lack of sleep, that's all.*

If her brain weren't so fried from fatigue, it certainly wouldn't have wandered to fixating on his hair, or ass, to begin with. If she were in her right mind, her focus would be where it belonged. Hunting Niko and the betrayers within her Order. Niko, she'd definitely kill, along with every single member of his filthy pride. The slayers who'd betrayed the Order and put people in danger was a quandary. Hauling them before the Tribunal was the correct course of action but not a satisfying one. They could make pleas, argue on technicalities, and glide off, untouched. Unpunished. No. The Tribunal would prove far too lenient for their crimes. It'd be much more satisfying to feed them to the very creatures they'd set loose, piece by bloody ass piece, suffering the same deaths as the innocent folks suffered due to the slayers' indiscretions.

She also needed to figure out a game plan to fulfill her promise to Cerise by finding Lars. Assuming Cerise was right and he was alive, not dead as the Order assumed. What if he, too, was a victim of the conspiracy and he was out in the Rockies alone? If so, he might not have a lot of time left on his clock.

Between those very real, life and death situations to deal with, plus contending with the rampaging creatures, who had the time or energy for romance?

Of course, that didn't mean she couldn't admire. What was life without taking a moment to enjoy the beauty?

She tugged the keys out of the ignition, plopped her head against the headrest, and closed her eyes to curb her spiraling thoughts. It didn't work. Without the lovely scenery called Brahms to focus on, the image of the fiery church and rectory blazed through her mind, searing it in her memory. With no reprieve in the darkness of her soul, she stared at the fading stars.

The priest hadn't made it out of the rectory. Of that, she was sure. There was simply no plausible way. The fire started too fast and burned too aggressively for him to have the slimmest hope of survival. Harley couldn't help but wonder if her actions had accidentally triggered the priest's death. Everything seemed peaceful there until she'd arrived. Sure, the creatures had been set loose, but that'd been weeks ago. Had Francis's friend, Fr. Martin, met his fate at their claws? Would they have eventually murdered the temporary priest to cover their tracks? Or had they been content to leave it alone until she'd plugged in her code at the sanctuary?

She'd never know for certain. She'd been able to push the anger and guilt aside as she drove because shamelessly eavesdropping on Brahms's calls to Cerberus while concentrating on staying awake kept her mind occupied. Here in the pre-dawn hush of a nearly empty parking lot, the implications of the blaze crashed upon her.

Her quest for answers, for the truth, might have cost that priest his life.

Brahms opened the door and grabbed his bag from the back. "Ready?"

"Yeah." Feeling numb, she reached behind her, yanked out her overnight bag, and slid out of the truck. "Where's my key?"

A hot shower and bed would be as close to heaven as she was ever going to get, so she may as well take them now. Instant gratification was undeservedly maligned.

"I have the key to our room." He flipped the plastic room key in his fingers and showed her the room number. "Safety in numbers."

"I'm safe on my own." Staying in the same room as him was not smart and not safe. Not at all. It'd open too many opportunities for her to act on her misguided impulses. She'd gotten close enough to him already, thank you. Getting closer would be a distraction she didn't need or want.

He canted his head and wisely didn't argue. Instead, he said, "We also have to talk. That's easier to do if we're in the same room. You heard my side of the conversations during the drive, but not the entire story."

Damn him. He knew just how to set a hook and yank it through flesh to get her to agree. Ugh. She hated that. Had fate set them on the same course purely to drive her insane?

He took a step closer, watching her with open concern. "You okay?"

"If you define okay as wanting to beat the shit out of you and then strangle you, then, yes, I'm so okay I can barely contain it."

He had the gall to laugh. The urge to both deck him and kiss him rose simultaneously and warred within her. Thankfully, her will power won.

*Iron clad, baby.*

Now, it needed to keep winning, particularly in such close quarters.

She settled on a deadpan look and swept her arm toward the motel. "Whatever information you have better be worth it."

He smiled, and she wished he hadn't. It was dastardly charming. "You could get your own room and I can keep Niko's whereabouts to myself."

She didn't even attempt to keep the surprise off her face. "You found him? How?"

"He's about as good of a liar as you are." Brahms led the way to the door.

Once inside, he dropped his bag by the ratty, caramel-colored couch dotted with coffee stains and other fluids she'd rather not dwell on.

"Which is about as good as the way you answer questions." She shut and locked the door. It was too flimsy to be much of a deterrent to a human let alone any sort of beastie, but it was better than sleeping in her truck. Slightly. At least in her truck, they could make a fast getaway if the situation called for it. Downside would be that they'd be cramped even closer together.

*How can he still smell like the forest?*

He dropped into the corner chair and toed off his shoes.

She studied him. His bronzed face. Warm brown eyes. Hair still restrained. "Spit it out and take that damned elastic thing out of your hair."

"Switching to a career in fashion? Don't. You'd get bored." He tugged the band off and his hair fell around his shoulders. "That better?"

*I hate you.*

Why couldn't he be boorish or pushy or an ass?

"Worse, but better." Because now she definitely wanted to kiss him. *Niko. Must find Niko. People are dying and losing their souls. There's no time for this shit.* "Now, where's that damn cat?"

She'd have to have a chat with Cree the next time she saw her. Women were supposed to stick together, do the whole united sisterhood thing. Out of feminine courtesy, Cree could have warned her about Brahms and his sneaky, underhanded way of weaseling into hearts.

To buy herself some time and to have an excuse not to dwell on those dark eyes of his, she untied her boots and tugged them off.

"The swamps of Louisiana," he said.

She glanced up at him. "That's vague. Have you ever seen a map of those swamps? There're rivers and bayous and crap everywhere. Like a damned watery maze."

"Says the person who snuck out of her room to investigate a breech in a sanctuary's security without backup."

"Ah. You think I'd mosey out of here without you and the help of Cerberus to take down a pride of werepuma?" If it'd been a handful of weres then yeah, she would have. "Hell, do you have any idea how many people he could have turned by now?"

"Enough Fain is sending most of our agents within the surrounding states. But I still wouldn't put it past you to attempt confronting Niko alone." He held her in his gaze. "Because I'd rather you live I'm not giving you anything more specific."

"You think I can't take him?"

"Weres don't fight fair."

"Neither do I."

"And you can't go blowing up half the swamp."

"Sometimes I hate you."

He chuckled and switched the subject. "So, who let the creatures out at the sanctuary?"

To delay answering, she rubbed her face and then scooted

back on the bed, plumping the pillows for a backrest. Once she admitted what she'd found there was no going back. The strangest thing was she didn't think she wanted them to go back to the way they were, even if they could, because what she'd once known as truth was just a candy coating over a plump ball of lies. "The last person who logged into the sanctuary was Ian, one of Germaine's favorites. He's been doing the inventories for the last year, so he knows the layouts and contents of most of the sanctuaries east of the heartland."

"How do you know?"

"His code showed up on the log."

"Are you sure he did it, though? Couldn't someone have used his code?"

She pondered that for a moment. "It's a possibility. There are ways to infiltrate our security, as Thayer so aptly displayed. But there are additional layers of security within the sanctuaries themselves that prevent the release of creatures, particularly entire rows of them, without the proper clearances. Whoever released them was someone within the Order. Someone who'd not only knew those security features existed but also how to bypass them. No one else would've been able to activate those systems without initiating a total lockdown and setting off the alarms."

"What do you know of Ian?"

"Besides he prevented me from killing Niko to begin with? I'd still love to strangle him for interfering in that."

"That aside."

"Francis doesn't trust him, which is odd. Frances trusts nearly anyone. It's really kinda dangerous but it's who he is, I guess." She shrugged. "Whenever Ian shows up for inspections or other Order business Francis finds some way to worm out of the area. Until this last time, when Cerise and I were investigating the caves. Francis thought Ian was lying about Cerise and my fates. Which is weird. He's not one to go about accusing people of lies or much of anything else."

"His slayers cross," Brahms said, "is like the one burned in Livia's flesh?"

"Yeah, his is a chunky ring like mine but he wears his. I've never seen him without it. Even assuming he released the creatures from the sanctuary, it doesn't mean he killed Livia or anyone else. Not directly."

"No, but it's enough to warrant investigating."

That she couldn't argue. When someone walked the path of the dark side, where did they draw the line? Was outright, hands-on murder that far-fetched for someone who betrayed his Order and set loose creatures that'd kill, maim, and devastate others?

"And someone in my order killed that priest. Purposely. Maliciously. And it wasn't Ian. He'd never have mistaken your car as mine."

Brahms sat on the edge of the bed next to her. She wished he'd go back to the chair. He was so close she could smell the outdoorsy scent of his skin. Fresh. Earthy. Irresistible.

"So," he said, "if Ian is involved in this, he's not working alone. There've been too many releases, too widespread for it to be the actions of an individual. Whoever, wherever they are, we'll find them and stop them or die trying. I promise."

"I believe you." She grabbed the second pillow off the bed and shoved it into his chest. "Now, go sleep on the couch before I do something I'll regret in the morning."

His dark gaze penetrated deep into her soul. Cerberus's folks boasted many different talents. Lord forbid his was mind reading. He'd get several eyefuls.

"I wouldn't," he said. His voice was even lower than its normal warm timbre. "But if you want to banish me to that disgusting couch, I'll go."

"Baby." She pulled the corner of the comforter up and handed it to him. "This'll protect you."

With an exaggerated, fake sigh, he left, taking the comforter with him.

Watching him spread it out neatly on the couch and plump up his pillow before settling in, Harley wondered if he'd been serious. Either way, separate sleeping areas was safer all the way around. Even if she wished he wouldn't have been quite so agreeable.

"Coward," she muttered and slid under the sheets.

"What?" he asked.

"Nothing." If anything, the word aptly described her. When had she ever had issues bedding a guy she was interested in? Never. Until now. That made her all sorts of shades of coward. Or something worse.

Far, far worse.

# CHAPTER SIXTEEN

After a few hours of sleep in the motel's lumpy bed, Harley sat at a booth in a quaint diner, finally inhaling the delightful scent of the fat deluxe cheeseburger she'd ordered. Complete with onion rings instead of fries and French dressing on the side because onion rings were not onion rings without the tangy orange dip.

They'd arrived at the diner during the relative lull between the lunch and dinner crowds. They'd had their choice of table, so Harley picked one with a view of the parking lot so she could monitor her truck and the weapons within. It had an advanced security system but there was no system better than her own observation.

"Happy now?" Brahms asked.

She hadn't eaten anything since the avocado protein shake the evening before. The foodless hours added up to one hungry, cranky woman.

"Still haven't been able to get a hold of Francis," she said.

"He could be out." Brahms dumped the small container of

tartar sauce onto his plate. He'd ordered the fish and chips basket with a side of coleslaw.

"Today is his catching up on accounting and editing through the church bulletin day." She squished the top of her burger down so it'd fit better in her mouth. She didn't want to look like a complete pig in front of him.

"Think he'd still pick up if he didn't recognize the number?"

Harley poked at the burner phone to wake it up. No new messages or missed calls. "It'd be unusual for him not to. People call him from bunches of different numbers. And I can't leave a message because someone might get nosey."

If Francis was helping a parishioner through an emergency, he might hold calls until he saw them through whatever issue they were experiencing: births, deaths, marital freak-outs. Still, his prolonged silence bothered her, even though she could find excuses for it. It was that nameless feeling deep in her gut, not like a ping, but something elusive, some smoky thing she couldn't quite grasp and couldn't quite shake.

Brahms said, "Won't take us too long to get back when we're done here."

"Yeah. And it won't do any good for me to arrive all hangry." She wrapped her hands around the burger. Grease slid off a curled piece of lettuce and plopped onto the stark white plate. "It's a thing of beauty."

"Yes, yes, it is." Brahms watched her, ignoring his battered fish.

"I'm not giving you my burger." She took a big bite, marking it as hers. Lovely steaming meat. Crunchy lettuce. Juicy tomato. Pungent onion. Sharp cheddar. Who could ask for more?

"Wasn't talking about the burger." He winked and dragged a fry through a puddle of ketchup.

She would have smiled if her cheeks weren't crammed with food. Brahms was tough and sweet, an irresistible combination.

She was proud she'd slept in the same motel room with him without caving into the impulses that urged her to do questionable things, like kiss him. He'd been close enough several times where she could have clearly seen she wasn't the only one experiencing feelings of attraction. She could have tormented him and then gone through with the flirtations, but she'd chosen the better part of valor and restrained from any involvement, other than those that involved their current quests.

To his credit, Brahms caught on to her mood, or lack thereof, and had made no moves, either.

Though she alternated between disappointment and approval of his decision. Sleeping with him would have complicated things. She didn't care for complicated.

*But isn't it already?*

Maybe. But at least it wasn't tangled up with the additional baggage of them having kissed or slept together.

She wondered if he realized how much willpower that neutral facade had sucked from her storage banks or if he'd simply fallen for the act, taking her feigned disinterest at face value. Some men, like Max, didn't peer deeper than the surface, but Brahms wasn't one of those. He probably already had her figured out and in his quiet way was giving her the space she needed, which didn't help her cause because that was damned heroic of him.

After swallowing her huge bite of burger, she said, "You're just charmed I didn't kick you out of the room."

"I was expecting it and wasn't looking forward to waking the innkeeper again."

She tossed everyone out of her room before she went to bed, as in to sleep, that is. Even dating Max, she never spent the night at his place or let him stay with her. She'd never felt comfortable sleeping with anyone else in the room, not even Cerise, until now.

Then again, Brahms knew her more than any man she'd dated. He stared into the darkness that lurked in the shadows, fought creatures few knew existed. Just like her. He knew she was a slayer and was neither intimidated by her strength or skills nor turned off by her dubious choice of career. Because of those things and the fuzzy feeling churning in her heart, she'd slept better with him nestled on the dirty couch during in those few hours in the motel than she had in her own bed.

"I can always kick you out next time." Testing her willpower again wouldn't be such a bad thing. Keep it honed and all.

He grinned, dark eyes glowing with a strange warmth.

She wanted to think it meant what was growing within her might also be growing in him, that their strengthening friendship meant more to him than the mere convenience of having an extra warrior around. Lord knew he was beginning to mean more to her than she'd expected or even wanted. Maybe after they stopped Niko and whoever it was in her Order who'd released him, they could act on their feelings, assuming he even had any for her. It would be tricky with her working for the Order and him for Cerberus, but she when she wanted something, she found a way to get it or make it happen. For now, though, she'd keep her realizations to herself, so the only thing they needed to do was to decide their next course of action.

A few muted conversations in the background threaded with that of the TV tuned to the news station mounted on the wall behind Brahms. The babbling bauble heads were spewing theory after theory about the motives behind the latest mass shooting and interviewing people on the street for their opinions on how to prevent future tragedy.

*As if it's even possible.*

"Sad," she said, nodding at the TV

"What is?"

"That we've allowed ourselves to become so removed from the natural world that most people forget violence and aggression are integral parts of nature. Trying to rid the world of natural instincts is as pointless as attempting to thwart the sun from rising."

Brahms cut a piece of his crunchy fish. "When I was a kid, I used to wonder why religious and government leaders of the world kept people ignorant about the existence of monsters. I thought it was an unfair and dangerous decision."

"Now?" she asked.

"Hearing peoples' opinions, I know why leaders choose deceit. Why it's necessary."

"Yeah. People can't handle the violence inherent in our own race without devolving into fits of panic, riots, and knee-jerk reactions." Harley shuddered to think what would become of society if they ever discovered there were far worse, far more vicious things in the world than human psycho and sociopaths. Creatures that would make serial killers look like cuddly teddy bears. She lowered her voice so that it'd mingle with the din. "Any news from Cerberus?"

She'd heard his phone ring when she'd been in the shower that morning, but he hadn't mentioned who it was, not that his phone calls were her business.

*Hell, who am I fooling? Yes, they are.*

He nodded. "Cree and Thayer are almost ready in the swamps. Now, our next step begins."

"And that is?" She stuffed another bite of burger into her mouth. The faster they ate, the faster they'd be on Niko's trail, and the sooner she could kill his fuzzy ass and sink it in the swamp for the critters to feast on.

"Attracting him."

She tried to hide her disappointment. "How are we going to do that, let alone corner him? It's not as if we can tempt them with a boatload of catnip or anything. And we're talking hundreds of miles of swamp. We need his exact position or–"

"We don't need that when we have you." His grin was decidedly sly.

"What's that supposed to mean?"

"If there's anyone Niko wants to get his claws on, it's you. Once he realizes you're on his turf we won't have to find him. He'll find us."

"You'd use me as bait?"

"You can take it."

She laughed, ridiculously pleased he had enough confidence in her he'd be willing to try such a tactic with a pride of were-pumas and the lives of his fellow agents at stake. "I can't wait to inject some lead between his eyes."

"Thought you'd like it. Cree and Thayer have a contact in the area, so we're to meet up with them at his cabin. The other agents are already there, but they'll be spread out, so we don't arouse too much suspicion and blow our cover."

"A deadly net to catch the stragglers." She approved. The only thing that would make the plan better was if she could invite some of her fellow slayers to the party. Given she currently didn't know who she could and couldn't trust, that was out of the question. Once she ripped the betrayers out of the Order, she'd have to push some policy changes on the powers that be.

For years they'd taught slayers Cerberus wasn't to be trusted. That they were a rogue, motley group which partook in dark rituals that negated any measly help they gave. The Order's decision makers had lost track of the whole "Judge not" part of the bible. From what Harley experienced, the people of Cerberus were stellar, talented people who strove for the same cause just from different angles. They embraced different religions, even magic, in pursuit of their goals.

And why not? It made sense to use every tool available when the enemy was doing the same and then some.

If she could get the hierarchy to accept working with Cerberus or even agree to joint task forces, they could become far more effective at protecting the innocent. Also, altruism aside, it'd make it easier for her to continue working with Brahms. She wasn't comfortable with the idea of him working with a different partner. The thought was discomfiting. She'd rather watch his ass than trust someone else to. Besides, the view was worth getting territorial about.

Testing the waters, she said, "Is Fain sending a partner for you?"

"I told him I already have one." He tilted his head toward her.

"He was okay with you working with a slayer?" Good God, if Germaine ever found out she'd picked her own partner, let alone one outside the Order, he'd be furious, and she'd be without a job.

He laughed, a deep and warm, uplifting sound. "Not even Fain argues with Celeste."

"I thought Fain was the head of Cerberus?" She argued with Germaine occasionally, and sometimes he yielded, other times not. It depended on each of their moods and how attached they were to the subject at hand.

"Celeste is his sister. Cerberus has been in their family for generations, each entrusting it to the next. I guess you could say she's the brains and he's the brawn. Not that Fain isn't smart, mind you, Celeste is just smarter."

"I like her already. Will they be in the swamp, too?" She polished off her cheeseburger.

"Only Fain goes into the field, and he's occupied with something else at the moment."

"That's sexist." She scooped up some fries. "I bet she can take care of herself just fine."

"Oh, she can. She's a nasty mage to cross, even to other agents. But they're the last of their bloodline. If they're killed, the future of Cerberus is questionable."

"I still don't see why..." She caught a glance at the TV screen.

Her throat constricted, and she nearly choked. "That's...that can't be."

She vaguely noted Brahms turning toward the TV where an over-makeuped reporter stood in front of St. Ambrose's cemetery. Where the rectory and church had once stood, there was nothing but two charred black stains.

Harley blinked hard to clear her eyes.

*It can't be true.*

No matter how many times she blinked, the stark image of blackened ground against the green of the cemetery grass remained.

Nothing.

There was nothing left of the rectory. Not a shingle. Not a half-burned stud. Nothing.

*Francis.*

Fear clawed at her heart and the world around her dimmed, narrowing into a pinpoint focused on the newscaster's face. Only the reporter's voice broke through the buzzing that flooded her head, drowning all other sounds. A voice that seemed to come from a vast chasm in a nether realm that was never meant to communicate with this one. "... late last night, St. Ambrose was the second Catholic Church that burned to the ground in the same night. According to our sources, police are ruling it arson and, most likely, a hate crime."

"Francis," Harley whispered. Her onion ring fell from numb fingers. "Where's Francis?"

The image shifted to the newsroom and a pasty-faced newscaster took over. "We've secured an interview with Cardinal Germaine in Chicago, who has been outspoken in the alleged war against Christians. This is what he has to say."

Germaine filled the screen decked in his finest of red cassocks, his balding head capped with a red zucchetto that couldn't contain what remained of his wispy white hair. Then, the camera panned out to show the reporter beside him. They opened with inane dialog and niceties, considering what had happened and considering there was a priest yet to be accounted for, *her* priest, before getting to the meat of the story.

"It's not about the buildings," Germaine said. "We can rebuild structures, even St. Ambrose, which was a historic site. What we cannot replace are the lives of the two faithful priests killed in last night's blazes, Fr. Bestio, who was serving as a temporary pastor at St. Mary's, and Fr. Francis of St. Ambrose." Germaine crossed himself, and tears brimmed in his eyes.

They looked fake, forced.

Harley wanted to reach through the screen and rip his eyeballs out. Squash them with her bare hands. How could Germaine not have known what was going on in his own Order, the Order he led? How could he not have foreseen and stopped this?

Germaine said, "May they rest with the Lord."

*Francis. Oh, God, Francis.*

"I wasn't there," Harley said. "He needed me and I wasn't there."

The dimness in her vision turned to a dark, creeping black, and the world fell away beneath her feet. Adrift in the abyss of guilt. If she and Cerise hadn't gone off to the caves, if Cerise hadn't died, if they hadn't discovered the treachery within the Order, would he have been spared? If she'd stayed home last night and hadn't plugged her damned code into the damned sanctuary computer, would Francis be alive, doodling about in his garden? If she'd have returned last night instead of wimping out at some gross motel, could she have saved him?

"Do you have any leads or suspects on who might be responsible for last night's tragic events?" the reporter asked.

"We do," Germaine said. "We've released the security footage to the police and are showing it to your viewers, asking anyone with information regarding these individuals to call the number at the bottom of the screen."

As the white letters giving the contact information scrolled the security footage rolled. In grainy full color, it showed her and Brahms outside of St. Ambrose's. She recognized the path they'd taken. It'd been after they'd buried Cerise but the timestamp read about the same time that they'd blown up the stone golem at an entirely different church, which meant someone must have meddled with the security footage there, too.

Didn't the reporter and most of all law enforcement wonder how the hell they managed to set fire to two churches simultaneously? What did they think she had, a fucking teleporter? And if both the churches and the rectories were destroyed, did they not wonder, did they not see that there was a much larger game in motion?

"That son of a bitch." Anger consumed Harley's sorrow. "That lying, filthy, murdering son of a bitch."

Brahms was out of the booth seat and grabbed her arm before she'd even realized he was no longer sitting. "We have to go. Now."

"That fuckhead killed Francis." She allowed Brahms to pull her to her feet and then slapped his hand away. "I'm going to gut him. With chopsticks. Blunt ones."

"Save that thought for later," his whisper sounded more akin to a quiet growl. "We need to get out of here before someone recognizes us and we end up behind bars."

"Still going to kill him," she muttered. She turned away from the TV before she acted on the rising desire to rip it off the wall and smash it to itty bits.

"You won't find me standing in your way."

Harley and Brahms drove for hours, and the day turned into night. A two-lane rural highway stretched out before them. The Tahoe's headlights illuminated the nearly unbroken line of trees that flanked each side like ghostly sentinels.

Normally Brahms felt at home near the woods. They filled him with a sense of peace and reminded him that he was a part of a much larger scheme.

But not tonight. Tonight, he felt edgy.

The grizzly stirred within him, its protective nature extending to Harley. The Order and beasts had taken so much from her over the past week. Losing Francis on top of it all would have devastated a lesser person.

*A less stubborn one, anyway.*

Germaine's betrayal didn't surprise him. But it'd hurt Harley deeply. She'd never admit it, but he'd seen that second of pain gash across those lovely blue eyes. He hated Germaine for causing it.

*Germaine isn't ours to kill,* he thought to the grizzly, trying to calm it. *He's Harley's. She'd never forgive us if we took that from her.*

The grizzly's growl hummed through his body, but it reluctantly backed down, hunkering, alert, and ready within him. It knew its time was close. It'd be needed and when called upon it'd rend their enemies to shreds.

He turned the Tahoe left, heading south again.

Since the lie-stuffed story of the burned churches had aired, they'd stuck to the back roads, crossed several state lines, and switched plates in small towns along the way, just in case. Brahms wasn't fond of stealing but the alternative was worse, not only for him and Harley, but for the public as well. The number of deaths or turning of innocents would continue to grow until they stopped Niko and the rogue slayers. Besides the werepuma pride, who knew how many more beasts they'd have to hunt and kill before they could confront the source of the chaos, Germaine and the tainted slayers who did his dirty deeds. Thankfully, not all slayers agreed with the Cardinal's atrocity, so perhaps Cerberus could locate and ally with slayers like Harley to thwart Germaine's plans before he tossed civilization into a waking nightmare.

He glanced at Harley.

He'd taken over the wheel an hour ago and told her to grab some sleep while she could. With their faces plastered over TV screens, police channels and descriptions broadcast over the radio stations, they couldn't pull over to rest or rent a hotel room, even in the rural areas, without the risk someone would recognize them or notice the truck.

Sleep, if it came at all, would have to be taken on the go because if Thayer's latest report was accurate, all hell would break loose in the swamps and Harley would be the focus of that maelstrom. She needed every wit about her when they lured Niko into their trap. If she were tired or lagging, she'd be hurt, or worse. Brahms shook his head, not wanting to ponder those thoughts. He needed Harley alive for reasons that had nothing to do with weres or rampant creatures or the Order.

Harley, however, didn't seem inclined to rest. She sat in the passenger's bucket seat, using a flashlight to study maps of Louisiana, hunting for a back way into the swamps that didn't use major highways where most of law enforcement's efforts to find them would be.

Even in the harsh light of the flashlight, she was beautiful. Her strong cheekbones and jawline reflected the strength he felt in her spirit. The intense, sheer determination in her eyes infused him with confidence. In her, in their cause, and in the future. Considering the hell crashing around them, Brahms wished he could say that he felt guilty finding pleasure and maybe something deeper, something stronger than friendship or comradery with Harley, but he didn't, even if it defied logic. Since meeting her, he'd become a fugitive and still he'd rather be on the run with her than anywhere else. Besides, if they hadn't met, she'd be going through this disaster alone. Although he harbored no doubts about her tenacity or prowess as a warrior, the emotional turmoil Germaine's treachery caused was something no one ought to navigate solo.

She'd said little since they'd left the diner. He let her brood hoping that the presence of someone she trusted would offer her a small measure of comfort. If she needed time to get a grip on her emotions, then time was what she'd get. Brahms wished he could shield her from experiencing any more pain. Unfortunately, that wasn't within his powers to do. The best he could do was to be present for her, support, and encourage her. Kill Niko with her. Help her right the wrongs of her Order because in accomplishing that perhaps she'd right the turmoil within herself.

"If only we'd stayed." She traced her finger along the map, her lips skewed to the side.

He didn't have the heart to tell her she was most likely the target of the attack on St. Ambrose. That she was the one they'd wanted to kill, and that Francis was acceptable collateral damage. It was one thing for her to deal with Francis's death. It was another for her to think it was her fault. "If we'd stayed, then whoever killed him would have just waited until we left. He'd have died a day later."

"How the hell did we get blamed for this?" Harley thrust the map away from her. "I mean, what the hell? The police aren't bothering to check the times? What, do they think we can be in two places at once?"

"That's assuming no one fiddled with the stamps. They never showed footage from the stone golem church." From what he'd learned from Thayer, in the digital world, there were many ways to rig video to show precisely and only what you wanted shown. Even if there were slight glitches, the police were under a ton of social and political pressure to find and crucify the culprits who'd burned the churches and killed the priests. Because he and Harley had been so easily offered as the sacrificial lambs, he doubted law enforcement would bother to consider other suspects, or consider the possibility they might be innocent, let alone summon the gumption to investigate the church itself.

"Still," she said. "The investigators would have estimated the times by now. It ought to be damned apparent that the fires erupted too close together for us to have started both."

He glanced at her then back to the winding road. When other women he'd dated were upset he'd tried to smooth it over, make everything appear okay, safe, within control. He didn't think Harley would appreciate the attempt, so he opted for brutal honesty. "Won't be the first or last time they assumed innocent people guilty of crimes they didn't commit all in the name of making the public feel safer and dousing the heat on officials. Law enforcement doesn't care about logistics, truth, or facts right now. With the Church breathing down their backs and the public in an uproar they need people to take the fall and we're it."

She muttered a stream of curses. Her arsenal of cusses was impressive. "They're supposed to find the real bad guys."

"Ideally, yes," Brahms said. "My uncle is a cop. He's an honest man, but even he will tell you that—"

"Sometimes, you have to bow to politics."

"Yeah, something like that. He calls it mollifying the public with lollipop lies."

"You'd think the public would want the actual criminal caught so they'd actually be safe."

"They just want to *feel* safe regardless of if it's true or not. If the police and politicians can produce that illusion for them then they can go back to the humdrum of life and forget an innocent person might pay the price for their misguided comfort."

"Meanwhile, the danger is still out there." She swiped her

hand at the window. "God only knows what Germaine and Ian and whoever the hell else is in on this is planning next."

He nodded. "But as long as the cops and politicians don't need to worry about the clamoring public it's all good in their books."

She crossed her arms over her chest and sank back into the seat, staring out into the night. "Sometimes I wonder why we protect them. We should just let Germaine release all the beasts and kick back as they rampage through the streets. I don't know. Maybe even munch on some butter-slathered popcorn while we're at it."

He wanted to reach out to her, to take her into his arms and hold her tight, but they couldn't spare the time to stop, and she probably would deck him this time. "Because if we don't protect them, who will?"

"That's the point. Maybe we shouldn't. Maybe no one should. If they don't value the truth or care if innocent people are prosecuted as long as they get to keep their safe little world views intact, do they even deserve it?"

Arguing with her would be moot, and besides, she presented a valid point. "I don't know."

# CHAPTER SEVENTEEN

Harley's head banged against the Tahoe's window. Pain jolted across her skull, waking her with an unwelcome start. "Hey, watch it."

She rubbed her throbbing head and squinted out the once clean, now filmed with backroad grime, window. Gentle morning sunlight bathed the world outside in a hushed orange that offset the bright green brush and trees that huddled on either side of the bumpy two-track road. Now and then, glimmers of sluggish muddy brown water peeped through the leaves, only to be hidden again by the dense growth.

"Why didn't you wake me?" she asked. They'd agreed to switch drivers at 2:00 a.m. so he could get rest. How could she have slept so long cramped in the passenger's seat?

"You needed it more," Brahms said. Though he maintained steady control of the truck, his eyes were bleary, lids heavy. Letting her rest had taken its toll on him.

"Next time," she said, "pull off to the side somewhere or into the woods. It'd be safe for us both to sleep in here." She rapped the glass with her knuckle. "Doesn't look like it, but it'd take several whacks of a mighty troll's hammer to crack this glass."

He raised a dark eyebrow. "Seems like regular glass to me."

"Fern is amazing that way."

"What?"

"She's a friend. One of the good ones, I know it." Harley shifted in her seat, scooting up. "I'll give you her contact info later. If anything happens to me—"

"It won't."

"She'll help you. If she needs some bribing, try anything sharky. She's wonky obsessed, especially with megs. Or wine. Dark, dry reds. Works every time."

"You'll be there with me," he said. "So, I'll let you worry about bribe items."

"Personally, I prefer dark chocolate. With coconut is even better. Or rum."

He chuckled and shook his head. "I'll remember that when I'm in trouble."

"Best you do." Threading her fingers together, she pressed her hands forward to stretch. The road dipped. Mud splashed across the doors. "How much do you want to bet this road floods?"

"I don't take bets I know I'll lose. Hang tight. It'll be rough going from here out." Brahms slowed the Tahoe to a crawl to avoid unnecessary jostling. "The cabin shouldn't be too much farther."

She rolled her shoulders and tilted her head from side to side, working the kinks out of her muscles. She'd used her wadded jacket as a pillow, but it hadn't been comfy. God, she needed coffee, bad. "Think Cree and Thayer are already there?"

"Yeah, and Thayer will have breakfast going. I sent him a text at the last gas station so we wouldn't catch them by surprise."

Her stomach growled at the mention of food. They hadn't eaten anything since the diner other than quick bags of chips and candy bars picked up from tiny gas stations along their covert route. "Coffee. Tell me there's coffee. Could use some eggs and bacon, too. Or pancakes. Waffles with strawberries and cream. Slabs of ham."

"A woman after my heart."

*Oh, yeah.*

He was closer to the truth than he knew. But on the verge of battle was not the time to light the passions of romance. Once they'd crushed the werepumas and made good on her promises to Cerise and yanked that foul betrayer, Germaine, off his lofty, slimy perch, then there'd be time to consider getting involved with a guy. Until then, dealing with a relationship would add too much hassle and drama, not to mention that it'd fracture her focus. Brahms was distracting enough as just a partner.

As he'd predicted, they soon pulled into a dirt driveway marred with divots, potholes, and random weeds. In testimony to the seasonal floods, the cabin stood on sturdy, water-stained wooden pillars that allowed the river to rise without seeping into the house through the floorboards. The weathered wood siding probably hadn't seen stain in a solid decade. The single-paned windows wouldn't offer much protection against the cold, or anything else, but that far south, cold was hardly an issue. A covered porch wrapped around the plank sided cabin that sat right on the bank of a wide swath of lazy river, the monotony of the tannin-tinged water broken only by thick patches of floating plants. The bones of old trees poked from the surface, snaring debris that floated downstream, creating interesting eddies and swirls on the surface.

Free-range chickens moseyed around the small, cleared area near the cabin, pecking and scratching at the dirt in search of plump bugs for their morning meal. The ramshackle coop was also built on posts with a U-shaped deck area the chickens could use for exercise when their normal hunting ground was submerged.

"I wonder how many of them become gator snacks." Harley hopped out of the Tahoe as soon as it came to a stop. Lamenting her numb butt cheeks, she stretched her legs and twisted, releasing the tension in her back with a series of pops up her spine. She studied the water. A swim would wake her up and normally she'd plunge right in. Not here. Nope. Not a chance. There were so many organic particles in the water that visibility was zilch. She couldn't see anything hovering an inch below the surface, and beyond that could be any sort of nastiness. A gator or venomous snake could lurk in there, unseen.

*At least they're not rats.*

She was fond of her appendages and wanted to keep them precisely as-is.

"Not as many as you'd think." A short man with feathered black hair lumbered out of the cabin. The screen door snapped shut behind him with a sharp thwap. He hitched his leg up and sat on the railing that surrounded the porch. "Territorial creatures, gators."

"Guessing you have one that's claimed this area?" Brahms grabbed his bag from the back seat.

"Ole Nessie." He inclined his head toward the river. "She snaps up smaller gators like bait worms. Had to store the trash bins in the shed or she tips them over and rips through the bags, dragging garbage everywhere. Brings in even more rats."

Harley froze. "Did you just say rats?"

"Nature of the beast out here." He settled his blue gaze on Brahms. "You must be Brahms and Harley. I'm Nash, owner of this fine outpost. Cree is getting some coffee on, and Thayer has breakfast going."

"There aren't rats in the cabin, are there?" she eyed the cabin, warily.

Rats could squeeze their pudgy bodies through quarter-sized holes. The graying cabin boards fit together in a loose fashion. She'd bet her pretty hollow points there were holes big enough for those twitchy-nosed bastards to infiltrate. Sleeping in her truck was looking to be the best option. At least she knew that was sealed beyond all sealdom. Nothing would get in there. Not wispies, not zombies, and not rats.

"Nah," Nash said. "I've sealed her up tight. They stay outside."

"With?" she asked.

"Hardware cloth. They'll have a tough time chewing through that."

"I don't know." Harley wasn't sure she could trust his word. It'd take time for a werepuma to rip through her truck's metal, but it was possible. How long would it take the Cerberus agents to realize she was under attack and respond? Besides, Brahms might insist on staying out there with her because of that possibility. Her willpower had held out so far but cramped together in the back of her truck just inches away from him, she wouldn't place a bet on those odds. "Fine."

She retrieved one of her bags from the back seat and followed Nash and Brahms into the cabin. It was bigger than it appeared from the outside and a hell of a lot cozier than the exterior would lead one to believe. Golden hardwood walls matched the golden hardwood floors, made even warmer and richer with a set of dark chocolate colored couch, loveseat, and fluffy reclining chair. Thayer dominated the open tiled, floored kitchen, which flowed right into the living room to create a large central living area that offered hiding spots to only the smallest of creatures.

"Hope you're hungry." Thayer kept his attention on the stove, his broad back to them.

"Starving." Brahms lifted his bag and turned to Nash. "Where do you want us?"

"Caffeine." Harley inhaled a lung full of the beautiful scent of coffee. Actual coffee. Not the gas station atrocity they labeled as coffee but just might be disguised alien piss.

"If you don't mind sharing a room with the lady," Nash said, "then down the hall second door to the right. If either of you object, then you get the couch, and she gets the room."

Brahms turned and hauled the bags down the hall.

Cree stopped, the coffeepot in her hand hovering above the empty mugs. "You two, um..."

"Guess he wants to think so," Harley said.

She followed Brahms, leaving Cree and Thayer to draw their own conclusions. She was too hungry to care what anyone thought. Her foremost concern was to dump the rest of the bags in the room and get to the table before Thayer started dishing the breakfast. From what she'd seen, Cerberus agents could devour food fast as any slayers.

The bedroom they'd been given was the size of a glorified closet but cute in a Cerise would have loved it sort of way. Flimsy sheers filtered the view of the backyard. A wooden bowl filled with potpourri sat atop a dented five-drawer dresser wedged between the foot of the metal framed bed and the wall. Piled on the floral draped mattress was a mountain of pillows in varying pastel shades.

Where in the hell were they going to put all those? The hallway?

Harley dropped her bag by the bed. "Something tells me Nash didn't decorate this particular room."

"Cree said he's only had the cabin for about a year. He's probably working his way through the upgrades and this room is last on his list."

She tilted her head and eyed him. "You're awfully brave or stupid to stay in the same room with me again. Never know what I'll do."

"I've been wanting to do this."

Before she could ask, "Do what?", he tugged her into his arms and kissed her forehead. It wasn't a friendly brush of a kiss, nor was it sexually passionate. It was comforting. He was there with her, sticking by her side. He cared for her as more than just a partner. She felt it in his stance, the way he leaned toward her but didn't quite touch. He wouldn't force her into a situation she might not be ready for. Her heart did a disturbing flip in her chest.

His hands slid to her waist, and he pulled her close against him.

So much for the miniscule distance.

She nestled her cheek on his shoulder. Even though they'd spent the last twenty-four hours in the truck, he still smelled of earth and pine, sky, and sun. Slowly, she embraced him, running her fingers over the taut muscles in his back. Solid. A rock to hang on to in the chaos and upheaval around her.

After a moment, he pulled back.

Her stomach sank, afraid he'd try to kiss her on the lips. She didn't want to get closer. Didn't want to know what his lips would feel like on hers or what he tasted like. He smelled too damned good. She imagined he'd taste better. That wasn't what she needed. Not yet not now. Later, yeah, sure.

When she looked up at him, his gaze was troubled, not impassioned.

"Don't tell me," she said, "you're going all gallant and having second thoughts about using me as bait." She narrowed her eyes at him.

She usually didn't stay in relationships long enough for the guy to form a close bond with her, but the rare time or two that she'd let time slip away from her and stayed too long had taught her men exhibited possessive streaks that were mostly annoying and slightly endearing. With those guys, she hadn't cared enough to bother sticking around and working through it. It wasn't as if she could ever tell them the truth about her real life, anyway, so what use was the whole reconciliation thing when it'd always be a lie? With Brahms, she'd need to work through it. Didn't seem like too awful of a thing. And the make-up sex. That'd have to be phenomenal.

"No, you can handle Niko." He cupped her face and ran his thumb over her cheek. "But there are things I want to tell you, must tell you. Things you need to know before this goes much further."

She rocked back on her heels. "All right, what?"

She couldn't imagine anything he could have to tell her that would cause him so much concern. "You're not married, are you?"

If he was, she'd have to do more than just deck him. Feeding him to Nessie would work. Maybe Nash had a way to call the gator to him like a puppy or something.

He blinked, shocked, then shook his head. "No. But now isn't the time to go into it, so you'll have to trust me a while longer. Once Niko and his pride are dead, we'll talk."

Weird. He wasn't the type to keep secrets. Curious as she was, she let it drop. He was right. They had to deal with the current threat first, and then they'd have time for more delicate matters. "Breakfast, then shower and then prep. I call dibs on first shower."

"Perfect."

Leaving their bags in the room, they returned to the main living area to join the others for a breakfast of delicious spicy scrambled eggs, jumbo shrimp in the shell, and the best coffee Harley had ever laid lips on. As they ate, they discussed the events that happened since they'd left St. Ambrose until they reached the swamp.

"We saw you guys on TV," Nash said. "Some people from that diner called in tips but they lost you after that."

"They theorized you'd head north," Thayer said, "toward Chicago."

"Germaine's idea, no doubt," Harley muttered. "Afraid I'll find him and skin his slimy hide."

"A valid fear," Cree said, "I'd say."

Germaine had been as close to a father as she'd ever had outside of her own. Could she kill him even after what he'd done? She wanted to say yes, yearned to have the courage to dole out that sort of justice for the souls his actions had slain, but she hated lying to herself. "If I don't find irrefutable proof that he's behind this there's no way the Tribunal will put him on trial. He'll waltz away in that froofy red cassock of his, free and clear. I'll be the one whose head they'll want on a pike."

Cree said, "His actions might become his own noose in time."

Did they have that sort of time? It was already too late for those people whose bones rested in the werepuma cave. How many more would die before they could end this?

"Meanwhile," Thayer said, "Niko and his cats have been busy."

"Been losing track of friends." Nash hitched a thumb toward the old radio on a small desk near the side door. "We normally keep in contact over the radio. Out here, it's just us. Emergency services, the law take forever, if they even decide to show up at all."

"I'm sure that pleases Niko to no end." Harley poured herself a fresh cup of coffee.

Nash continued. "Over the last week, people haven't been responding, or when they do, they act different. Odd."

"He's turning them." Cree deftly deshelled a plump shrimp. "If Fain hadn't sent as many agents as he did, we wouldn't have a prayer."

"We might not have one now," Thayer said. "We can't create Cerberus agents like he can turn people into weres."

"There's no need to be hasty about our deaths." Cree wiggled the shrimp at him.

"How will Niko know that I'm here?" Harley asked.

Nash turned to Brahms. "You followed the directions Thayer gave you, didn't you?"

"To the letter," Brahms said, "including driving through town. Main street, no less."

"Then, he'll know," Nash said. "Your truck isn't that hard to identify."

"And when he gets here," Harley said, "he'll regret it."

After breakfast, Harley snagged a shower, using most of the hot water in the cabin's small tank.

Then, she spent most of the day with the others plotting their course of action, helping prepare the surprises they concocted for Niko and aiding Cree in setting wards that would alert them when the weres trespassed onto Nash's land.

After that, she helped Nash set traps around the perimeter to catch a few of the weres before they converged on the cabin. If even half the traps caught their furry prey, and Cree's wards fired accurately, it'd even the odds. That was, of course, assuming the Cerberus agents forming the net around the swamp caught and destroyed their share of werepumas. It was odd working for a team that wasn't composed of slayers whom she'd known for years, or at least had met. Putting trust in strangers, particularly when her life depended on it, wasn't Harley's gig, but if the rest of Cerberus' agents possessed the talent and moral compasses of Brahms, Cree, and Thayer, then she supposed she was okay with it.

*Not as if I have a choice in the matter, anyway.*

Because Brahms was in town and his fellow Cerberus agents were in a phone meeting with their boss, Harley took a midafternoon break to clear her mind. Entering battle with a cluttered brain was the equivalent of suicide, and she planned to live a long life full of hunting monsters.

Plus, she still wanted that tropical vacation with rum and

cabana boys. Toasty sand. Turquoise seas. Exotic foods. No way was she going to die without that experience.

Nash chose not to attend the meeting, so he was wandering around the grounds somewhere. Cree and the others seemed to trust him, but she was leery. She couldn't stick a label on why. He was nice enough. Hospitable enough. Knew his land, knew the swamps. Put forth valuable ideas during the brainstorming session and made stellar coffee. She couldn't think of any logical reason he'd cause her ping to sound.

Yet he did.

Maybe it was the way he'd slip off without a sound or pop in out of nowhere. And he disappeared a lot. Still, none of that added up to anything more than that he possessed a graceful stride and would make a fantastic hunter.

She considered telling Brahms her suspicions but there wasn't enough time and even less of it spent alone. Besides, if their plan panned out and they destroyed Niko's pride, she'd only have to tolerate Nash for a day and then she'd be off on the next part of her mission of finding Lars or Ian. She hadn't yet decided upon which would come first yet. Doing both at once would be optimal, and unfortunately, impossible. She'd need irrefutable proof against Germaine to present to the Tribunal. To get that she'd need strong allies.

Because she wasn't certain if Cerberus would help her after they'd annihilated the werepuma threat, her best bet was to find Lars and other slayers she trusted.

*Maybe Fern. Fern would never agree to help in Germaine's idiocy.*

Then again, she'd never thought Germaine would do anything this insane. Never thought he'd betray her. Now that he'd thrown her under the bus to the media and law enforcement, chances were that he'd placed a kill order on her. She'd have to approach fellow slayers, even those she'd considered friends, cautiously.

Who knew what sort of lies Germaine was spinning within the Order.

*Fern wouldn't believe a word of it.*

Next to Cerise, Fern was one of her closest friends.

*If she's still alive.*

No. She wasn't going to go there. Fern was smart. She'd figure it out, and if she felt she was in danger, she'd either be packing to get out of Dodge or she'd already left.

*Cerise had been smart, too.*

Stifling a yawn, Harley stretched her legs and lounged on the grassy shore next to the wooden dock that jutted out behind the cabin. The wood seemed sturdy, even if the surface begged for a fresh coat of sealer. The river lapped gently against the pillars, lulling her into a sense of lethargy. She wished she could kick off her boots, soak her feet in the water, and take a nap. However, having listened to with rapt attention as Nash elaborated on what sort of hungry nasties lived in those seemingly placid waters waiting for something with soft flesh to plop in, she kept her boots on and feet a healthy distance from the waterline.

The lazy current eddied around the skiff's hull with a barely audible swish of water brushing against metal, the creak of the rope that tethered the boat to the dock and the drone of a multitude of insects combined into an insidious lullaby.

Harley's eyelids drooped and her mind wandered to pleasant, dreamy subjects like Brahms's lips and the taut stretch of his skin over muscle. She leaned back, planting her elbows on the ground to stretch her shoulders. She let her head tip back, hair swaying softly in the humid breeze. What would it be like to have an entire week off with no obligations, no weres, no creatures, not a single thing to do other than lay on a warm white sand beach with Brahms? Oh, yeah. Heaven. When this debacle was over, she would take the backlog of vacation time she'd stored up over the years and head to the Keys or the Caribbean or Bahamas or some other tropical, lackadaisical place where her only obligations were to drink, sleep, and swim. With Brahms around she could skip the whole cabana boys thing because–

A sudden chill ran up her spine. Her skin tingled from her toes to her scalp. Someone, something, was watching her, and it wasn't Brahms or anyone with fluffy good intentions. No. This felt malicious. Murderous. The gaze of a predator stalking its prey.

*Niko?*

Odd as it'd be for him to attack in the afternoon it wasn't out of the question, especially if he was aiming to surprise them. They'd expected him to wait until dark before daring to approach. Not that weres needed to attack at night, like Hollywood movies suggested, but night was their preferred hunting time because their eyesight was superior to that of humans. In the darkness, they were less likely to be seen, and they could hide in the deep shadows as they crept up on their victims. Being the sadistic creatures they were, werepuma would make just enough noise at just the right times to instill the primal fear that beat in human hearts when confronted with an unknown threat in the dark. Werepuma delighted in fear. They loved to watch their prey tremble and sweat, knowing death lurked in the night and that there wasn't a damned thing they could do to stop it.

By attacking in the day, the werepuma lost those benefits. If Niko attacked now, with the sun still hovering on the horizon, he must be as impatient for their violent reunion as she was.

*Miss me, kitty?*

Harley faked a contented sigh and pretended she was lost in her daydreams, blissfully unaware of his presence. Let him come closer. Let him attack and experience the sting of her vengeance.

*For Cerise.*

She resisted the urge to glance toward the cabin. Did they know? Had Cree's wards fired? If so, why hadn't they told her? Surely, they'd have let her know or they'd be out here with her.

Which left her with one conclusion. They didn't know the weres were here. As much as she wanted to yell a warning to them, she couldn't without losing the element of surprise. She and Niko had been disturbingly matched the last time they tangoed. She'd need every advantage she could muster so she could not only win this time but kill him. Dead, dead. As in, would not return as anything type of dead. Not even a zombie or animated plaything for some sick necromancer. Anything less than that was unacceptable. So, the others would have to figure out that they were under attack on their own and take care of themselves until she was through ripping Niko into bullet-ridden shreds.

*One. Two. Three. Ready or not, here I come.*

In one fluid motion, she hopped to her feet and drew her Smith & Wesson, swinging the sight into focus on the skulking predator, her finger applying steady pressure on the trigger. But it wasn't Niko who filled her sight, nor was it one of his werepuma lackeys.

There, standing only ten feet away, was the largest gator she'd ever seen. Hell, it was the first gator she'd seen up close and all personal. Definitely an experience she didn't want to repeat. Its curved claws bit into ground. Dark, rumply scales ran across its sides and back, with several rows of taller triangular scales rising from its back and along its thick tail. Its enormous mouth gaped open, and it hissed, actually hissed. Yellowed teeth protruded from its gums at strange, wide intervals that would have been comical if they weren't so damned deadly.

Knowing her bullets were unlikely to penetrate its thick hide enough for a kill shot, Harley dropped to one knee and took aim at the fleshy, pinkish-white mouth and gullet.

"Don't." Nash ran out of the cabin and onto the porch.

"Better call it off then." Harley kept the pistol pointed at the gator, ready to shoot if the oversized lizard moved forward. "Before it suffers from massive lead poisoning."

Crinkling sounded from the porch. "Nessie. I have your favorites," Nash said, followed by more crinkling.

The gator turned faster than what Harley thought possible for such a bulky, stubby legged creature and ran toward the porch at an amazing clip. It glided into the water, whipped its powerful tail, and swam in front of the porch near the dock, waiting with its head above the surface, mouth hinged open, an ancient beast expecting a sacrificial offering.

Nash opened a container of Oreos and unceremoniously dumped them into the gator's mouth. It snapped its jaws shut on the dark, sugary treats and sank quietly below the surface as if it had never been there, as if it wasn't even there now.

*Creepy damned lizard.*

"You feed that thing?" Harley holstered her pistol and stalked to the porch.

"Nessie loves her Oreos." Nash wadded the plastic into a ball. "And chicken, and steak, and anything else she finds."

"So do I. Got more Oreos?"

"In the pantry, can't miss 'em."

"I can't believe you keep feeding that thing."

He raised his eyebrow. "What would you have me do with her?"

Harley glared at him and stomped up the stairs. "I don't know. Boots. Belts. Nifty bullet-proof vest with matching holster."

She wasn't for killing animals that weren't an overt danger to people. But creatures as lethal as gators who were trained by jerks like Nash to expect food from humans were a special sort of dangerous. One minute, they expected food from you, the next you became the food. If life were fair, Nessie would eat Nash. Chomp him down like a big, juicy steak. Problem was that life wasn't anything close to fair. Chances were that the gator would snack on some little kid fishing along the riverbank, or random jogger, or innocent person in their own yard minding their own business, never suspecting a gator would snatch them up on dry land right next to their house.

Nash shook his head and remained on the porch as she went into the cabin.

She yanked the pantry door open and stared at the Oreo packages that filled an entire two and a half shelves. The top shelf housed full packs and the second individual tubes of the luscious black cookies. "What the hell is he planning for–the gator apocalypse?"

How in the hell Nessie hadn't blown up or died of sugar overdose was beyond her knowledge of all things reptilian. Which wasn't saying much.

"Take a few." Cree measured ground coffee into the filter. "Nash won't mind."

"It'll be my good Samaritan act for the day." Harley grabbed a few of the tubes, stuffed two into the inside pocket of her jacket, which hung off the back of a kitchen chair, and ripped open the other. "Saving that hulking reptile from diabetes."

Harley popped a cookie into her mouth, relishing the gritty chocolate and cream explosion.

"Nash is," Cree hesitated, using the time to finish preparing the coffee, "different."

"I'm okay with different. What I'm wondering is if we can trust him. The guy has to be addled to keep a gator that size, talk to it, and feed it cookies. He's creating a monster out of an animal and we have enough monsters wandering amok as it is."

Cree glanced out the window to see where Nash was then took a seat at the table near Harley. She wiggled an Oreo out of the open bag. "Souls that have seen too much darkness tend to be a little addled. We shouldn't judge. We might all end up that way, eventually."

True enough, Harley supposed. But she'd worked beside

people irrevocably damaged by the shadows before and they hadn't set off her ping. Nash did. "And you trust him why?"

"Ties between partners don't easily break."

"He's still in Cerberus? Thought Brahms said he quit."

"We like to think he is," Thayer fiddled with the wire that connected his laptop to the landline, "regardless of what he wants us to think."

"Nash was your partner?" Harley asked Cree.

She nodded. "He retired a few years ago after his father died. Got out of the dark to tend the land and in return tend his soul."

Harley found the idea of retirement strange. Slayers never retired. Those who survived the field stayed in the field until their effectiveness at fighting wore thin. Then they returned to the strongholds to teach new generations of slayers, or to work at sanctuaries, or help the white coats with the beasts they kept in the labs.

And she didn't think Nash left the dark when he left Cerberus but arguing the point with Cree would prove moot.

"Fair enough," Harley said. "Is everything set?"

Tires crunched in the driveway and came to an abrupt halt.

"Brahms is back." Thayer opened the screen door for him. "People in town see you?"

Brahms strode in. "Yeah. And I took my time on the way back. Sightseeing. Pictures. If Niko didn't already know exactly where she was, he does now."

"How many people do you think he's turned?" Harley tucked the remaining Oreos into her outside jacket pocket, as she'd already stuffed her inside pockets. It'd be a long night. She needed chocolatey snacks to keep herself alert.

"Hard to say." Thayer lifted the lid off the pot that simmered on the stove and stirred the contents. "He's been here a couple weeks, depending on how many weres he had with him to begin with."

"He could have turned the entire town." Harley drew a deep breath, delighting in the spicy, mouthwatering scent that wafted from the pot. "What is that?"

"Dinner," Thayer said. "Fresh gumbo, shrimp, crab, crays, chicken, the works." He measured out a teaspoon of a powdered green substance. "And it isn't real gumbo without sassafras leaves."

Thayer's phone rang in his pocket. He took it out and stared at it as one would eye a rampaging venomous snake.

"She wouldn't call tonight without a reason," Cree said. "Answer it."

The sour look Thayer gave Cree indicated he believed whoever was on the other end would, indeed, call for no reason other than to annoy him. He answered, anyway, and listened, walking out the door for privacy.

"Who is it?" Harley whispered to Cree.

"Celeste. She's a wonderful woman. Thayer is just a jackass."

Shocked, Harley stared at her. She hadn't heard Cree swear before.

Cree chuckled then said, "Sometimes no other word works."

Thayer returned. His chiseled face taut with anger. "We're too late."

"What do you mean?" Brahms asked.

Thayer prowled toward the TV, pent energy coiled in him like a spring. For a second, Harley thought he'd punch the screen. Instead, he turned it on then stood back so everyone could see.

All the coifed hair and makeup couldn't detract from the newscaster's confused, uneasy expression. His lips ticked as if unsure if he should frown or laugh or panic. "Only one day since the arsonists burned two Catholic churches to the ground and emergency lines across the United States and the world are flooded with reports of," he glanced down at his papers rereading a segment, "sightings of mythical creatures. Already, several deaths have been blamed on these," he lightly cleared his throat, "creatures, in what skeptics, including the president, have claimed to be an attack by the same extremist group that set fire to the churches, killing two priests. In a special address this morning, the president urged people not to panic, not to believe the antics of these vicious tricksters who, he assures us, are very human."

The image gave way to a close if grainy shot of a red-scaled devil clinging to a roof by its black claws. It peeled off the shingles, one at a time, attempting to infiltrate the house. "Is this really an elaborate hoax?" the newscaster asked. "Or is it, as some religious sects are saying, a sign of the end times?"

Then there he was again in his full red wardrobe. Germaine lying his soul away.

"We've handed evidence to law enforcement," Germaine said, "regarding the Cerberus Foundation's involvement in this catastrophe."

The reporter asked, "Who or what is the Cerberus Foundation?"

"They're an enigmatic cult we've been tracking for decades. Very, very dangerous people."

"Why didn't you bring them to the attention of law enforcement before?"

Germaine gave a soft laugh. "We've been attempting to get law enforcement's attention onto this cult ever since we became aware of their activities. But our concerns were never taken seriously."

"I'm not sure," the reporter glanced around as he didn't feel quite safe in his surroundings, "I'd have believed you until, well, until now."

Germain nodded like a sage confirming a just now realized truth spouted from the lips of a neophyte. "They've lost faith.

Many have lost faith. The Bible teaches of these threats and many people have forgotten them."

"What is your advice to people so they can stay safe in these trying times?"

"Keep your neighborhoods safe by reporting anything unusual immediately. Report anyone you know who might be working with Cerberus. They'll be those of alternative religions. Pagans. Witches. Anyone not walking the way of faith is or could be a danger. Stay indoors at night, lock your house, and keep everyone, including pets, in after dark. See your local parish to acquire holy water and crucifixes. When in doubt, or if you are frightened in any way, seek out the Church. We've already begun staffing our churches twenty-four-seven so the doors will be open to anyone in need."

Harley's fingers itched, yearning for the trigger of her pistol. Wherever he was, he ought to give thanks to every saint in and under heaven he wasn't anywhere within shooting distance from her.

Thayer turned the set off as soon as the news switched to other events.

For a while, no one spoke. The simmering gumbo and buzzing insects were the only sounds in the cabin. Harley glanced to Brahms and found him studying her from across the room. From the steel in his gaze, she guessed he was placing his bet on the same outcome as she was. The events might not mark the end of times, as the fear mongers would have the public believe, but it would certainly mark the entrance into a darker, tumultuous time. A time unlike any since the dark ages, where shadows and fangs ruled the night in a bloody reign of violence. No one would be safe. Not mundanes, not Cerberus agents, and not slayers. They'd all be under attack in this chaotic new world. Civilization would fall. Governments degrade. But in the chaos, there was hope for them. Humanity could rise from the bloody ashes. She had to believe that, or fighting was only a fun but ultimately useless pastime.

"They've released hell on earth," Cree whispered, "and the innocent will pay a heavy price in blood and terror."

"Looks like humanity will have to rediscover the real purpose of shutters," Harley said. Not that they'd deter anything like weres, but it'd be some protection against other beasts. It'd give families a few extra moments to prepare their defenses. Or wake up if they failed to realize that in these times someone would need to post watch after darkness fell.

Nash strode into the room. "And a healthy fear of what prowls in the night." He peered out the window. Apparently satisfied nothing was out there, he turned back to them. "When we're done with Niko and his crew, I'll talk to the sheriff. Tell him the truth to clear your names. But..." He let his words trail off.

Harley took it up. "But it'll be pointless. Only a matter of time before the news networks and communication systems go down. No one will be concerned about a few fugitives when they're busy keeping their kids safe from the all too real monsters under the bed."

# CHAPTER EIGHTEEN

Night fell and plunged the swamp into a Cimmerian darkness impenetrable to the human eye. Harley leaned her hip on the porch railing as she attempted to peer beyond the first line of trees into the woods, but everything past the light that pooled from the cabin windows was a sheet of black. She drew a breath of the stagnant, humid air and turned her attention to the river. The cabin lights glimmered off the gently rippled water, giving her a better view of the river and the edge of the opposite shoreline. Beyond that, utter darkness.

"See anything out there?" Brahms shut the screen door lightly behind him, joining her on the back porch.

She dug an Oreo out of the package in her jacket pocket and nibbled on it to give herself a moment to think. She wasn't used to sharing her feelings, except with a select few. Cerise, dead, Francis, dead, Germaine. Oh, he'd be dead soon enough. Everyone she'd trusted with her, with her innermost thoughts and emotions, were either dead or a foul betrayer. Would Brahms be the same? He could die tonight because the odds, frankly, weren't in their favor. Even if he lived, men were fickle beings. His interest in her could wane once they defeated the werepumas. And regardless of his feelings for her, he was a part of Cerberus. His loyalty was to them, not her. When they left, he'd go with them, and she couldn't follow even if she wanted to.

Hell. They all might die tonight. Including her. What harm was one night of hope? In believing in the possibility of a "them"?

"The future," she said.

"That's bleak." He slid his hand around hers and studied her face. He wore his hair down. Maybe it made him feel as wild and dangerous as he looked. Or maybe he'd let it loose because he knew she preferred it. She hoped it was the latter.

"But true. Centuries of bloodshed to make this world even quasi safe destroyed by the depravity of one man. All for what? A power trip?"

"I doubt he sees it that way."

She scrutinized him. "How else could it possibly be seen?"

"The old adage, 'The road to hell is paved with good intentions'."

"Meaning?"

"Few people become villains on purpose. They don't see what they're doing as being wrong. They believe, truly, that what they're doing is right. Justified. By bringing people back to the Church, back to faithful lives, Germaine thinks he's saving souls. A noble, if misguided, goal."

"So, because of his arrogance, everything the Order has done, everything we've sacrificed and lost, everything Cerberus and groups like us have suffered has been for what? To stand by and watch the world shatter?"

"People aren't like what they were centuries or even a hundred years ago," Brahms said. "Maybe in some strange, cosmic way this current darkness is necessary to unite humanity. To show us once again our neighbors aren't our enemies. It's given us a common goal that transcends country, race, religion. Survival. To reclaim civilization, for us, for our families, and the future."

Harley wished it were that simple.

Brahms possessed a faith in people that she lacked, and she envied him for it. She'd seen too much. Sometimes, she felt that her heart would forever be beyond repair. That, like Nash, the darkness would never lift from her soul.

*Some stains are permanent.*

"People haven't changed that much," she said. "Oh, we have nifty little gadgets. Technology. All sorts of toys to keep our minds off important things. Most people have learned to put on polite masks like good little puppets because it made life easier. It made them seem nicer. More politically correct. The world we're entering, the world that will be our new reality, isn't nice. It isn't political and it sure as hell isn't correct. The world never was any of those things. We just believed it was so we could enjoy our vacations and days off without worry. Leave the kids home alone without the fear of returning to a bloodbath. So few will survive this. So few will know how."

"That's not true. Not if people like us don't allow it to happen. Not if we step up and defend them, show them, teach them."

"There's not enough of us out there, Brahms. Even if Cerberus has as many people as the Order there won't be enough. We only have so much blood in our veins, and luck holds only so long. We can spread ourselves only so far before we break. Before we all die."

"There're others." Brahms turned to gaze at the skiff that bobbed gently in the current. "Not everyone succumbed to the complacency of the modern world or forgot the tenuous edge civilization has danced upon since its conception. They will rise. They will fight."

"And for every group," Harley said, "that strives to protect the defenseless with some code of honor or ethics there'll be another that strives to enslave, to bully, to take advantage of the weak and their need for food and protection." She laughed but it lacked joy. "Don't you see? With no laws, no repercussions for those base behaviors we'll be fighting ourselves and everything else. The mages, the weres, the vampires, the ghouls, the devils, zombies, and demons, imps and elementals, fae, and goblins, everything. And since man turns against man so easily, who will we trust?"

They lapsed into silence.

*Whom can I trust?*

Brahms. He'd fight for those who couldn't fight for themselves. So would Cree and Thayer. With or without her, they'd shed blood. They'd die to defeat the creatures that would feast upon man.

If they were to form a resistance, it would make sense to start with loyal members of Cerberus and those within the Order that remained steadfast in their oaths. Before they parted ways, she'd have to rely on their word to decide which of their fellow Cerberus agents were trustworthy and which were not.

"I'll weed through Francis's list," she said, "of slayers and their contact info. Make sure you guys have a copy of those slayers that should be trustable." Not every slayer was honorable, Ian being a prime example, but some would be. Fern. "Definitely Fern. Plus, at least two dozen I can vouch for."

*Like I once vouched for Germaine?*

"How did I let him fool me for so long?" she whispered, not expecting an answer because there wasn't one.

"Cerise had precognitive powers," Brahms said, quietly, "at least at the end."

"What do you mean?"

He dipped his fingers into his pocket and pulled out a glimmering piece of jewelry. Silver. Cerise's cross.

"You've had this the entire time?" She thrust her hand out, palm up, demanding he fork it over. Why had he hidden it from her? He'd known she was searching for it in the Tahoe at St. Ambrose's, yet he'd said nothing about having it in his damned pocket.

He carefully coiled the chain in her hand, laid the frilly cross on top of it, and closed her fingers over it. "I would have given it to you when you regained consciousness at the safe house but before Cerise died, she made me promise to keep it until you had need of it. Until you had a need for her strength. I think this is that time."

She opened her hand and ran a finger over the lacy, delicate silver cross. He was right. She did need Cerise. If anyone could have made sense of this chaos, she could have. She could have explained why Germaine would turn against her, against the Order, and against the people they'd vowed to protect.

*If only you were here, my friend.*

"Circumstances might become as dire as you say," Brahms said, "but forests regrow stronger after a fire." He gently pressed his lips to her cheek and returned to the cabin and leaving her alone on the porch.

Part of her wished he would have stayed out there, even if he did nothing except stand quietly beside her. As his foresty scent faded she felt suddenly bereft. Alone.

If the world plummeted into chaos and violence, perhaps now was the perfect time to let the fires of love blaze. Maybe the light of love would be the only magic powerful enough to destroy this coming dark. That and a great deal of lead, stakes, and fire.

Surrounded by the incessant drone of insects and soothing gurgle of the river, she felt a strange click of connection deep within her. As if someone, something, was watching her, reaching out. It wasn't malevolent. It was comforting, as if someone were offering good juju from beyond the grave.

*Cerise? You were right again. But don't gloat too much or St. Peter will kick you out of those pearly gates.*

She sighed, closed her hand over the cross, then held her fist against her heart.

*You'd see the bright side of this, wouldn't you?*

That something positive could come out of Germaine's treachery if they worked hard enough to make it so. That civilization would survive, albeit differently, with their eyes wide open to the existence of other beings.

Cerise would believe such notions and Brahms obviously did but Harley didn't buy it.

*I'm sorry. I just...I can't. There's too much —*

A bump from behind her in the cabin. A thud. Followed by a muffled cry.

Harley whirled. Behind the screen door, the interior lights outlined the thick frame of a man. It wasn't Brahms, Thayer, or Nash. There wasn't enough light outside to make out his facial features. But his stance. The set of his shoulders.

The haughty tilt of his chin She recognized him, all right.

"It's been a while, Harley," he said, his voice smooth as a purr. "Why don't you be friendly and come in before something nasty happens to one of your friends?"

Ice skittered across her skin. Her hand hovered above her holster.

*Niko.*

"I wouldn't draw that if I were you," Niko said, "unless you want the blood of the druid woman on your hands."

*Fuck. Fuck. Fuck.*

The enemy was in the cabin. But how? How had they gotten onto the property let alone infiltrated the house without tripping Cree's wards or Nash's traps?

*And what the hell am I going to do about it?*

## CHAPTER NINETEEN

"I've been waiting for our next dance." Harley said. She reluctantly dropped her hand from the butt of her pistol. She didn't know if Cree was alive, as Niko words indicated, or already dead. The only thing she'd expect Niko to keep his word on was a threat of death because it was his area of expertise.

Devoid of any sense of compassion or guilt, he'd tell her anything he thought would lure her to a more advantageous position for him to successfully attack her.

If Cree or any of the others were alive, ordering their murder would be as easy for him as ordering a burger at a drive-through. The only conscious their deaths would stain would be Harley's. She didn't know how many more deaths she could carry before she broke. So, until she got a better grasp of the situation inside the cabin there wasn't much she could do without putting the others in mortal danger.

For the moment, she must let Niko call the shots.

"I mean," she said, "seeing as we were so rudely interrupted last time."

He leaned against the doorframe as if he were waxing poetic with an old schoolmate about playground tussles. "How is our mutual friend, Ian, by the way? Wanted to thank him for his generosity in shortening our sentence."

Too bad a were's word couldn't be used as proof during Tribunal trials or she'd torture the information out of Niko, record it, and then kill him. Though, Cerise would point out this gave her even more reason to serve Ian his dose of justice personally instead of bothering with the arduous Tribunal system.

*If it still exists.*

"Busy, from what I hear," she said.

Niko laughed.

Harley clenched her hands into fists, struggling to contain the overwhelming urge to slip her boot knife out and hack his lungs out.

He said, "Have I told you I love that glower of yours?"

"That just turns my heart to goo. Truly." She'd love to make his heart gooey all right, with a barrage of bullets. Though she supposed that'd turn out more like chewy Swiss cheese.

"Ditch the grenades and the gun. Slowly."

Harley wiggled the grenades off her belt, one at a time, and set them on the porch planks near enough to the door so that if she broke away, she could reach them. Then she did the same for the pistol and even the spare magazine she kept on her belt just to show him how sweet and cooperative she was.

"Now, come inside nicely." He opened the door and stood aside for her to pass. "Try anything underhanded, and your friend dies."

Harley stepped past Niko, resisting the urge to pummel his smug face into a meaty, unrecognizable blob.

*Weapons. Weapons. Need weapons.*

Her entire body was a weapon, but physics was a real bitch. A human body, no matter how well trained, was fragile compared to that of a were.

She kept her eyes forward, remembering the layout of the kitchen without giving her plans away by glancing at the counters. There were knives in the island counter drawer if she could get to them. The maple cutting board had potential. Two lamps in the living room. The TV. Suffocating him with a throw pillow had its merits but it'd take too long.

*Glass coffee carafe...it'd suck for that to shatter in your face.*

Her thoughts trailed off as she absorbed the scene inside the cabin.

Cree stood frozen with the barrel of a hefty .45 pressed into her temple by none other than their good pal Nash. Apparently, Cerberus was no better at identifying traitors in their ranks, or ex-ranks, as she'd been in the Order. It comforted her in a twisted sort of way. Corruption ran rampant everywhere. Not surprising. But she'd hoped there was at least one group they could count on.

*Now how will we know who to trust?*

The simplest answer was to trust no one, but that wasn't how she wanted to live.

Her gaze flicked to Brahms. He stood relaxed and calm despite the werepuma in human form a safe ten feet away who had him pinned within the sight of his pistol. A 9mm. Deadly if the shooter had good aim. Power wise, it paled in comparison to Nash's .45.

The two should have switched weapons.

Thayer shared Brahms's fate. The werepuma covering him also kept a healthy distance from the Cerberus warrior.

Harley released a dramatic sigh. "How cowardly. Letting the muzzles of your pistols do the threatening. Scared, kitties?"

They didn't so much as look at her. Disappointing. Usually, werepuma were easier to rile.

Harley glanced between Thayer, Cree, and Brahms. She didn't know them well enough to guess their tactics or how they'd react to the situation if she gave them an opening. Was she willing to take a gamble on them? Did she trust them with her life?

She gazed into Brahms's deep brown eyes and her instincts decided for her. She couldn't deny the way her heart hitched every time she saw him. The warmth that spread through her, offering hope. Offering another way. A life with more than just fighting.

Even if she couldn't trust anyone else, she could trust Brahms.

*He'll fight. He'll win. He has to.*

"Let me guess," Harley skewered a glare at Nash, "you dismantled your traps and, as Cree's ex-partner, you knew how to disable her wards. Sneaky."

"Why, Nash? At least tell me why." Cree's voice trembled.

Nash scoffed. "You don't understand what you're missing—"

Niko cut him off with a sharp motion of his hand.

Then he circled Harley. His golden eyes filled with a fiery hunger as he spoke. "Who in their right mind would refuse what I offer?" His gaze swept up and down her as she angled her body, keeping him in sight. "Strength, freedom, the power to heal, to crush. Illnesses, pish, a thing of the past. Longevity. Decades from now I'll still look like this," he turned, showing off muscles in their bulky prime, "while human men of my age will have withered into useless old men. With our brethren across the globe are released from their prisons. Humanity will die off sooner rather than later and the strong will once again rule the world as nature intended. You don't want to be on the losing side, do you, Harley?"

"Is that a rhetorical question?" she asked.

*Come on. Why isn't he attacking?*

He could have, should have. It was within his best interests if he wanted to keep breath in his lungs. He must know that.

With the advantage Nash gave him by turning against Cerberus, it surprised her the agents were still alive or at least not already infected with the were virus, adding to Niko's already considerable pride. Why keep them hostage? Why not kill them?

On the porch, why had he announced his presence by talking instead of initiating a silent attack from behind?

*He's planning something, and none of us are going to like it.*

"You killed my mate," he said, his voice strangely matter of fact as if losing his mate didn't upset him anymore.

That was unsettling.

Other than Niko, the Order had no record of any werepuma taking a lifelong mate. The species mated and parted on whims, rarely sticking with the same partner for more than a season. Niko and his mate, however, stood in stark contradiction to everything the Order had known. The two had fought together, hunted together, and rarely wandered far from each other's sides. Lethal as they were to others, they'd displayed strong affection for one another. Perhaps even love. For Niko to disassociate himself from his mate's memory confused her but didn't stop her from poking at him.

*One little attack, Niko. You know you want to...*

"Ah, if only I could do it twice," Harley ended with a wistful sigh, while watching him closely, searching for any sign of anger or attack. There was none.

"It only seems fair," he canted his head to the side, lips turning up in a sly smile, "that you replace her."

Her throat constricted. Eyes widened.

*He didn't just say that did he?*

Surely, she'd misheard him. Yeah. He'd meant that it'd be fair to torture her. Or kill her. Or something.

"Come again?" she asked. Her heart thumped in her chest, threatening to crack her ribs, and burst through her chest like some gory scene out of Aliens. He hadn't meant were'd. No. Not even Niko would dare to turn *her*. Not when she'd killed his mate and a solid portion of his original pride. He certainly wouldn't want her playing on his team when he could try to avenge his dead mate.

"I need a strong mate," Niko said. "Because she was the strongest of my females and you bested her in battle, you will replace her."

"You won't touch her," Brahms said. His energy shifted and bristled. It tingled across her senses feeling much akin to what she'd felt from him before in the garage at St. Ambrose, though she still couldn't figure what the energy was. It was familiar and strange at the same time.

"Ah, a kindred spirit." Niko flashed Brahms a self-satisfied grin. "A pity you won't join our side. You'd be a valuable ally."

Harley glowered at Niko, attempting to rip his attention away from Brahms. "Don't put yourself on too high of a pedestal, Niko. I hear the tumbles off those things are a real killer."

"I figured," Niko turned back to Harley, "that you wouldn't see the benefits of my offer right away. You are rather stubborn. So, I'm prepared to barter."

She clamped her mouth shut, forcing back the laughter that bubbled up in her throat. She wanted to let it out, to tell him off with a grand, scathing torrent, but she was afraid she knew exactly why he'd kept her friends alive.

It wasn't the time to poke the kitty. Not when he had the upper hand and could order the death of her friends with a mere signal. She needed a different, more creative plan now than just pissing him off.

"What sort of barter are you proposing?" she asked.

"Interesting wording." Niko chuckled and then motioned to the Cerberus agents. "Consider them a wedding gift. We mate, they go free."

A ball of tension formed in her stomach, and she fought the urge to vomit. He was serious. He wanted her were'd.

*Better dead than were'd.*

Better that she died, yeah. But them?

She glanced from Brahms to Thayer to Cree and then back to Brahms. Did she have the strength to watch him die if she refused Niko's offer? Could she live with herself if any of them died based on her refusal? Besides, if she refused Niko would turn her, anyway. Her friends would die, and she'd still end up turning into a filthy werepuma.

She felt the color drain from her face but found her voice. "They don't just go free. I —"

"We." Niko interjected. "Mates are one, united in purpose."

Her stomach churned.

*I will not vomit.*

She swallowed, forcing down bile before continuing, "We will see them safely out of the swamps. No one in your pride—"

"Our pride."

*Good God, this is a nightmare.*

"No one in our pride will follow them or attempt to stop, infect, harm, or kill them. Not tonight. Not tomorrow. Not next week. Not ever."

"Agreed," Niko said.

*Too quick.*

"Harley, you can't agree to this." Brahms took a step forward, his hands bunched into fists at his sides.

The werepuma covering him cocked the hammer back on his revolver.

Harley raised her hand for Brahms to stop.

"Yes, she can," Thayer said, "she's strong. She'll do what's right."

Brahms shot him an incredulous look but stopped. Anger pulsed off him in palpable waves.

Could she really agree to Niko's terms? She searched Brahms's eyes. Even for him? She was strong. Stronger than Niko suspected.

"All right," she said to Niko, "we have a deal." *Yup. Going to hell. Wheee.* "A few parting words to my friends and I'll be ready."

"Don't get too close," Niko warned.

"Jealous?" Harley grinned.

Niko flexed his fingers. "Don't test me."

"If you don't get used to teasing," she winked, "we might have marital issues."

She turned from Niko and went first to Cree. She tilted her head toward Brahms. "Take care of him for me, will you?"

"I promise." Cree blinked, rapidly, holding back tears. Or was it anger? There was definitely a firestorm brewing in there, ready to lash out whenever Cree's control snapped, which would be soon.

Harley searched the druid's eyes and buried the sorrow in her heart. If anyone was most likely to die in this, it was Cree. She hadn't known Cree for long, but the woman was as sweet-hearted and wise as they came. Now, she was headed toward a too-early grave.

*Like Cerise.*

"I'm so sorry," Harley said.

"As you said," Cree gave a trembling smile, "this is the beginning of a new world, and births are bloody by nature. This is no different."

Harley forced herself away from the druid before she lost control of her temper and did something stupid that would endanger all of them.

Next, she went to Thayer, carefully counting the distance between him and Cree, assessing the druid's chances. No. Even if Thayer was panther quick, there was no way he'd make it to Cree before Nash's bullet impacted with her skull.

Harley said, "Thank you for your confidence, Thayer, though you'll need more strength and courage than me, as your trial may cut deeper."

Sadness deadened his gaze, lamenting the eminent death of his partner and friend. Threaded within it was a steely resolve that tweaked Harley's satisfaction. If Cree died, Nash would follow shortly after, and Thayer would as many weres to the grave as he could. "I've a feeling our sacrifices have only just begun."

"An unfortunate truth," she muttered.

Finally, she stood before Brahms and smiled while committing his face to memory. If she died out there, she wanted his face to be the last thing she saw, even if she had to conjure it in her mind.

He pointed to her empty belt. "No grenades."

"Tisk, such lack of faith. I don't have to blow everything up."

"Don't do this." Brahms said.

Kissing him in front of Niko would be his death sentence. Instead, she flashed her most impish smile and said, "Some things are worth the sacrifice."

THE ONCE COZY cabin walls crushed in on Brahms, a wooden vice that threatened to pulverize his heart and soul. Harley couldn't, wouldn't, allow herself to turn into a were.

Would she?

She knew weres and the wreckage the virus did to the soul. She had to know Niko lied. He had no intention of setting them free. Once Harley became infected with the were virus, she would never be the same person. Weres weren't like his kind, the shifters, who maintained the essence of their being even during the transformation. The were virus was a disease, a heinous twisting of nature. Once it flowed through someone's blood it would ravage the most altruistic person until they were nothing more than a vile, malicious beast lacking in compassion, love, or even kindness. What remained would be an empty shell living to conquer and kill. Whoever and whatever the person once loved in their human life would be nothing more than tools or food.

He wanted to argue with Harley but that was pointless. She was doing what she felt she had to, for them.

*Four of them, four of us.*

Brahms's mind whirled, desperate for a plan that'd help Harley. She needed an opportunity to strike at Niko before he could turn her, and it was up to them to provide it or she'd be lost to them, to him, forever.

With the werepumas in their human forms, it evened the odds from a physical standpoint. If they changed into their were form, those odds would change fast. Dodging claws and teeth wielded by insanely powerful beasts was more problematic than dodging bullets, and currently bullets were the only advantage the weres had on them.

Because he and Thayer were both trained in combat, they could negate that advantage and possibly destroy their respective weres before they had the chance to change. Cree, however, was at a severe disadvantage. Though trained in advanced self-defense, her prime power was her magic and Brahms wasn't sure what spell she could cast when in such close confines with an enemy. He'd worked with Cree and Thayer on several occasions but not enough to know her abilities or how they operated. Though Nash relaxed a bit after Harley's acceptance of Niko's offer, he still held Cree tight against his chest with the barrel of his .45 aimed at her temple, giving her precious little space to maneuver. No matter what Brahms or Thayer did or how fast they did it, he couldn't foresee any scenario that didn't involve a fatal blast to her face.

Cree caught him studying her, and she gave him a confident smile as if she knew what destiny planned and accepted it with the same dignity that she'd accept any other burden she bore. But her acceptance and grace in the face of death didn't make him feel any less heartbroken about what they must do and the blood it'd cost.

"I won't forget this," Harley said to Nash. Her lips curled into a wicked smile that promised torment and death. "When I embrace this change and turn, I'll be faster and stronger than you. Since no one taught you this lesson before, it'll be my pleasure to teach it to you myself. If an offer sounds too good to be true, it is. Asshole."

Nash's eyes narrowed. "You—"

"Nuh-uh." Niko ticked his finger at Nash. "She will be my mate, your alpha. You will show her the proper respect, even if she orders you to lick the shit off her ass."

Nash gritted his teeth. The barrel of his gun slipped a little lower, hovering closer to Cree's cheek than temple. It was no less of a fatal shot, it'd just take longer in the dying, but maybe Harley had given Cree that tiny edge she'd need to survive.

"Well, that's one thing I have to look forward to." Harley turned on her heel and strode past Niko into the kitchen area.

Brahms stiffened, his muscles tensing.

*Don't take him outside.*

If Harley left the cabin, he wouldn't be able to monitor her safety or help her if she needed it. She'd survived the werepuma attack in the caves, barely, and she survived Niko before, barely. Yet he worried. In her, he'd found a piece of himself he hadn't realized was missing. He couldn't lose her. Not when he finally felt whole.

She passed the island counter and stopped, letting her fingers trail across the countertop where they'd earlier shared coffee and congenial banter with Nash the betrayer.

She turned to face Niko, her back to the rear screen door. Even in his human form, Niko stood a solid foot and a half taller than Harley and out-bulked her by even more. How in the world she'd fought him evenly in his full werepuma form was beyond Brahms's imagination. Yet, he had no doubt that she had.

The grizzly's energy rippled within him, rising in a protective wave that washed his entire body with a desire to act. Now. To stand in front of Harley. To kill Niko and put the threat to her down forever.

*Not yet.*

In shifting to grizzly's burly form, he'd be vulnerable, unable to defend himself when the werepumas attacked. Besides, there was an even greater risk to himself in allowing the grizzly out. Harley herself. She hated weres with valid reason. Without the ability to explain his nature to her, without the ability to show her the other side of him in a controlled, peaceful environment, she might mistake him for a were. It wasn't wise to spring that sort of surprise on her in the current situation. Yet he might have to do exactly that to save their lives.

*If I must lose you to save you, it is worth the cost to know you live, that you continue the fight and remain as you are.*

HARLEY TOOK a deep breath to steady herself. The next few minutes would determine her fate. Brahms's fate. The fate of her friends. She preferred to live, but if she had to die, she'd make damned sure she took Niko with her.

*Straight to hell, kitty cat.*

As much as she wanted to relish the sight of his face for the last time, she didn't dare glance beyond Niko to Brahms for fear she'd lose her nerve. As long as she dragged Niko with her to shove up the devil's ass she could accept her death. It was a mite bit harder to accept Brahms's.

But she couldn't allow Niko to live. He was the only thing holding his vile pride together. Once he died, the pride would fall apart. The remaining individual werepuma were far less a threat than a pride acting in unison. They'd be easier to put out the world's misery.

*I can do this. I will do this. One. Two. Three.*

"The night's wasting," she said to Niko.

She figured he'd planned activities for the night. For after he infected her with his filthy virus. Plans he'd enjoy and she'd loath. As long as he kept his mind focused on that, he might not realize that he stood in front of her, between her and the others, which left the route to the weapons she'd left on the porch clear.

"You are *mine.*" He slid his finger up her arm, his eyes brewed with lust.

*Yeah, you just keep thinking that, precious.*

Harley waited quietly, neither confirming nor denying his assertion. Timing was crucial. If any of them made their move too fast or too slow, the only one who'd survive this night would be her and she'd wish for death. Spending the rest of her life as a were, and worse as Niko's mate, was not on her bucket list.

*Patience is a virtue.*

Maybe it'd shave some time off her stay in hell.

"No need to make you wait any longer," Niko said.

"My heart is all aflutter." Harley leaned her hip on the counter and canted her head to the side with casual insolence.

Niko's face reddened and his body trembled, readying for the change that would transform him from human into the beast he really was.

Harley shifted her stance ever so slightly, getting ready to pivot toward the door.

*Wait for it.*

Harley had witnessed weres changing more times than was healthy for her sanity, but she still found it morbidly fascinating, in a despicable sort of way, how the virus contorted the human body and the soul.

Niko's arms and chest bulged. Too much muscle under too

few clothes. Cloth tore, seams popped and rent. Wild tufts of golden hair popped between the seams. His facial features distorted. His nose elongated and flattened.

*Come on. One of you guys make your move.*

She needed the werepumas distracted or she'd never make it to the door without a few bullets in her back.

Niko's mouth widened. His lips blackened. Blood drooled from his gums and plopped onto the floor in thick splats. The formerly straight rows of human teeth jutted from the reddened gums at disturbing angles. They peeled upward and fell out, tinking across the kitchen tiles. Thick, curved, cream-colored fangs popped out of gums where the human teeth had just vacated. His shirt and pants fell at his paws in tattered rags and his skin prickled and swaths of tawny gold fur sprouted between the tufts until it covered his entire body.

*Too bad they don't stay in were form when they die. He is hide would make an awfully fine rug.*

A gunshot blasted through the cabin and buffeted her ears.

Niko whirled away from her and crouched, ready to meet an attack from behind.

*Now.*

Harley couldn't spare the time to assess the scene to see who fired the shot or if it'd hit anyone. There were no guarantees her friends could distract Niko any more than he was currently distracted.

She darted out the door, onto the porch, and grabbed her weapons. She snagged her gun and almost had her hand around a grenade when Niko burst through the screen door. Pieces of doorframe flew outward in shards that pelted off the railing and plunked into the river.

*Damn it.*

She'd hoped for enough time to get all her toys.

Niko growled.

"Changed my mind about the whole mate thing." Harley shuffled backward, down the stairs, and into the yard to put more distance between them as she chambered a round. She locked sights on him and slid her finger on the trigger. "Cold feet and all. It isn't you, it's me."

He hunched down, his muscles gathered beneath him. Then he leapt from the porch in a flying charge.

A flash of gold streaked toward Harley from the left. Green eyes blurred in the dark. Before she could pivot to switch targets, it rammed into her with the impact of a freight train. Pain raced across her side and punched into her abdomen. She hit the ground with a harsh exhale. Her Smith & Wesson jolted out of her hand. She vaguely heard it splash into the river.

*Son. Of. A—*

The female lunged toward her.

Harley coiled her knees into her abs. She took the brunt of the were's momentum on the soles of her feet then used all the strength in her legs to propel the were up and over her. The were flew past and crashed into the rickety shed. Wood planks cracked and caved in on top of it.

A pack of hunchbacked rats flooded out of the demolished shed, squealing in fear as they dodged around the flailing werepuma.

"Oh, shit." Harley scrambled to her knees, popped to her feet, then backed away from the fleeing rodents.

Seeking high ground, three rats climbed up Harley's boots and onto her jeans.

She yelped and brushed at the rats, trying to dislodge their claws from the fabric. In the background, boards clattered, and garbage scattered across the yard like stinking confetti.

Harley flung two rats off her.

The female werepuma charged again.

Harley cringed, grasped the last rat by its plump sides, and threw it at the puma. The were's claws shredded through it, strewing chunks of ratty bits atop the garbage. Harley stood firm, letting the were get within arm's reach. Then she pivoted and thrust her leg out.

The were tripped and toppled forward, landing on all fours.

Niko snarled and prowled closer to them.

The female were snarled back and shook the dirt off her fur in a sneeze worthy rain.

*Damned mate wars or some shit.*

She'd have to remember to burn these two together in a cute little pyre.

Whatever the social dynamic was, Harley wasn't interested in playing. She grabbed a jagged board, held it tight to her side, and charged the female while it was still down.

The were turned just before the sharp tip of the board could make contact with its flesh. Its claws swiped down, throwing the board wide and putting Harley off balance. If she was going to fall, she was going to do damage as she did. She swung her elbow up, enjoying the satisfying feel of the puma's cheek cracking under her elbow.

The female were twisted. Its crushing weight landed square on Harley's chest. The heavy stink of musk invaded her nostrils. She swallowed the rising bile and, ignoring the stench and the pain in her side, tried to heave upward to buck the were off. But the were didn't budge. It glared down at Harley with a fierce green gaze that she immediately recognized.

"You." A wildfire of fury burned within Harley's core. Adrenalin rushed through her body. Her muscles throbbed, aching to use their extra strength.

This bitch had led the werepumas that'd attacked her in the cave. The ones that killed Cerise.

The edges of the green-eyed puma's black lips curled back in a mockery of a sneer. Its shattered cheekbone knit together, drawing the bones and muscles closer, already healing.

*Payback time, fuzz ball.*

The werepuma raised her wickedly curved claws and splayed out her wide paws, readying for a lethal swipe.

Harley exhaled and expelled all the breath from her lungs to give herself wiggle room. The instant she felt the opening, she slid her heel up and thrust her hand down at the same time. Her fingers curled around the hard handle of her boot knife. Then she yanked free of its sheath.

The were's claws arced toward her.

With the knife locked in her hand, Harley hooked her fist across her chest and sliced deep into the were's corded throat. Fur, muscle, and tendon peeled back, releasing a shower of blood that splattered across Harley's chest and face. Following the energy of the were's momentum, Harley rolled, barely avoiding the dying female's claws as she broke free. The female werepuma struggled to stand but its wobbling knees couldn't support it. Rivers of blood drained from the were's neck, staining the dirt, flowed down the bank, and into the muddy water.

More gunshots exploded from the cabin. Shattering glass crescendoed in the night, underscored by a deep, guttural roar.

*Brahms.*

These filthy cats had taken Cerise from her. She'd be damned if she allowed them to take Brahms from her, too. She would get there in time to help him. To save him. If she were certain there were only the three werepuma in the cabin she'd be less concerned. But if this green-eyed bitch had been lurking in the shadows there'd be more skulking out here ready to pounce.

Harley planted her hands on the ground and pushed herself to her knees. Her ribs screamed in protest, but she refused to show weakness. Refused to allow either of these weres the satisfaction of seeing her pain.

The female were attempted a hiss. It came out as a garbled gurgle.

"Merry. Fucking. Christmas." She stabbed the blade into one of the puma's dimming green eyes, wiggled the tip in its brain, and then yanked the blade back. The female puma's one remaining eye glazed over, sightless. Harley kicked its limp form into the river as a tasty teat for Nessie. The gator needed some healthy protein instead of sugar overload.

Niko stalked toward Harley with an egotistical curl to his lips, looking like the proverbial cat who stole the cream. A pleased purr vibrated up his throat. In his twisted mind, Harley had defeated yet another female in a bid to be his mate. The only thing Harley wanted to be to him was the very last thing he saw on this Earth.

She rolled forward, away from the hulking, aroused were. She came out of the roll, hopped to her feet, and dropped into her knife-fighting stance with her blade clutched in front of her.

*Strike fast, strike true.*

There were only a few knife-friendly areas she could hit that would prove lethal to a were. Niko knew of each one and would viciously guard them.

*What I wouldn't give for a gun, or a grenade, or a bazooka.*

"Let's play rough." Harley winked. "See who wins this time."

Niko's lips peeled back in a heinous, toothy smile. He lunged, muscular arms extended, claws ready to slash and grab.

Harley pivoted, lashed out with her knife, and used his forward momentum to cut a deeper, longer swath across his upper arm and down his ribs.

He snarled and spun, smashing his elbow into her chin. Her teeth clattered together, her vision dimmed, and she felt herself propelled backward. Her spine jolted as she hit the ground hard. Blotches of light swam in her darkening gaze.

A streak of movement. She rolled to the side just as Niko

lurched at her. Blood trickled out the side of her mouth. Her ears rang.

*Pain is temporary, will is forever.*

As he passed, she skittered to her feet and readjusted the knife.

*The pain isn't real unless I allow it to be.*

She whirled to face Niko. Pain lanced through her head, the world tilted, swayed, and threw her off balance.

*So much for that theory.*

His hand thrust out. His fingers encased her neck and closed around it. The tips of his claws dug into the back of her neck and base of her skull. He snapped her close to him.

*Oh, no, you don't.*

She flipped her knife, reversing it, and then punched upward toward the soft underside of his chin. He caught her wrist in a vise grip and squeezed. Her wrist felt as if it'd shatter into a thousand tiny shards. She cried out. The knife dropped from her hand.

He pulled his furry face toward hers and emitted a sound that was half purr, half growl, as if asking her to submit to him.

Her body ached. Her head felt as if an ogre were on the verge of popping her skull and using her brains for jelly. One bite and the were virus would whisk it all away. She could slip into a beautiful oblivion for a while. Pain be a mere memory. The sorrowful void left by Cerise's death. Francis's death. It'd all fade away. She'd slip into that void, make it her own, become it.

*No more tears.*

# CHAPTER TWENTY

Brahms flew through the rear window. Glittering glass sprayed into the night. As he plummeted toward the ground, he tucked his knees to his chest and rolled. He hit with his leading shoulder. Glass crunched under him. Shards cut through his shirt and sliced into his skin. He leapt out of the roll. Chunks of glass fell from his hair and landed in the sparse grass. Brahms functioned best in the outdoors but would have preferred a smooth exit through the door rather than an abrupt toss through the window.

He shook the remaining shards from his clothes, turned toward the cabin, and crouched, ready to defend.

Nash stood in the center of the shattered window. Moonlight grazed across the barrel of his raised pistol. He took aim at Brahms. A dark shadow slammed into Nash from the side, the gun fired, and the bullet went wildly astray, hitting somewhere in the woods.

For now, Thayer would keep Nash occupied.

The grizzly within Brahms stirred then raged to the surface.

The acrid scent of gun smoke twanged up his nose. Then, the musky, decidedly feline stench of werepuma invaded his nostrils.

*How many?* he asked the grizzly.

*Too many.*

His weapons were in the cabin, taken from him when the weres had infiltrated. Without them he would die unless he allowed the grizzly to shift into its formidable self. If he did, would he be able to change back before Harley saw him?

She was on the opposite side of the cabin fighting with Niko but that didn't mean she'd stay there. Their fight could spill over into the backyard. Or she'd finish Niko off then come this way when she heard the battle.

If Harley saw him like this without realizing it was him, she'd perceive him as the enemy. She'd attack him as ruthlessly as she'd attack the werepuma.

Branches cracked and creaked in the distance.

Niko's pride was coming.

If Brahms wanted to live, he had no choice. Sometimes to fight the beasts one must become a beast.

He inhaled, filled his lungs with the swampy air then slowly exhaled, relinquishing his conscious hold on his body to the grizzly. Warmth emanated from his core and then spread through his limbs, licking its way down his arms and legs all the way to the very tips of his fingers and toes.

The grizzly burst from him with a primal roar, and none too soon at that.

All around him the woods teemed with werepuma. Their golden eyes flickered in and out of the shadows like mini will-o-wisps. Brahms needed to keep them occupied and kill them off before they could attack Harley or get into the cabin.

He huffed and scratched at the dirt with the grizzly's mighty paws issuing a challenge. Feline weres fostered incredibly large egos, and the werepumas were no different. To maintain status in the eyes of their comrades, each of them must answer his challenge or they'd be forever belittled and relegated to the weak fringes of the were society.

Other than that Thayer had been alive at the time he'd tackled Nash, Brahms didn't know how his friends in the cabin fared. He didn't know if Cree was alive or dead. If Thayer fought on, or if he at this very moment, was falling prey to the weres inside. As much as not knowing the fate of his friends bothered him, what gnawed at his gut was the silence from the other side of the cabin, where Harley and Niko were. No gunshots. No trademark explosions. Nothing to indicate Harley was alive and fighting. So far, he'd heard some crashing and her pained yelp.

*I must get to her.*

If Harley discovered she couldn't beat Niko, she'd enrage the were enough to kill her in the heat of fury. Whether she died or Niko turned her, she'd be lost to him forever. The thought was intolerable. Grizzly balked. It wanted to go to her, to help her, protect her, and destroy the threat against her. But he'd never make it to her alive if he turned his back on the surrounding weres. Even the grizzly's thick hide and resilient muscles could take only so much.

In eerie, trained unison, the werepumas darted out of the brush and leapt down from the trees in streaks of deadly gold and rushed toward him.

Brahms rose to the grizzly's intimidating full height and roared. Tonight, he'd face his toughest battle. Tonight, he'd win despite the odds. Because tonight what he fought for was more powerful than all the weres that disgraced the Earth.

Energy drained out of Harley's muscles, and she went ragdoll limp. It didn't take Oscar-winning acting to feign being tired and sore. She just allowed it to show. It was a blow to her pride to show weakness in front of an enemy but better that, better anything, than being infected with the were virus.

Niko's claws relaxed a bit, taking the sting off the back of her neck. His pleased purr rumbled through his body.

*Poor kitty. He'll be so tragically heartbroken.*

Ian wasn't there this time to stop her from killing Niko and kill him she damned well would. Or die trying.

*For Cerise. For Brahms. For the slain innocent.*

A light splash to her right caught her attention. Drawn to the shore by the tasty werepuma blood, Nessie rose from the river. Water drained off her murky thick, raised scales, leaving a trail of rivulets in her wake. Her wide pink maw gaped open in a territorial hiss, warning were and human alike she laid claim to the female werepuma's corpse.

*Have at it, Nessie. I'll have my own corpse to play with soon enough.*

Harley groaned and tilted her head to the side, letting it hang so the side of her neck showed in a sign of submission.

Niko thrust her upward in triumph and held her aloft, showing off his prize.

Now she was up higher and not clenched tight to him, she had just enough room to attack where every male, regardless of species, was weak.

She pulled her leg back and kicked at his balls. The top of her foot impacted with his soft, squishy parts.

He yowled. His grip abruptly loosened.

She fell to the ground and landed in a crouch.

Niko doubled over and cupped his fuzzy balls in his hands.

As soon as his head dipped, she struck with a kick to his face and felt the lovely crunch of his nose breaking under the sole of her boot.

*Weapon, weapon. Knife isn't cutting it.*

Her grenades were on the porch but there was no way she'd get there before Niko recovered.

*So close, yet so far away.*

The Tahoe was closer. Yes. She had a few fun toys in there that would light up his night.

*Time for some fireworks, baby.*

She sprang past Niko, dashing toward her truck and goodies hidden in her trunk trove. It wasn't locked so within a matter of moments she'd have–

Burning pain slashed across her scalp. Niko yanked her backward. Her feet flew off the ground. He tangled his claws deeper in her hair and pulled her to him.

"Ever hear of 'no means no'?" She twisted. Blood oozed down her head and dripped onto her neck. Biting back the pain, she aimed a punch at his throat.

He deflected and rammed his knee into her stomach.

Harley gasped and gagged.

He hefted her upward and threw her.

She landed facedown, a foot from the shore. The Oreos in her jacket pocket crunched and crinkled beneath her.

*Oh, shit. Nessie.*

She struggled to her elbows and glanced toward the river.

Sure enough, the gator had heard the siren call of its beloved chocolate treats. It released the partially submerged werepuma corpse and whipped its tail through the water, heading straight for Harley.

*Liars, gators, and weres, oh, my.*

Harley flipped onto her back and used her heels to push herself farther from the river's edge.

Niko, either unaware of the gator or failing to deem it a threat, strode toward her. His chest puffed out, his clawed hands opened and closed in agitation.

She dug into the inside pocket of her jacket and grabbed one of the crushed Oreo packs. The cookie chunks had poked tiny holes in the plastic, releasing the beautiful scent of chocolate and cream. Given Nessie's voracious appetite, she doubted the lizard would care the cookies weren't whole.

Harley kept the package hidden. "You know what makes humans better than weres?" she asked.

Niko snarled and lunged at her.

"Cookies." Harley wiggled her fingers, making a ruckus with the Oreo package wrapping. She tossed the Oreos at Niko then pressed her back into the ground, making herself as small as she could.

With stunning speed that belied her large size, Nessie launched herself at the package. The gator flew over Harley's prone body in a dripping mass of solid muscle covered in tight, thick scales.

The Oreos hit smack into Niko's chest.

Nessie opened her wide maw and twisted to the side. Her jaws wrapped around the sides of Niko's chest, and she slammed into him with every ounce of her considerable weight, bringing him down as she clamped her teeth into his flesh, successfully snaring both him and her precious Oreos.

Niko's high-pitched feline scream of pain echoed through the swamp. He writhed in the confines of the gator's mouth, scoring deep gashes into his arms and sides as he tugged to break free from the jagged teeth. But the only thing he did other than mutilate himself was piss Nessie off. She thrashed her head back and forth as she backed toward the water. Her teeth punctured deeper into his flesh. His bones snapped. Blood oozed down his sides, dripped onto the ground then followed the slope of the shore to diffuse into the river.

With Niko clamped in her jaws, Nessie slid into the blood-stained, muddy water with a grace that didn't quite fit her ferocity.

Eerie.

Harley didn't want to take any chances Niko would, by some unholy miracle, survive the attack. She crawled to her knife, closed her hand around its hilt, and took aim.

Just as Nessie was about to submerge with her dinner, Harley threw the blade with a deft flick of her wrist. It spun through the air and thunked at an upward angle deep into Niko's cheek. The steel shattered his cheekbone and punched into his brain. Niko's body jerked and flopped then went limp.

Nessie sank, leaving a soft wake behind her and then nothing. As if the placid water had never seen death.

"Hope he doesn't ruin your dessert, Nessie," Harley muttered.

Dead. Niko was finally, blessedly dead.

If the Order would have allowed her to kill him before, none of this would have happened.

*That's not true.*

Germaine, Ian, and whoever the hell else was with them had released many other creatures, not just Niko and his pride. Even if she'd killed Niko during their first tango, she'd just be fighting something else somewhere else.

*Better the devil I know, I guess.*

Between the green-eyed bitch's tackle and Niko, she felt like a breathing mass of bruise. She wanted to plop into a comfortable, fluffy chair, tend her wounds, and down a vat of rum. Forget the coconuts. Just the rum. Hell, forget the glass. Straight out of the bottle worked.

The sounds of fighting behind and inside the cabin broke through any illusion she'd snatch a moment's reprieve.

She pulled herself to her feet and jogged toward the Tahoe.

*Whoever said whatever doesn't kill you makes you stronger was a damned liar. Whatever doesn't kill you hurts like a sonofabitch.*

She popped the hatch and dug into her stash. She made a

habit of taking all her stash anywhere and tonight proved to be an excellent example of why.

*Hmm. What toys to bring to the party?*

As much as she loved her explosives, they weren't safe to use with friendlies mixed in the fray who weren't aware of her tactics and didn't know to get down.

Then she pressed on the Tahoe's ceiling. A panel dropped down, displaying several high-powered firearms. She spotted Fern's latest greatest rifle. Its matte black finish didn't glimmer or produce any sort of reflection. Whatever paint Fern had used seemed to take on the same hue as the shadows around it. A perfect assassin's weapon.

*Ah, yes, it'll make some lovely holes in naughty weres.*

"Cuz death is in the details." She grabbed her rifle and slung the strap over one shoulder then chose a machine gun and slid it over the other. She quickly shut the hidden stash and pushed on the other side of the trunk, releasing a secondary, smaller cubby. Inside was her Things Just Went to Fuck weapon, a Glock .45 already loaded with a full magazine of hollow points laced with silver and imbedded with rowan wood. Other slayers might fiddle around with the lower calibers or skimp on the extras, but when Harley shot, she wanted her target to drop with faster being better.

She took a second to tuck another knife into her boot and then assessed the cabin.

*Start inside or outside?*

If Brahms were alive, and he had to be because she'd accept no other option, he'd fight outside where he felt more at ease, more in control. Decision made, she crouch ran toward the other side of the cabin.

"Let's put the rest of you furballs down." She kept close to the cabin's log siding, ducking beneath the windows in case any weres watched them. As long as they thought she was still playing with Niko they wouldn't have any reason to think she'd show up to crash their fun.

When she reached the back corner, she stopped, flattened her back against the rounded logs, and inched her face around the edge.

There in the center of the weed-riddled clearing was a huge grizzly. Its lips snarled back, and it took a vicious swipe at a lunging werepuma. The bear's enormous claws dredged deep into the puma's throat. It severed its head, leaving a mangled mass of muscle, tendon, and other stuff sticking out of the were's shoulders.

*Well, shit.*

That was no ordinary bear. That was a were. She stepped back a bit for better cover and strained to see.

*What the hell is a werebear doing out here?*

It couldn't be turf wars. Grizzlies didn't range that far south. Though, she'd prefer dealing with weregrizzlies to the bears that inhabited the area, black bears. At least weregrizzlies had reasons for attacking that were fathomable. They only attacked to protect turf, mates, offspring, or rip those very things away from others, particularly humans, in bids of supremacy.

Wereblackbears, however, were unpredictable. They attacked for reasons that might even mystify themselves.

Judging by the amount of gored werepuma bodies scattered around it, the grizzly had tipped the odds of winning the battle in their favor because, at least as far as she could see, there weren't any left.

*And it's only polite to repay a favor with a favor.*

She quietly tugged her pistol out and sighted it on the bear's massive chest.

*Like putting it out of its misery.*

# CHAPTER TWENTY-ONE

Brahms huffed, expelling a breath from the grizzly's lungs to clear the foul stench of werepuma blood from his nostrils. With a sense of smell keener than the best of bloodhounds, the grizzly was sensitive to odors. He exhaled again and shook his massive head. Droplets of werepuma blood shook free of his thick fur and rained on the ground around him.

The grizzly's hide was thick but not thick enough to stand up against the claws and teeth of werepuma. Claw marks raked down his shoulders and sides. Bites stung along his neck and hind legs, punctured deep into his flesh. His powerful muscles ached from the battle, but it wasn't over yet.

He rose onto his hind legs, standing as tall as he could, then lifted his nose to the sky, sniffing for signs of werepumas and Harley. He caught her scent mingled with that of her blood. Anger tore through him and invigorated his tired muscles with energy.

He must find her. Help her.

A rustling in the brush near the cabin caught his attention. The light scent of gun oil carried on the breeze.

*Harley.*

This was not how he wanted to introduce the grizzly to her. There were details he needed to tell her first so that she could recognize and accept the differences between shifters and weres instead of automatically hating him. Hating what he was.

Muzzle flash lit the night. A shot cracked through the drone of insects.

Brahms dropped onto all fours and prayed the bullet passed over his head and not through it.

HARLEY'S BULLET smashed into a tree flinging shreds of bark several feet above the werebear's massive head and shoulders.

*Damn.*

Strange. It didn't run off into the woods as it ought to, nor attack as it should have. Given how it'd decimated the were-pumas, she couldn't seem like much of a threat to it.

*Unless it's afraid of guns.*

It was also wounded. Maybe it didn't possess the strength to run.

Instead, it stood amongst the werepuma corpses and stared at her, through her, into her. Something about its eyes tugged at her, called to her as if she ought to know it. A strange recognition of sorts. But that was impossible. Weregrizzlies were wise enough to stay off slayer radar, and this was the first one she'd encountered in person.

So why did it seem familiar?

Harley didn't have time to play detective with a were. Some things she could live without knowing, like why this werebear seemed familiar. Why it wasn't reacting as it should.

Other things she couldn't tolerate not knowing, like where Brahms was and if he was okay. If Thayer was all right and if Cree had lived. Those questions needed answers, stat, and though the weregrizzly had shown no aggression toward her yet that didn't mean it wouldn't attack the instant she turned her back.

She raised her Glock, took aim, and slid her finger on the trigger.

Instead of charging, the bear loped toward the cabin stairs, its torn muscles bunched and stretched under its thick, shaggy reddish fur.

She needed a kill shot. A wounded werebear of any kind was a lumbering juggernaut of destruction. Where she stood, the angle was wrong for a heart shot, and if she tried to get through the chest from the side while it was moving, she risked the bullet hitting its leg or shoulder, deflecting the impact. A head shot was her best option.

She sighted in on the bear's bulky head.

*Make it count.*

Her finger pressed on the trigger. A flash of bright orange filled her sight.

*Cree?*

She immediately released the pressure on the trigger and swung the muzzle down, pointing it at the dirt.

Cree and Thayer stood between her and the weregrizzly, their arms stretched out to form a human shield.

*The hell?*

Why were they defending a were? They'd seemed keen enough to hunt Niko and levelheaded enough to know trusting a were was as stupid as trusting a rabid raccoon in a baby's crib. And where was Brahms? Surely, he'd back her call on this one.

"Wait," Cree said. Blood splatters marred the druid's face and dotted her clothes. She took a tentative step toward Harley's hiding spot as if she wasn't quite sure that Harley wouldn't shoot her to get to the bear.

A valid concern.

"Cree," warning hedged Thayer's voice. The sleeve of his shirt was torn to shreds. Blood seeped along the edges of the fabric, plastering it on his arm. A swath of blood, not his, ran from his temple, down his neck, and onto his chest.

Harley kept her gun down but at the ready as she strode from the brush into the open. She scanned for an opening to hit the were without injuring Cree or Thayer, but they weren't leaving her one. At least not one that'd offer her a kill shot. If Harley only injured the bear, it could provoke it into attacking the Cerberus agents while their backs were turned.

That wouldn't end well.

"I'd heard the nasty rumor," Harley said, "that Cerberus worked with weres. I didn't believe it until now."

"He's not a were," Thayer said, "he's a shifter."

Behind them the weregrizzly shrank and writhed. Its fur thinned, disappearing into its hide. Its claws retracted as its paws shortened.

"Uh-huh," Harley said. "Same difference. Now, move out of the way." Harley circled toward the river, forcing Thayer to move with her to keep her in his view, widening the space between him and Cree.

*Patience. Just takes one opening.*

Thayer said, "Even the Order had to teach you better than that."

"Yeah, yeah," Harley said. "They mentioned there might be decent weres. It's bullshit."

"Shifters aren't weres." Thayer sighed in frustration. "I'll let him explain it to you."

Harley shook her head. "Fat chance. Move."

"What happened to Niko?" Cree asked.

"Alligators and cookies, they're a deadly combination," Harley raised her pistol, "just like the medley of lead and herbs in this baby."

A growl behind them, near the cabin, broke her concentration. Harley glanced toward the porch just as Nash, in his werepuma form, leapt from the railing toward Cree.

The druid tore one of her pouches off her belt, ripped the tie off, and threw it at Nash. Three lengths of black string burst from the pouch, within a second each one elongated and widened. Brownish black scales rippled into being faster than what ought to be possible, turning the strings into three eight-foot-long lethal black mambas.

The snakes' mouths gaped open. Their milky white fangs stark against the night. They hit square into the werepuma, sinking their wicked fangs deep into his chest and neck.

Nash screamed and grabbed at the thick, wiggling snakes, attempting to yank them off. The snakes clamped their jaws tight, ripping gashes into the were's muscles.

Harley sighted her .45 in on Nash's forehead.

"Oh, no, he's mine." Thayer's pistol barked, and the back of Nash's feline head exploded, splattering the porch and grass with a motley mix of brains, skull shards, and blood-matted fur.

The snakes released their preys then slithered with creepy grace in and around Nash's corpse, reveling in their kill. They didn't seem to mind their prey's sudden demise.

Cree whispered something and the snakes mutated into undulating lines of black smoke that whirled and faded until they disappeared entirely, leaving only the glaring puncture wounds and gashes on Nash's chest as evidence that they'd ever been there at all.

"Impressive," Harley said. "Maybe you can teach me that one."

Cree chuckled. "Magic will never be your strong suit."

"Ah, well." Harley shrugged. As awe-inspiring as magic could be she preferred her weapons. There was nothing quite like the smooth feel of a grip and the smell of gunpowder.

"I'm sorry," Brahms said.

Surprised to hear his voice and confused as to why he was apologizing, Harley glanced behind Thayer where the weregrizzly had been. There, back lit by the glimmering river, Brahms stood naked with a heap of rumpled bear hide at his feet.

The strength left Harley's arm, and it dropped to her side, her pistol pointed at the ground. Her mind tried to reconcile the brewing conflict within her of seeing Brahms in his glorious nudity, his long hair playing against his shoulders and chest, with the fact that he was the enemy.

"You. You're a were?" Her voice sounded as hollow as her heart felt. How could he do this to her? How could he have hidden this from her? Especially when they'd been getting so close. He'd had plenty of time. Plenty of opportunity. And she'd have thought he had plenty enough courage to do it. She'd been wrong. "And you didn't bother to tell me?"

"I'm a shifter." He kept his tone quiet, soothing as a breeze, and made no move to approach her. "Not a were. The grizzly is a gift. A spirit that lives within me."

She squeezed the grip of her pistol and fought the urge to raise it again because she never took aim unless she intended to shoot. To kill. Part of her wanted to do exactly that. To put a hole right through his head but she doubted she could pull the trigger when he looked like...like Brahms. The man she loved.

*Correction. Loved.*

"You lied." Anger flooded through her. Betrayed. Once again. First Germaine, now Brahms. Maybe she ought to aim for his heart. Blast his out like he'd just blasted hers.

"I wanted to tell you but—"

"But you knew how I'd feel about it." She stalked to him, stopping a few inches away. Well within fist range. "What I'd think. Yet still you chose the coward's way."

He winced as if she'd slapped him, and she was damned

tempted to do that, too. Or plant a solid right hook smack in his face. That'd make her feel better and she wouldn't have his death on her hands or conscious.

*Or heart.*

But he'd feel pain.

Still, as she glared into his sorrowful eyes, she couldn't bring herself to lift her fist to him let alone her weapons.

*Damn you to hell, Brahms. Damn all of you.*

"How about this," Brahms held his hands up, palms toward her, "you go your way, we'll go ours. It'll give you time to think. To understand."

He yearned to touch her. To wipe the blood from her face. To pluck the debris from her hair. But she was one wrong action away from attacking him and he didn't want to fight her. Didn't want to hurt her any more than she was already hurt. He wasn't sure he could stop himself. That he possessed the willpower to create the distance she needed.

She looked about ready to interrupt him with a barrage of cussing. Without thinking his actions through he reached out to touch her lips.

She slapped his hand away and the storm brewing in her blue eyes burst into an all-out hurricane of swirling emotions. She wanted to do a lot more to him than slap him and none of it would be good.

"Don't. Touch. Me. Ever," she said.

Pain lanced through his heart. As much as she needed to understand the difference between shifters and weres to survive the violent new world her Order had unleashed, he had to accept the scars of her past and why she'd fight her feelings for him because of what he was. What he reminded her of. Why she'd hate him.

He understood her reaction. He didn't accept it, didn't like it, but understood it. He'd have to draw heavily from the bear's patience because his was out. Brahms took a step back to give her space and stay out of her striking range.

"Then," he continued as though she hadn't interrupted, "we'll meet you in Kansas, and we'll go to Colorado together. It'll be safer with the four of us."

Even if she spent the entire time glaring at him and refusing to speak to him, it'd be better than knowing she was out there fighting the monsters alone. With everything, everyone, that she'd lost, he couldn't be sure that she wouldn't resort to suicidal tactics.

"Don't do me any favors. I don't need you there and I don't want you there. Besides—"

"The difference between failure and success," Cree's soft voice interrupted Harley's tangent, "is knowing that sometimes we have to do what is necessary, not what we want."

Brahms said, "Now that Germaine has released the beasts from their prisons his next move will be to eliminate those who can stand against them. Then he and whoever has joined with him will be the only saviors people can turn to for help. For protection."

"Even Germaine wouldn't go that far." Harley scowled, but she glanced away, unable to meet his gaze.

He hated hurting her and forcing Harley to accept a truth she didn't want to see was futile, so he dropped it. She'd discover it on her own as time passed. Besides, it seemed as if she were trying to convince herself Germaine's betrayal had limits as much as she was attempting to convince them. So maybe she was fighting the idea more because he'd said it than her belief.

"Even if he doesn't," Thayer said, tucking his pistol back into its holster, "finding Lars in the mountains by yourself will be nearly impossible. Given your status with the Church, which from what I read in the current alerts is 'capture or kill on sight,' you won't have their support. Without their help and their equipment, how do you expect to find one man in the nooks and crannies of the Rocky Mountains?"

Her eyes narrowed, and for a moment, Brahms thought she might explode. But after a second of stewing it over, she sighed and studied the shifting shadows around them.

"We're offering you help from Cerberus." Brahms wanted to hold her. To assure her everything would be all right but it'd only make the situation worse. As much as he wanted her beside him, she needed space. Time to come to terms with what he was and what feelings she had for him. If any. "We possess the equipment and the people to help you fulfill your promise to Cerise. Whatever you decide about us, about you and me, is secondary to that, isn't it?"

"Fine," she said. "We meet in Kansas. I better not even get a tiny glimmer of a suspicion you're anywhere near me until then." She stomped off, hesitating on the cabin steps. She didn't even look back at them when she said, "Don't be late."

The flimsy screen door shut with a slap behind her

Brahms flinched.

"It'll be safer if I work out the logistics with her." Thayer clapped a hand on Brahms's shoulder and squeezed. Then he headed into the cabin to join Harley.

"She shouldn't be out there alone," Brahms said. "She might not want to believe it but we both know Germaine won't hesitate to kill slayers who are a threat to his plan. Even her. Probably especially her."

"He'll kill anyone he needs to, including us," Cree said. She stepped beside him. The lingering scent of incense and herbs floated on the breeze. She handed him her bloodied orange shawl to cover his nakedness. “Harley is strong. She might be brash, but she isn’t stupid. By traveling alone, she might be less noticeable.”

Nothing could make Harley less noticeable, and if anything happened to her...his heart clenched into a tight ball. He could live with her hate, barely. He could, maybe one day, come to terms with the fact he was in love with a woman who’d never love him in return. But if she died, he couldn’t handle that.

“I pray that’s true,” he said. “Our world is dark enough as it is.”

Cocooned in the lush leather interior of his new SUV, Ian slid his laptop onto the center console and shut the screen so the monitor’s light wouldn’t interfere with his night vision. He’d had to switch vehicles twice now because he’d erred too long on the side of curiosity, and the beasts he’d released had attacked his cars, damaging them beyond reasonable repairs.

*Ingrates.*

He adjusted his night vision goggles, leaned forward, and pressed against the steering wheel to get a better view of the valley below his perch.

Nestled in a large clearing surrounded by a chain-link fence and jack pines was the next sanctuary on his list. Posing as a warehouse, the simple pole and metal structure held a vastly more complex and secure interior. It also contained some of the largest, deadliest creatures slayers across the States had captured for the white coats to study, hence his decision to watch from a distance. If some of these creatures attacked his SUV, he’d be crushed along with it. The angels had been with him, protected him, during his past too-close encounters with the creatures. He doubted they'd brook his stupidity a third time, especially when releasing beasts of this magnitude.

Behind the sprawling structure was a massive yard scattered with what any passerby would consider junk but what the slayer, Fern, one of their top engineers and designers, called her exterior stock room. Though she wasn't loyal to Germaine's cause, yet, he was disappointed when he spotted her sporty red Jag parked in the lot. He didn't want Fern to die. He wanted to try his hand at converting her to their side. She'd make a valuable and beautiful ally in the trying years that lay ahead.

The sanctuary doors flew open, and people burst out.

Ian chuckled. From his high vantage point, they looked like white-clad miniatures running in frenzied panic to their vehicles. The metal on the building's side bulged, strained, and broke in a screech that reverberated through the valley and up the mountainside. Sleek, jointed black legs poked out, followed by an enormous bulbous body that gleamed black in the perimeter floodlights. A giant black widow, female, according to his records. The facility also contained a male. It wouldn't be long until they found each other in the wild, mated and proliferated this area with a host of spiderlings, each capable of growing to the same size as their parents.

The elk and moose population in the area was about to plummet.

A car of indeterminable type sped past the widow attempting to get out of the fenced area before the rest of the creatures broke free.

The widow lifted one of her front legs and plunged it down. The tip shattered the windshield, impaling the car to the ground.

Dust kicked up in a billowing cloud from behind the building. A horn blared. The spider turned to face its new threat, a camouflaged amphibious vehicle of unique design.

*Fern.*

She and Harley were the only people allowed to play with her prototypes, and Harley was nowhere near here.

The widow yanked her leg free of the car and strode toward Fern's tank.

"Go," Ian whispered. "Get out of there before the others are free." If Fern played with the spider too long, too close to the building, even that tank of a vehicle of hers would be over-run.

*Why couldn't she have stayed home today?*

Fern cranked the wheel, doing tight doughnuts in the dirt lot, kicking up an even thicker cloud of dust. The widow slunk through it. Fern straightened the vehicle and floored it toward the woods, away from her fleeing comrades.

*Good girl.*

The widow followed closely behind.

Ian liked to think Fern had heard his thoughts. That there was an unspoken bond between them. She'd always talked to him and smiled when he was at her facility for inventories or to get reports on her progress with various weaponry she'd been tasked with designing.

He'd solidify that bond soon. He'd never cared about the idea of a partner but for Fern he'd make an exception.

Though he would have to teach her to stop playing hero unless, of course, it was his life or Germaine's in question. She'd given the fleeing white coats a bit of a lead on the creatures that, even now, teemed in the corridors, seeking the way out of the sanctuary but she'd ended up with a lethal predator on her tail.

*Stay safe. I'll find you.*

His phone rang. He plucked it up and answered.

"Is it done?" Germaine asked.

"The releasing is complete. What would you wish of me now, your Eminence?"

"Hunt those who'd thwart us."

"What of Harley?"

Germaine hesitated, and for a moment, Ian thought he'd decide to spare Harley. That he'd get the misguided notion to sway her to their side. Harley wasn't the swayable type. It'd be a disaster.

"Kill them all."

# CHAPTER TWENTY-TWO

Harley splayed her fingertips across the cold glass of her upper-floor hotel room window. A hungry imp hovered on the other side, flapping its black leathery wings, and marring the otherwise beautiful view of the rugged Rocky Mountains.

"What are you doing?" Fern asked. Static crackled over her voice. It wasn't the speaker on Harley's phone, it was the connection. As close as Harley was getting to her friend, they were still a day or so apart and Fern was way out the wilds. Not great reception out there.

Or anywhere, now-a-days.

"Playing with an imp," Harley said.

The imp's flying saucer shaped face split into a wide, sharp-toothed grin. It lunged at her fingers and hit the glass with a muted thud. It hovered away and shook its head.

"It's called glass, you little gnat," Harley said.

Fern chucked. "I hope you're talking to the imp."

"What have you found out?"

The imp flew closer. It tilted its head. Its tiny, rimmed horns created a strange frame for a white cabin set precariously on the mountainside beyond. The imp bobbed even closer. A brief flash of confusion crossed its face. It reminded Harley of a demented dog trying to figure out the mystical workings of a sliding glass door.

"I checked," Fern said, "and triple checked the reports on Lars' disappearance. Combed through the data from his chip and they all led here. Problem is, no one in town is fessing up to seeing him."

"Could the data have been tampered with?" Harley pulled her fingers in then slid them back out across the glass in a silent dare to the imp.

It planted its paws on the window, its small black talons screeched across the glass.

"Hm," Fern said, "maybe."

"Maybe you can learn, imp-san." Harley swiped her hand in an arc to the right. "Wax on."

"I work with gadgets. Machines. Engines. Weapons. Not computers."

"I was talking to the imp."

"I see." Fern sighed. "I'll keep looking and keep asking. Hanging around. Maybe something will kick up. But I think it'll take your style of tactics to pry information from these guys. Assuming they know anything. If the data was tampered with then Lars' last known location could be anywhere."

The imp followed Harley's movements, its needle-sharp teeth bit at the glass.

"Wax off." She moved her hand in an arc to the left. "If Cerberus wouldn't have slunk away, I'd have the perfect person to look into the computer meddling thing."

*Damn them. All of them.*

Fern humphed in disapproval. "No word yet, then, I take it?"

The imp's thin lips smeared a trail of yellow saliva across the window.

"It's for the best," Harley said. "I don't know how I'd react to Brahms if we ever run into each other again."

An explosion rattled the glass. A ball of fire whooshed into the air far behind the imp. Flames licked up the trees and began to spread.

"What was that?" Fern asked.

"Something on the north end of town exploded."

With a grotesque grin of glee, the imp turned away from her and flew off toward the fire, more interested in instant chaos than a target tucked safe behind an invisible shield.

*Yeah. Colorado.*

Flames tendrilled into the fading blue sky.

*A skier's paradise.*

Harley plopped onto the bed and propped pillows behind her back before settling in with the TV remote.

"They put me so far behind," Harley said. "I wanted to get to here before things went to total shit."

"At least you can say you gave them the benefit of the doubt."

"Is waiting two extra days enough time to claim that?"

"Not too long ago it would have been more than plenty." The sound of crisp paper being flipped through came across the phone. "Now, though, I really can't say. I've been stuck out here in the boonies since everything went south at the sanctuary. Searching for Lars. Don't get me wrong, I'm glad you called to ask. I just could really use some sushi right about now. And more bug spray."

"Cowards," Harley said. "They lied. Abandoned the mission."

*Abandoned me.*

"Are you surprised?"

Harley twirled the remote in her hand and gazed out the

window. "A little. I figured that Brahms would show up, at least. Maybe not Cree or Thayer."

"I thought you didn't want to see him."

"I'm not sure." Though Fern couldn't see her, Harley shrugged. In the fight filled days and restless nights since leaving Brahms behind in the swamps, she hadn't decided what to say to him if she ever saw him again. Or what she'd do. "I'm leaning toward not killing him, if that means anything, but that also changes with my mood."

She definitely wanted to kiss him, which probably wasn't a good thing and would end in more heartbreak. Yeah. Shooting him might prove the better of the two options. For her, anyway. For him, not so much.

"That's progress," Fern said. "Better than blowing him to smithereens."

"I'd serve him right. Liar."

"It'd be very messy." The sound of crinkling paper filled the line. "There're some trails to the west, here. Rough terrain though. It'd be difficult for me to navigate but I'd bet Lars would."

"If he'd even been there."

"Excellent point."

Outside, inky smoke billowed upward, blending into the darkening sky, smudging the newly born stars. Once upon a time, Harley would have slapped on her gear, rushed to the scene, and kicked whatever's ass needed kicking to put the world back in order. Now, the demons were loose. And the weres, golems and vampires. Along with murderous apparitions and the creepers. Giant bugs and aberrations. And everything else that went bump in the night. There was no order left to put back.

The fabric of society was torn. With most police officers busy defending their families, there were precious few left to patrol the streets and keep the populace safe. The military concentrated its protection in areas populated by the political authorities, Washington, and the homes of prominent politicians.

Everyone else was on their own. Including her.

*And so, the fragile words of law that once held anarchy in check have fallen. What do you think if that, Cerise?* She glanced up at the ceiling tiles, wishing she could peer into heaven. *Bet even you didn't see it coming to this.*

Fern said, "I could try, though. If Lars had been here there has to be some clues, right?"

"Not on your own you won't." Harley wagged her finger at the phone. Criminals and gangs were out there running rampant making the human threat just as much of a danger as the beasts Germaine released. Even more so because they could gain the trust of unsuspecting families and groups of survivors, only to turn on them, destroying them from the inside.

If her Order hadn't fallen to just such a deceiver, the slayers would be out there, fighting, united, putting beast and criminal back into their graves.

"Hello," Fern said. "I'm a slayer just like you."

"I wouldn't go into that situation alone, either."

Fern laughed. "Now who's the liar?"

"Well, the Cerberus Foundation might be okay breaking promises, but I am not."

"Cerise wouldn't want you to die trying to find Lars."

"I can't fail again." Harley hadn't been able to stop Germaine from creating hell on earth. She'd be damned if she failed to fulfill her promise.

"We need more equipment. There's a sanctuary not far from here."

"You'll wait until I get there." She refused to fail Fern, too. Yes, Fern was a slayer, but fighting wasn't her strong suit. "I scrounged some stuff that should get us by for a while."

"Okay," Fern said. "I figure that once we find Lars, we'll focus on finding other slayers."

"And sending the monsters that get in our way back to the abyss."

"That, too."

There was a light knock at the door.

"Expecting company?" Fern asked.

"Shh." Harley drew her .45 Smith & Wesson she'd reclaimed from the river while Nessie mowed on Niko and Oreo delight.

Brahms had been right. Germaine had loosed his dogs on her. She'd, unfortunately, had to kill several slayers whom she'd once fought beside. Of course, she'd tried to talk sense into them first, but people believed what they wanted to believe, and no amount of logic could shake those beliefs once embedded.

She stalked to the door. There, standing in the distorted view of the peephole, was Brahms. Dueling emotions surged through her. Relief that he was safe, excitement that he'd not only kept his word, albeit late, but had tracked her here, and anger. That he'd lied. That he'd made her worry about him to begin with.

She tamped all of it back. None of it would do her any good and all of it would lead her down a path she didn't want to tread-.She disengaged the door locks, leaned casually against the wall, and flung the door open, not bothering to holster her pistol because she still might use it on him.

"Look what the wizard dragged back from Oz," she said.

He cocked an eyebrow and walked in. "Wizard?"

"When you didn't show in Kansas, I figured you got sucked into a tornado." She kicked the door shut. "Or were too afraid for your life to run into me again. Either or."

"That must be Brahms," Fern said. "You're late."

"And you are?" he asked.

"That's Fern. She's been busy helping. Unlike someone else I know."

He reached out to touch Harley's hair, but wisely stopped short. "Why didn't you at least try to disguise yourself and your truck?"

He smelled of pine, earth, and cypress. Damn him.

To put distance between them, Harley plopped back on the bed and crossed her legs. "I'm inherently lazy. If the bad apple slayers are willing to come to me then it saves me the energy of hunting them down. Not to mention figuring out who's on who's side."

"The better question," Fern said, "Brahms, is where have you been and why didn't you meet Harley when you'd said?"

*And why am I still attracted to him*?

He dropped his duffle and backpack at the foot of the bed. "That's a dangerous tactic. What if they decided to gang up and take you out?"

She hitched a shoulder up. "Good luck with that."

He glanced at her gear and the map of the mountains.

Harley said, "Fern tracked Lars' path to his last known location. It's marked in black."

"But," Fern said, "I'm not allowed to do anything else until Harley gets here. As if I can't take care of myself."

"Lars was a fully capable slayer," Harley said, "and he had a partner."

Fern grumbled something incoherent.

"Okay, then," Brahms said, "we'll leave at first light."

"You don't have to help," Harley glowered up at him. "You can skulk your way back to Cerberus."

"You can't expect me to leave you here alone," he said softly.

She arched an eyebrow. "I don't want to hear it. Where's your cohorts?"

"Downstairs. I asked them to wait a few minutes."

"Why?"

"I thought we should talk."

"That's my cue to go," Fern said. "Might try my hand at fishing. MREs are getting dull."

"No," Harley said. "You stay in or right by that tank of yours."

"It's not a tank. It's an amphibious assault vehicle."

"Same difference."

"No, no not really."

"I can't have you disappearing on me, too. Promise you'll stay there until we reach you. If anything attacks, seal yourself in there. We should be to you by tomorrow night."

Fern blew a resigned sigh. "I guess another day of eating out of bags won't kill me. But if you see a sushi place or happen by some doughnuts, pick some up for me, will you?"

"Fine."

"Oh, and bug spray. Lots of it. Napalm, too."

Harley shook her head and chuckled. "I'll see what we can do."

"Night, guys," Fern said. "And Harley, be nice. We need all the help we can get. Brahms, don't let her fool you. She's read all our files on shifters."

"Snitch." Harley pushed the disconnect button with more force than necessary. Then she skewered Brahms with a glare. "Don't think that means you're off the hook."

"I'm sorry." He sat near the foot of the bed, a healthy distance away.

Now, what was she supposed to do with that? It was sincere. She might not have known he was a shifter when she'd fallen in love with him, but she did know he wasn't the type to intentionally lie or make false apologies.

He continued, "I should have told you early on but I didn't want to compromise our trust when facing something as dangerous as Niko's pride."

"You do realize hiding the truth doesn't go very far in building trust, right?"

"I thought it was the lesser of two evils." He ran his fingers through his hair. "Maybe it wasn't."

What would she have done differently if she'd known? Would she have stayed and worked with them to destroy Niko and his cult?

She groaned. Then said, "As much as I hate it, you were probably right. I don't think I'd have worked with you guys. I'd have gone after Niko alone or trusted in the wrong slayers and likely ended up dead. Watching this shit show from the sidelines of hell."

"I wish there'd have been another way."

"Me, too. I—"

Thayer burst through the door, muttering under his breath.

"Nice manners." Harley waved to the open doorway. "Close that before you let in the imps or some other marauding creature."

"You have no idea." Thayer lowered his bulky body into the padded chair and rested his head in his hands, as if suddenly too weary to hold it up without support.

"This isn't fifteen minutes," Brahms said. "We were in the middle of a conversation, Thayer."

"Hey," Thayer said, "I did my best."

"Where's Cree?" Harley asked.

"At the compound," Brahms said.

"What?" Harley asked. "I didn't figure Cree as someone to sit out a fight."

"Indeed, she isn't." A tall, broad-shouldered man that put even Thayer's impressive physic to shame strolled in. It seemed like an angel had just materialized out of the Dungeons and Dragons monster manual and straight into her hotel room. His chiseled face was only vaguely softened by shoulder-length shanks of blond hair. No warmth graced his golden eyes which seemed to take in everything, everywhere, all at once. They were riveting in a reptilian sort of way. He moved with a terrible grace that came from power barely leashed. "However, it was imperative that she learn the magic that the river spirits wished to teach her. There are many coastal and river towns we will need to protect in the coming years."

"And," the man turned his cold gaze to Thayer, "she had the wisdom not to argue."

Thayer withstood the man's stare for a few seconds, then he looked away and plucked at stray fibers sticking out from the hotel chair.

Harley glanced between Thayer and the disturbing newcomer. "So, you're his new partner?"

The man raised a blond eyebrow.

"Harley," Brahms motioned to him, "this is Fain, head of Cerberus."

Fain gave a crisp nod of his head. "Cree and Brahms told me of your adventure in the swamps. Killing a werepuma with an alligator. Fascinating tactic."

Interesting. Fain left Thayer out. She found it weird that Thayer wouldn't have told his part of the story. Then again, he did tend to be quiet.

Harley said, "I wouldn't have thought that a hunt for a missing slayer would catch Cerberus' attention."

"We have other interests," Fain said, "in this area. That aside, I hear that you're angry with Brahms."

"Not that it's your business," she said.

"It is when his tardiness is my sister's fault."

Thayer abruptly stood and paced the far end of the room like a caged tiger.

"The compound is safe," Brahms said to Thayer. "It's the best place for her to be."

"No where is safe now." Thayer continued to prowl the room. "And if communications go down, then what?"

Harley crossed her arms and said to Fain, "You must mean Celeste. The sister you keep imprisoned."

Dark anger slashed through Fain's eyes. His face hardened and he looked exactly like a statue of an avenging angel. "You know nothing."

Brahms held his hands out. "I need that fifteen minutes with Harley that the two of you promised."

Thayer strode out without a word. Between his anger and Fain's, she wondered how long it'd be before the two came to blows. Hopefully it'd be when they were out in the open with less furniture to break.

"Very well." Fain turned on his heel and headed to the door. He hesitated on threshold and glanced back. "Celeste sends her apologies for delaying your warrior."

Harley sputtered and straightened her back. A jumble of emotions flowed through her, top of which was shock, followed closely by annoyance that this newcomer would make such a wild assumption. "Brahms isn't my warrior. He isn't my anything."

*Was he?*

Fain stared deep into her eyes. Harley wondered if this is what it'd feel like when she was judged at St. Peter's gates. It felt as though Fain was scathing over her soul. Seeing everything that had been and was within her. The tips of Fain's lips quirked up in what might be interpreted as a smile.

"The worst lies," he said, "are those we tell ourselves."

Then he left, closing the door quietly behind him.

Harley tilted her chin upward and glanced to Brahms. His face remained stoic and unreadable. Damn him. He'd lied to her and that still stung. Okay. He didn't exactly lie but hiding the truth was a version of lying.

Still, she was no saint, either.

She changed the subject. "Thayer is afraid of him."

"Anyone with a healthy sense of self-preservation would be."

"Point." Harley turned toward Brahms and curled her legs under her to set him at ease. She didn't want him thinking she'd kick him or anything. "Can he read minds?"

He shook his head. "Not minds."

"But people. Souls?"

"When he's inclined."

"He's eerily accurate."

"Why do you say that?"

"If I hadn't lied to myself. Had believed Cerise. She'd be alive. I just...I didn't want to believe something like this could happen. That there were people I'd worked with, trained with, that I called friends who'd be so..."

She let her words trail off, at a loss for what to call Germaine and the slayers who'd abandoned their oaths to unleash death and destruction on the world.

"It's not as if we suspected Nash, either," Brahms said. 'No one wants to believe the worst of their friends."

"Cerise is dead. It's too late to apologize to her."

"I'm sure she knows."

But he didn't. What good was she doing for herself or him? *Cerise, you best be watching.*

"I don't want it to be too late for us." She scooted close to him and put a hand over his. "It's not really you I'm angry with. It's this damned feeling I get every time I see you. Or think of it. It's a liability."

"Love makes people stronger." He turned his hand over, threading his fingers in with hers. "Not weaker. Think of a mother bear. How much more strength she wields when protecting her cubs that she might not otherwise have."

"But that also leaves her open to attack. Not fully thinking of what she's doing."

Not that she was prone to planning things out anyway.

"I'm no cub." He rubbed his thumb gently on her chin. "Whatever openings you leave, I'll cover. That's what mates do."

"You don't think it's wrong to want this, to have this, when the world is falling apart?"

"When has the world ever been safe?"

Harley laughed. "Got me there."

He raised his eyebrows. "Really?"

"Yeah," she said. "Really."

He leaned in and kissed her. Tender. Sweet. An electric heat swept through Harley from her head down to the tips of her toes. Belonging. Love. Contentment.

The door burst open again. "There, see," Thayer said. "They've had enough time."

"You are being ridiculous," Fain said.

"Me?" Thayer's voice sounded incredulous.

Harley chuckled and nuzzled Brahms's nose. "They need to stop doing this."

"Really." Brahms said, glowering at Thayer.

"What?" Thayer grabbed the remote and pushed the power button. "I thought you'd find this interesting."

They all turned their attention to the TV. A bauble-headed reporter was centered in the frame against a background of burned, gutted buildings. According to the text ribbon below the picture, she was in Chicago. The reporter gushed through several theories regarding what she called the "uptick" in violence and rampant reports of monsters live in the streets.

"Not one mention of the Church being involved," Harley growled. "Because really, who'd have thought the Church would toss us into another dark age?" She would have continued the tirade, but Fain held up a hand, demanding quiet.

The reporter said, "Here is our own Cardinal Germaine on the current situation."

The camera cut to the interior of Germaine's office. Plush.

Velvet chairs. Polished bookshelves. His burly desk with its characteristic bowl of candies. Untouched by the violence in the streets. Yeah. Harley bet he was protected out the wazoo. He had nothing to fear from the beasts and death he'd unleashed. Not like the people he was supposed to serve.

*Asshole.*

Oh, but he should fear her. Somehow. Someway. She'd get to him.

The pompous propaganda that spewed out of Germaine's mouth was enough to make her want to puke. Chunks. Big juicy chunks.

"Remember, no matter how dark the world," Germaine said, "the Church is here for you. Together, we will find the light. We must set aside these conspiracy theories that point blame and instead bind ourselves together in strength, unity, and love under the protection of our Lord."

The camera cut back to the reporter, "In the meantime, Church authorities are asking you to keep an eye out for these two," Harley's face appeared on the left of the screen and Brahms's to the right, their names stamped below the photos, "who are linked to the recent violence that—"

Harley blocked out the rest of the reporter's blather. She threw the remote across the room. It hit into the wall and bounced on the carpet.

Thayer turned off the offending TV, and the room fell into silence.

"That's it. Truly it." She glowered at the dark screen.

She couldn't give life back to the dead. But she'd take Germaine down. Way down. To the pit of hell herself if necessary. Along with every single slayer who had helped him commit this atrocity.

"He can really put a shine on bullshit, can't he?" Brahms said.

"To even the odds," Fain's gaze flicked to Thayer, "someone

started an online rumor there is conspiracy within the Church itself. The theory has caught hold in some groups. Perhaps more will join."

"Just because it's a conspiracy theory," Harley clutched Cerise's frilly cross, which hung from her neck on its silver rope chain, "doesn't mean people aren't conspiring."

"We'll stop this," Brahms said. "I promise."

"Hell, yeah." Harley brushed her fingers across his cheek. "Because we have much more important things to do."

"And what are those?" He pulled her in closer, enveloping her in the soothing scent of a peaceful forest.

"Life. An actual real life with everything that goes along with it."

# ABOUT THE AUTHOR

Raven lives in remote northern Michigan creating and causing chaos in several fictional worlds. She lives with her husband, son, bat dog, a furry mammoth, and a flock of demons(aka angelfish).

Made in the USA
Monee, IL
03 July 2023